REBIRTH ON XARBO

DIANE DE PISA

Cover design copyright © 2023 by Kelley York
sleepyfoxstudio.net

Published by Water Dragon Publishing
waterdragonpublishing.com

ISBN 978-1-959804-15-4 (Trade Paperback)

10 9 8 7 6 5 4 3 2 1

FIRST EDITION

*I dedicate this sortie into afterlife adventures to the
friends who have shared my speculations about them,
and who have taken that final trip themselves:
Elio De Pisa, Franco Guidone, Anthony Calabrese,
Lou Fonseca, Jean Needham, and Mildred Waller.*

ACKNOWLEDGMENTS

I thank Kelley York for tweaking my title as well as designing the cover of this book. I also extend much appreciation to Steven Radecki and editors at Water Dragon for their warm reception of my initial proposal and perseverance in publication.

Sincerely, Diane De Pisa

REBIRTH
ON
XARBO

1

NIGHT JOURNEY

WHEN THEY TOLD Adam he was dying, he was not surprised. For over a year, he'd felt it coming — and it was his own doing. Even earlier, since Althea went, he began to let himself die. Nothing gave him pleasure, and work was a futile exercise. He withdrew from his limbs and organs and they became inert, alienated from each other. His heart grew weary of supplying lethargic limbs with blood. His stomach refused to process food he didn't relish. His arteries hardened with apathy. His lungs deflated with shallow breathing.

It began as avoidance of pain, of keening to his loss. He shut out music and sunlight and the odors of grass — became blunt to all experience. Vaguely, at first, he fought to ward off this deadening of faculties, but every sensation was wired to pain. Each time he saw Althea's straw gardening hat, moldering now on a bench, the floppy brim anchored with her shears, he felt a pang of deprivation. So many memories, and desires, had to be forever relinquished. Thus, imperceptibly, he gave himself over to the process of dying.

Psychosomatic self-annihilation tendency was treatable, but he refused therapy. His son Alther tried to persuade him to seek it, but they had never been close and the tokens of persuasion seemed half-hearted. Adam could not expect more from the offspring whom he'd never cherished. Besides, any gesture toward life seemed obscene with Althea dead. He reached a state, he imagined, like that of someone injected with those banned weapons that numbed nerves, making adversaries impervious to pain and incapable of defending themselves. He injected himself with the notion of death and watched without sympathy as his stomach labored in the toils of indigestion, his heart palpitated like a mouse squeezed in a fist, his calves and forearms atrophied.

His whole system was grinding to a halt; morbidity compression, the clinicians called it. Only at the final hour did he rally instinctively. Panic struck as death throes rippled through his organism. He tried to muster his dying faculties as one might career through a building to warn tenants of a fire. But his organs were too inert to respond — except his heart, which flailed awhile, like a fish cast up on shore, its spasms sending rays of pain through his body. At last, he abandoned that quivering entity to the abyss.

At the final moment, he leapt clear and saw his body sprawled alone, wondering for a moment what Alther would do when he found it, haggard but still handsome, aged by stagnation. He was freed of the constricted lungs, the heavy legs, and felt no impulse to flog them into function again.

He felt giddy with the release. The spasms now became waves that gently bore him away and off. Concentric eddies expanded softly from the hard impingement of his death on the universal pool, and he was borne ever farther from that stone-sure event. He dissolved and merged with the subsiding impulses, soon losing all definition as he flowed into a place without landmarks. Was he going forward or backward? Was he upside down or right side up? He had the same sensation once while walking with Althea in a blizzard. It was euphoric then, an adventure into a magical space without dimensions, and now he used that memory to keep loneliness and fear at bay. Remembering the blizzard, he let himself drift, heedless of direction or destination. He was helpless and knew it. Let the rescuers find him, if rescuers there were in this place.

After an indeterminate time, he seemed to pick up a signal in the featureless vastness. Something as yet indefinable was demanding his attention. He felt certain it was not self-induced, but coming from an outside source. Suddenly he knew it was Althea. She was near him, he was sure, although she did not emit any sound or light or scent. He recognized her presence — a heartiness without heat, proud and intact and pure, like a burgundy iris, sharing her queenly confidence to bolster him. Even devoid of shape, he sensed that he was cupped to her and together they were going somewhere.

Then he realized they were not alone. Other presences were all about them, but Althea stood out by contrast. She was delicate yet strong, while many of them were crude or heavy or decrepit. Some proceeded fiercely and seemed to clang through the space around them; others flagged, weak, and he could imagine they were about to disintegrate; several were lost or going in circles and recurred at odd intervals with an air of dismay and delusion; a few were so self-contained that he could scarcely detect their nearness except for a faint electric buzz that directed them to some destination.

The crowd around the couple was thick; travelers hustled and jockeyed for position. Many apparently were attuned to a purpose that Adam had not yet discerned. Perhaps Althea could recognize it and would pull him through. It seemed all were in a black night sky vibrant with speeding bombers en route to their targets, he and Althea like frail kites among ponderous, purposeful sky ships. The two seemed to float so lightly that they eluded all interference, floated as Althea's hair used to, buoyant and brown and sleekly clean, cutting a swath through the summer air.

Suddenly Adam felt a pang of nostalgia for every summer sun that had ever risen. He wanted desperately to see once more, to touch his fingers to the reddish freckles on Althea's upper arms. He remembered how the flesh felt, at once firm and soft; and the twin rounds of her breasts in sundresses; and her perfume as she moved, a bit tart, the fragrance of wild herbs. He felt something like a sob shake his being, with terror almost, so strong was his yearning for sight and smell and touch in this breathless place. Suffocating nostalgia disrupted his connection with Althea, and he lost her.

With her assuring nearness gone, this place without borders felt restricted and oppressive. The darkness became more opaque, murky as a smoke-filled street when a house is burning. He wanted to call her back but seemed to choke. And anyway, he had no voice, and she no ears. So he tried to lure her back with flattery: He thought of how beautiful she was and how much he needed and desired her. Although he did not know what for. What was there to be desired now — and what could she do for him in any way? Could she speak to comfort him? Shoot him her wise look to calm his doubts? No, none of this would she ever do again.

Adam was overwhelmed with a feeling of impotence such as he had never experienced. It was not like sexual impotence, when one has a desire but cannot fulfill it; nor like moral impotence, when one sees a wrong and lacks the courage to fight it; nor was it like intellectual impotence, when a problem looms too great to solve. Adam was familiar with all the earthly forms of impotence. But this was something different. He had lost not just one faculty, temporarily, but all faculties, perhaps forever.

His life had been a brew in a bowl and the bowl broke, letting the brew drain away, leaving no trace of him. The bowl had given him a shape that he called his own. But it was an illusion, an unreliable fiction. Now he was left without a form or vehicle for his energies and these were dissipating. Without a body, a voice, he could not even scream to Althea for help.

Still, he had something. He was thinking, wasn't he? He even had some compensatory faculties: He had felt Althea's presence without the aid of sight or touch. As he began to reason in this way and to spin a thread of optimism, he entertained a hunch that Althea pricked up her attention from an incalculable distance and was drawn to him.

As a fiber of strength built up in him, he sensed Althea more and more intimately, as a pulse that entered his own stream of thoughts and attuned them to hers. If he lost all and still had this, this sure and clear rhythm deep where his heart should be, then he need never fear, never regret the summer sun and shining hair. For didn't sun and hair and freckled arms, and the numerous warm, lovely things of the world — didn't they all conspire to give him just this: the assurance that all was well, that he was immersed in the flow of familiar elements? If the feeling was there without the stimulants, why should he feel any loss? He began to settle down, lulled and complacent.

But now Althea was gone again, leaving no clues to her whereabouts. He had leaned on memories as a prop and this support gave way. He began to doubt that she had ever joined him. Perhaps he had fantasized the encounters and separations. Perhaps he was alone after all.

But if he was there — wherever, whatever this place might be — why couldn't she be there too? He decided to experiment. He had called her back once; let him try again. Instead of compliments, he tried conjuration as he understood it: through identification with the desired object. He imagined he was Althea — and was shocked at the immediacy of results. Without a body of his own to impede the process, he configured Althea's form. He could feel her long brown fingers at the ends of his arms: slim, strong woman's arms with fleshy freckled upper parts, brushed by a soft broom of hair. He could feel his neck like a stem, sleek, with scarcely a bump of a voice box. He was amazed at the refinement and delicacy of the female organism, the tiny ankles, the beardless face and molded lips. He could feel Althea's features and limbs emanating from the hub of his will. But he knew it was not Althea. And she was not attracted to this ethereal imagined form.

Thus Adam began to suspect that Althea did not much identify with her body, and probably never had. Twenty-two years of marriage, and all that time she had a detached, take-it-or-leave-it attitude toward her body, which he adored and worshipped and labored to please in so many ways! He wanted to laugh ironically, bitterly, but nothing came out. He just felt a dry little rasp, like the slip of a latch as it catches on a hasp, a small metallic gasp of cold knowledge without satisfaction.

Then he began to wonder what Althea did identify herself by, if not her body. It occurred to him that he was having an unexpected second chance now to learn what he should have long ago. What, in fact, he was being forced to discover by the most desperate need he had ever felt. She had waited for him in this dislocated location, yet he had lost her again. To lure her back, he must find her from the inside, learn what she identified herself with or as.

He tried to remember a characteristic expression or gesture of Althea's, but failed. Patches of memory, it seemed, had gone blank. What if memory should fail him altogether? A patch at a time, snuffed out, leaving him in a void, perhaps unable to recollect even his name? And worst of all, unable to remember whom he loved, or why. Already, he fretted, love was wavering. Had he adored Althea's body only, and could recall nothing of her but the grossest details?

He was immersed in murk again, thicker now, like a fog that would blanket and enfold him until he dissolved, the last circuit of memory blinking out feebly. Panic clutched him where his throat should be. The fog seemed cold, as if it could condense and freeze and lock him in unyielding ice and no one would be able to hack him out. He felt a tightness where his jaw used to be, as if it were clenched. He had to save himself from locking into catatonic frozen hell. He made a deliberate effort to relax. He let himself be weak and drifted, formless as fog itself.

He cast about for some flotsam to cling to — something familiar and comforting and exalting. "Glory be to God for dappled things," he quoted an ancient poet, and repeated it as a rune against disaster while he kept the image of Althea's freckles before him. He floated on a tide of speckles, of lovely, sharp, contrasting disks and full moons and trout sequins: images that broke up the hideous homogeneous fog. And he felt a surge of gratitude to Althea for having had freckled arms.

It seemed now that Althea took pity on him, or his gratitude touched her. He could picture her eyes now, with flecks swimming in them, laughing at him. And again she was nested next to him and a feeling of lightness returned, and they were going somewhere.

Xzz ... he seemed to hear, and Althea gave her approval to the sound. It was like a buzz somewhere inside him, in his middle ear, vibrating its tiny bones. The voyagers around them echoed the syllable soundlessly, like bats agreeing on a destination by radar. Yes, that was it: Xzz was the destination. Althea prodded him to hurry, join them all in their rush to Xzz. Now it expanded, opened to Xzzaa. He scanned his memory for what it might mean but failed to recognize it. Was it a sound that belonged to any earthly language? An African Bush dialect, perhaps?

Althea almost slipped from him as he speculated. *She is impatient,* he thought. *She has no tolerance for academic questions.* He remembered with chagrin how he plied her with his intellectual gymnastics, thinking to impress her, never noticing that he bored her. She tolerated him merely, from a deeper love that was not based on his cleverness but actually persisted despite it.

Even back then she had waited for him. And now, with these flashes of insight, he drew an answering warmth. It was unmistakable. Althea was there. Without look or touch, she yet responded, her deep-rooted goodwill flooding him with courage and hope.

Xarr ... the echo seemed to resonate through his whole being, as if he were sheet metal shaking in a thunderclap. Xarrr-bo. Then quickly in succession, like pellets from a repeat launcher: Xarbo, Xarbo, Xarbo. Althea rejoiced, excited as never in life. Her joy induced a thrill or shudder as exquisite music used to produce in him. His hair should stand on end, he felt.

But what was this Xarbo that Althea and all the others streamed toward without wind or wake? As if he had accessed a universal data base, answers flooded him: Xarbo: prime goal of former Earth beings; super-conducting atmosphere. Completion guaranteed; everything happens fast there.

Completion, he thought. And the flow of information stopped. He had tried for Completion as all Ahims must. Tried too hard, all the guides told him — fixated on the idea that he had to please them, prove his ability, compete with the others. No amount of coaching could induce him to relinquish that extra bit of strain that kept him from entering the last lap. Althea had begun the last lap but hadn't finished it. She was like a jogger caught up in the joy and pride of her strength, glorying in her abilities, but not excelling them. Not trying hard enough, it seemed. No, maybe not following instructions precisely. Perhaps he respected the guides too much, she too little. Perhaps.

He lost Althea again as he petered out into speculations. *Keep your word close to your heart,* he thought, quoting some time-lost ancient philosopher. What did the heart want? Oh yes, Completion. And Xarbo guaranteed it.

But if Completion had been close enough to his desire, he would not have meandered into memories at this all-important juncture, where Completion was promised in a strange destination. In fact, on Earth he had been a dilettante, not seriously expecting to reach that high state that the ancients called illumination, enlightenment. Why had he tried so hard? All for show. To show Althea he was one of her type, a dedicated Ahim, to save face with the guides, to prove he was not a Technist despite his background. So he had been a hypocrite. And now he was not eager to reach Xarbo — if it was where everything happens fast. No; he had put on an appearance of haste, but it was all a shuffle to hide his inertia. He had really wanted only to stay at Althea's side, whatever the pretext, and have her approval, however unworthily.

He felt ashamed, and again marveled that she had stayed by him and waited for him. Here, the slightest feeling could not be masked. Nothing escaped unregistered or without a reaction. And he realized now that it had been so even in life, but there, one could be distracted, gaze at the freckles and the sun-combed hair and take a holiday from consequences. But every gesture and look, every word and — yes — every thought registered somewhere. Of this he felt sure, now that all the distractions of flesh and posture were gone. And yet the void proved so full of detail. He must be headed for a comeuppance. Why else did he have to remember his foibles and faking?

2

LESSONS OF MEMORY

ADAM SENSED THAT ALTHEA was still with him, although impatient to the point of frenzy. He wanted her desperately, yet a certain traitorous inertia made him lag. He could not keep his mind in line with Xarbo. Its promise of Completion meant little to him. He had cultivated his potentials only half-heartedly. If Xarbo was prime target for Earth beings, it must be so only for major achievers, not mediocre beings like him.

Suddenly Althea was gone, as if sucked into a vacuum chamber. The buzz and sense of urgency vanished. Like a swimmer who has survived rapids and craves rest, he gravitated to a quiet backwater. He enjoyed a moment of relief, of freedom from pressure, and rocked in torpor as if sedated.

Adam was drawn out of repose by a gentle question: "Have you rested? Are you restored?" Whatever induced the question in him registered as neither hostile nor friendly in the usual sense. If it was an entity, it was a most objective yet beneficent one. All this Adam could tell from the simple query. And he knew that more questions would follow, and that they would all be devices to make him confirm certain facts about himself, to crystallize what he already was or had been, and so establish what he was to be. There was no way to prepare for this exam. *He* was under scrutiny, not his knowledge, ideas, plans, hopes, or intentions. And what he was, had been, was already settled irrevocably. There was no going back to fix anything. It was almost comforting to realize that struggle, strain and, most of all, hypocrisy would be utterly useless. He was alone, formless, perhaps nameless. Yes, about to be nameless. He surrendered.

The examining entity now fired a series of voiceless questions directly into Adam's mind — although he was not sure that he literally had a mind at this point. In his new condition, everything was accelerated: Question and response seemed simultaneous. Often a phrase or word sufficed to trigger an insight. And that was the entire purpose of the procedure: to define Adam total. Then the old Adam would become dispensable. Once fully configured, he would become the pattern for a new being with a determined destination.

Better than questions, some fragments of memory triggered insights — and many proved painful. A recurring image from the past would float by and he tried to pin it down, to stop and focus on it to extract its meaning. Like electronic arcade targets, these were impossible to hit as long as one strained, because straining dislodged them from their trajectories. With a relaxed approach, he recaptured an image of Althea tossing her head and looking at him with exasperation. He replayed the image, as if recalling a dream scene, trying to place it in context. What had he said that caused her to look at him like that? The flop of her hair as she tossed her head impatiently was familiar. It was a signal or code, meaning something, sending him a wordless message. A semaphore with a flag of brown hair. What did it mean?

He recaptured the vision in slow motion, zoomed in on the eyes, the lips. The lower lip jutted out fast and in again, twice. She was saying, "Confidence." Then it struck him. Althea had told him once, "You have more self-confidence than anyone, but you act unsure so others will rush to help you." She told him this one night when he was whining about something. Oh yes, the speech that the Technist League had asked him to make. He wanted Althea to help him see the Technist viewpoint objectively. He couldn't do it himself. He insisted that his mind was frozen. She was calmer. He demanded that she outline topics for him. She refused, with that toss of the head. And he threw a tantrum, became hysterical, worked himself into a state where he really could not think, let alone prepare a difficult speech where utmost diplomacy was required. So she had to prepare the piece for him after all.

He saw now, under the probing of the inquiring entity, that the whole emotional build-up was a ploy he used over and over, always with the result that he got his way, enlisted help. And at the same time, gave the vicious circle another kick, convincing himself that without aid he was helpless. Mainly it was Althea whom he called on to save him — and he loved her when she gave in and hated her when she held out on him. He bullied her with ranting, pulled her down with his outbursts, blackmailed her: "If you loved me, you wouldn't ignore my need. Are you my wife or a stranger?"

Whenever he began to whine, she looked at him angrily, with loathing and loathness masked by an embarrassed, deprecating laugh. The shake of the head, sideways, the hop of hair: These signals told that he was straying out of bounds, that he should desist. Each shake was a count: first chance, third, thirty-second. He should have learned to stand on his own, but he masked his ineptitude with false confidence, until the next crisis arose. Then he resolved to be strong and face it himself. But inertia overtook him. It was easier to fall back on habit.

What is this? Adam wondered. *Some sort of crime for which I have to atone?* And he knew in a flash that rebelliousness was a phase, like adolescence. The sooner he got through it, the better. So he accepted the unspoken criticism. Yes, he was a chronic complainer and weakling masquerading as a know-it-all. A chink in the puzzle had been filled in. He replayed the image of Althea's tossing hair to be sure that he omitted no nuance.

Then suddenly a radical and unexpected change occurred. As he watched the ruddy wise head flicking in resistance, Althea began to metamorphose — into a red deer with antlers trying to shake off an arrow embedded in its neck. And Adam was a hunter, crouched in long stinging grasses, reaching for a second arrow from a quiver at his back. The arrows were stuck too far down in the quiver and his arm strained to reach them. His leg muscles were cramped from crouching. A hunt should not involve so much discomfort, so many difficulties. His body should be relaxed. And the deer should not shake its head that way; it should bow in consent. But he had not performed a ceremony of consent. He embarked on a wrong path in haste. He was too eager to have this deer, an especially fine one. Now that he had started on the wrong way, he was sweating and straining to get it over with, to kill the deer as fast as possible. But it was not giving in. It would have to be dragged down, dart after dart. It would punish him for his stubbornness.

Great galaxies, thought Adam, *must I go back to the ten-thousandth lifetime and rub my nose in superstition?* This, he recognized almost immediately, was another instance of futile rebellion. He knew with cold latch-hasp sureness that the deer hunter's convictions were not superstitions. He had grown very little in wisdom from the ancient time of hunting to the time of Althea. He still persisted in having his way, especially when it was the wrong way.

Next he relived moments when he had his way with women. At first the images flooded him with warmth and pleasure. He relished the re-imagined stages of seduction, slipping his hand under a hemline of the old woven materials or running his eyes lasciviously over the naked copper of a tropic zone woman. And each gesture led to another, to consummation of his desires — almost. For just as he was about to possess a woman she metamorphosed into another whom he knew in a different time and place, and he had to resume seduction from the outset.

If I have to relive all my conquests, that won't be too bad, Adam thought. Little thrills coursed through his being. *Perhaps I'm collecting the just deserts of a great lover.* He felt the covert joy of a school-boy receiving an unearned good mark.

He enjoyed now a small woman who squirmed as if trying to crawl out from under him, but he knew she was pretending. Her little body with its firm mounds of breasts was most enticing, but in his discorporate state he could not experience sexual pleasure. Instead he focused in greater detail, and more intensely, on the play of emotions. He felt a surge of power mixed with compassion as he took hold of the writhing woman. They were in a dwelling made of textiles, a soft luxuriant structure, with only objects of pleasure about them: food, drink, musicians somewhere near.

As he was about to reach a climax of power and exultation, the wild little figure dissolved and metamorphosed into a languid, tranquil woman of the modern stamp. A celibate, he sensed. He walked slowly into her chamber, luxuriant in the modern way with a carpet of tiny hybrid flowers. Larger plants joined their branches overhead, making a ceiling. A shrill bird screamed; a furry pet stared at him. The woman was eager to hear his news. Again he enjoyed a sense of control. He imparted a portion of his message and then a compliment. She was pleased but not beguiled. She was tall and slim like a daffodil, with a large open face. Her attitude, so candid yet self-contained, inflamed him with little prickling thoughts, like dispersions of electricity. Tiny forked lightning around his heart and in his head urged him to violate this sanctuary of self-containment. The memory was so vivid that Adam relived the sensations even without a body to conduct them.

He besieged her with compliments, wooed her hotly. When she objected, he pressed his cause as if it were an unavoidable act of nature to which he was only a helpless accomplice. Which was true at this point, for he had allowed his emotions to escalate until he was desperate for her. His motions became more pronounced, inevitable, mechanical even. He perceived that the daffodil woman put herself into a protective trance, abandoning her body to seethe with pleasure while her mind remained detached, exempt from damaging excitations. It was a difficult trance to induce, he knew. She must be very advanced, and must deem this a major emergency. He was flattered that she considered him so dangerous, and yet undoubtedly attractive, or she would have retired physically as well as mentally. Adam exulted in this forbidden fruit. Then she disappeared, and he found himself with another.

As women replaced each other at the moment of possession and Adam had to re-enact endless seductions, he realized that this was no heavenly respite. These scenes were signals reminding him of his habits, his weaknesses. The emotions replayed in each scene fell into a pattern: He was admitted into an atmosphere of purity, or of danger, either of which stimulated a desire to master the situation, leave his stamp on a clean slate. And the 'slate' was always personified in a woman.

Now, exempt from bodily sensations, reliving these scenes, Adam realized that desire had little to do with any of his seductions — although he always assumed it did: *How headstrong my body is,* he had gloated, *that it masters me so.* But this he now saw was a lie, no truer for having been repeated millennially. He had believed that desire arose in the senses and ended in them, expressions of irresistible nature. Now he saw that his were actually urges for conquest. He yearned above all to prevail and leave a mark. Not a physical desire at all but an exigency of the will. The body merely delivered plunder in the form of pleasure. His indifference toward the women's wishes was not the blindness of a proud beast of a body but the selfishness of a will that wants its way at all costs. A will so insistent, in fact, because only by marking others could it be assured of its power and importance.

As Adam replayed the seductions, shame crept in. These were not victories but defeats, where he gave in to habit and ambition. At first he would entertain an almost amusing inclination, then a positive drive to dominate, and finally he succumbed to a kind of hysterical craving. He heard himself whine and bully and flatter, never failing to inflame his partners to an answering urgency. He infected them with his lust, had his way, and left them. He played the role of tempter and seducer but never the faithful lover.

Not until Althea. With her, he had kept the faith in sexual matters. In his last lifetime he accomplished the transition from seducer to true husband. And for this, he intuited now, he was rewarded with her devotion. For this, she waited for him. Although he manipulated her in other ways, he never exploited her sexually. *"Unravish'd bride,"* he thought, recalling a fragment from the Age of Written Ciphers.

He enjoyed little time resting on his laurels, for the inquiring entity reminded him there was no loitering in this realm of dreams and memories. He had to choose a task or a way, a destination. And that meant birth in a body. *What do you want?* the entity pressed. Adam had to choose a situation in which to outgrow the accumulation of habits that had constituted his identity so far — the childish exploiter. *I want Xarbo*, he found himself confiding without being aware that he had thought it. Although things happen very fast there, he would take a chance. Perhaps he could be rushed along to Completion. Above all, he expected to find Althea there, somehow reconfigured.

Xarbo is out of bounds at this time, the entity replied. And Adam knew it was because he desired it wrongly, hoping that he would be promoted despite unworthiness, lack of preparation.

Yes, he was an upstart, unwilling to accept the lower rank assigned to him by right. He habitually aimed blindly for forbidden objects, but now a rein was placed on his ambitions.

Adam felt rage swell him, beginning where his chest should be and then throbbing in his head. Soon he was possessed by anger, the fury of a child thwarted. But how could he pressure the entity into granting his wish — which was not especially to be on Xarbo but to rejoin Althea? Now he was to be deprived of her, who was his only link to strength and rightness.

Unable to affect the entity, Adam turned his fury in on himself and sweltered in the hellish brunt of his tantrum. He could not endure it long. He had to find a channel for it before it burnt his circuits. He was plummeting like an aircraft out of control, letting himself once more be carried by emotion to some inevitable consequence far too late to avoid.

Adam spiraled with the impetus of his uncontrollable anger. He desired Althea, only Althea. And the impossibility of joining her frustrated him to madness. Something denied him Althea. Unable to target the denying power, his rage deviated into spitfire images of mangling and mutilating prey or enemy. He became a soldier, an executioner of ancient times, beheading victims with axes. In a dozen obsolete wars, he rushed enemies in cumbersome machines, crushing them with big-shelled vehicles like beetles. He tortured and maimed, he became a Technist chief and disintegrated his foes with ludicrous Technist weapons. As he entertained these images of violence, he veered Earthwards and knew in a flash that he would end his trajectory there.

There is still time, something whispered. *Save yourself from the worst disaster,* another insinuated. *Change your mental tone.* A blitz of encouraging suggestions inundated him, gifts of savior entities trying to help him. He saw saints who had been sinners, miraculously converted. He heard snatches of epics praising the great-souled ones in the modern way, orchestrated to inspire him, warn him from calamity. He tried frantically then to buffer his landing, find something of positive value to break his fall, that he might not arrive in a blaze of rage.

He tried to recapture an image of intimacy with Althea, his one key to virtue. He pictured their bodies laced gracefully as vines together. But the gentle picture would not stay in focus. The copulating bodies throbbed violently, began to pump ferociously, obscenely. His anger transformed into lust. But he had no body with which to feel it. Instead he saw others' bodies so engaged — actual couples now on Earth, he realized. He hovered around them, applauding in his enraged condition the vehemence of their contortions. Repulsed by their crudity, he was yet fascinated, as an unquiet being is drawn by conflagrations and public punishments. He flashed on one coupling after another, almost fainting with the acuteness of the images and his own unruly emotions. He made a last-ditch effort to pull his attention away from the grossest scenes and dwell on more tender ones. Just as he focused on a couple groping at each other intensely but lovingly, he lost consciousness and, with it, all claim to being, or having been, Adam.

3

XARBO

T O BE BORN ON XARBO, a planet both benign and perilous, is a privilege which the discarnate entities from Earth covet. Three Xarbian months earlier, Mother Zalda had brought her egg to the nursery, where it matured rapidly — a symmetrical oblong sheathed in a translucent membrane. After the first month, Zalda invoked an entity to animate it and watched anxiously as the embryonic being stirred within its enclosed bath of nutrients. Detecting what seemed to be abnormal signs of struggle, she called on rebirth experts to observe the movements, which at times seemed about to poke through the soft leathery skin of the ovum. The consensus was that yes, the being whom Zalda had invoked instinctively resisted its new embodiment, probably because of residual attachment to a previous existence on Earth. However, the specialists convinced Zalda that, once on Xarbo, the being would relinquish the disturbing memories of its former lives. Nonetheless, she should be prepared for emergence of some throwback tendencies as her offspring developed.

Now this Pearl of Time was about to emerge from its flexible casing. Zalda dressed in ceremonial garments and went to the nursery to bring the newborn home with an airborne conveyance that she drew after her through the breeze-less atmosphere. Fleecy karuners and downy palanthins snuggled in its depth: simple beings who consented to line it with their soft living bodies.

At the nursery the translucent casing lay flaccid, dissolving like sea foam into myriad little bubbles reflecting rainbows. The newborn sat amid the brilliant spume, scarcely less delicate than it, her flesh almost translucent like that of certain sea creatures on Earth.

"Mother Zalda," a Namer addressed her, and she bowed her head as was the custom, following this specialist into the Naming Chamber to listen with her inner yeldom, to cognize the name destined for the new being. Slowly the convoluted yeldom beyond her inner ear began to contract and expand and a soundless word was received. Later she would say it silently to herself, then speak it aloud to the child, bestowing it as a gift.

The little one was gaining already its phylane, the cartilaginous substance that serves in place of earthly bones. Mother Zalda stood by and admired as her offspring rose in beauty from the foam, first to a sitting position and finally to standing. Only when it took a few steps toward her did she touch it, for by walking it showed that it was fully formed and would not be harmed by her embraces. She lifted it into the air-conveyance and flew to her home, leaping joyfully over dwellings and low domesticated flora.

As she flashed through the brilliant atmosphere, she could glimpse a million rainbows all about her in the air of Xarbo, which presents no resistance to movement. No leap or bound of joy is diminished in this vast ocean of prisms refracting light into blazing colors — a light that seemed to Zalda a symbol for the intelligence of the rapidly developing being in her charge.

Now the little one was sitting up in the air-carriage, full of glee to be alive. Once home, the two entered vertically. As those gathered to greet them watched, the ceiling merely indented at first, then dilated to admit the pair, air-carriage and all. The matter then reclosed without a trace of a gap. Zalda had chosen her dwelling materials well; they were most obedient and efficient.

In the ovoid space, Zalda found a party of six, three masculine and three feminine presences. They were to be the baby's mentors;

her zildings in the Xarbian language, whose functions far exceeded those of earthly tutors — as the young creature would soon learn. Having sensed or heard that the child had emerged and, knowing that their skills were appropriate to her upbringing, these sages came to welcome her and make themselves known to the mother. Like most undertakings on Xarbo, this was done ceremonially; that is with full attention and deliberate gestures — and yet in the spirit of fun. The adults placed the baby, still in her conveyance, in their midst and sat in a circle around her, watching with restrained hilarity, anticipating the amusing event they knew would soon take place.

One of them saw before the others did and pointed: "There!" Then they all saw and began to bend and peer, to watch the little miracle in their midst. Fine gossamer fibers were beginning to stick out all around the pearl-like head of the infant, leaving only the oblong patch of the face free. The fibers shot out like minute fireworks. A few minutes later she had, like the rest of them, a quivering dandelion crown of shiny colorless filaments that flashed and hopped as she moved. This process was called the Sprouting Ceremony, and ended in shouts of joyous laughter.

The elders introduced themselves to Zalda and informed her of their individual responsibilities toward the child, who tossed her head of glistening sprouts impatiently. "She doesn't understand yet who you are," laughed Zalda apologetically to the zildings, as she recorded their calling codes in her mind. They departed through the curving side panels of the dwelling. When all had left, Zalda hugged her daughter in the Earth-being manner, holding her tightly against her chest. All Xarbians have lived on Earth and remember some of their previous life and customs, kept alive as a reminder of humble origins. Even a few words of Earth languages are preserved. One of these is 'Sol,' for the star around which Xarbo revolves.

Zalda adjusted her vision to see-through and noted that Sol was approaching the horizon. Even its most oblique rays are warming in the perfectly conducting atmosphere of Xarbo. However, the moment it is obscured by the horizon, heat is lost with frightening rapidity. Night and Death are synonymous in the Xarbian language. So, to ensure no unpleasant surprises, Zalda silently recited the locking incantation in four directions. Obediently the particles composing her walls crystallized with a faint crackle. Now no heat would escape the dwelling. At the same time, it would no longer be possible for visitors to come and go. On Xarbo, one settles in for the night.

Outside in the great moonless Xarbian darkness, other beings made their adjustments to the plummeting temperature. The minuscule forms of vegetation that carpet the soil like wiry mosses closed off their crevices, doubling over on themselves as their tiny blooms ducked for cover. The enormous mogdons and phenamons that soar toward the stars spread their leathery clumps of foliage for the night like the wings of giant bats. Folded and drooping during the day, the blue leaves of the phenamon and the brown of the mogdon interlace on high to shelter seedlings. Former humans, however, cannot endure a Xarbian night.

Zalda laid the child down among soft karuners and palanthins, the volunteer comforters. Having achieved Completion, Zalda herself did not need to sleep in the usual sense. She merely closed her eyes to rest body and mind. She was curious, though, to watch her child a while. At first its face was perfectly tranquil, even more like a pearl now that the eyes were closed and the tiny features relaxed. But after a few minutes the child began to sigh and turned on its side and soon rapid eye movements betrayed a dream. Zalda was tempted for an instant to monitor its contents. She possessed the xena, or esoteric skill, to do so and was curious about this new being entrusted to her care. Would the dream indicate her little one's lingering attachment to troubling connections on Earth? She recalled how a consultant had warned of disturbances carrying over from a past life. Her maternal instincts registered concern. But could she influence the past? Of course not. And idle curiosity can lead to fruitless meddling, as all Xarbians know.

Zalda removed her ceremonial garments before she lay down on her mossy floor. In the low arching space, all was dark except the two bodies, which glowed faintly with the inner Xarbian light. The tiny pearl-like being slept and sighed next to her mother, whose rainbow skin shone steadily and whose chest did not rise and fall with breath, for achievers of Completion expend no energy when at rest.

Zalda laughed when she opened her eyes next day to see the little one yawning, its eyes closed and mouth open revealing the first nubs of yavers, the quartz-like 'teeth' that would metabolize air and never bite anything else. Today Zalda would impart the delicious secret that she held in store for her offspring: the name given at the hour of hatching.

Ceremonies call for vestments, and now Zalda drew on a cloak and placed one on the baby, who already remembered that the garb was a signal for special attention and watched with iris-purple eyes, her little head bristling attentively. This would be their only private ceremony. Zalda closed her eyes and spoke to herself a silent chant that stilled her heart and breath and allowed her to hear very clearly again the name she was about to impart. Slowly she drew it out of the silence, heard it pulse in her inner yeldom once more, and whispered it into the child's ear: "Altherin, Altherin, Altherin."

The child absorbed the word gravely. She would never speak her own name, of course, but all would know it after the public ceremony soon to be held in her honor. She realized the word referred to her, but as yet did not know its connotations: the prismatic colors of the Xarbian air, or xaltherin, and thus the whole spectrum. It also suggests the Xarbian musical scale, or xin — not an octave but a sextave of wide-set, bold notes. Altherin thus connotes at once harmony, spectrum or rainbow, and wholeness. It was a good name, as little Altherin would appreciate in time.

4

SMALL LIES

YOUNG ABRAHAM'S DREAMS swamped him continually with images of half-remembered, half-imagined matters: a swath of reddish hair, a bizarre buzzing sound, a sense of fevered desperation. He felt emotionally ill-prepared as he rushed to meet his examining committee in a Rocky Mountain retreat. The group, composed of international scientists and shamans — — or, 'technicians of the sacred,' as an ancient had dubbed them — would oversee his initiation into psychic Powers. Apprehensive, Abraham hoped the committee would take his desires into account as well as his accomplishments. But he doubted it, and feared his insecurity would register as a sign he was unfit. The examining panel was intent on choosing the initiation best suited to him, not necessarily the level he hoped for — and resignation to inevitabilities was not his forte.

Abraham had a couple of hours to rest in his room before the ordeal. There, he practiced a relaxation technique, letting his body go limp, while Technist experts adjusted test equipment. One of them attached electrodes to his scalp for the electroencephalogram that indicated how much brain capacity he used and if the lobes operated coherently while the committee grilled him with questions. A tape on his palm recorded his galvanic skin response, to reveal nervousness and detect lies. A tiny set of vials ran continuous tests of blood chemistry, indicating his degree of vascular and neural efficiency while under pressure. All these parameters showed mainly his aptitude, no proof of what he might eventually accomplish. Technists, he knew, place their faith entirely in such physical tests. Abraham, however, aspired to the psychic Powers that only Ahims cultivate.

At length, Abraham heard the preceptors from many traditions chant the opening Sanskrit yagya, revived from ancient times, and felt its calming influence. The temperature of the room dropped a few degrees, as Abraham's older friends said it would. Then, while the chant faded, the eclectic who directed the examining committee gazed at him and inquired, "Are you ready?"

Abraham nodded.

"Are you Technist or Ahim?" The neurobiologist asked this and other preliminary questions with obvious answers to set a baseline reading for Abraham's functions.

"Ahim," he replied, and gained a dram of confidence.

The real interrogation began with an Algonquian shaman, purist of his tradition, adorned with hawk feathers and animal hides: "Describe your most profound experience in this life."

Abraham's friends told him he might be asked about such an experience, which should be meaningful in the context of any tradition. He chose to tell of a conversation he had as a child with a bluebird — an argument, in fact, over the rights to certain berries — his only extended communication with another species. He expected some cross-examination from the Inuit seer or the Dogon wizard, but they seemed satisfied with the story. However, the metabolism expert from Austria had a query: "How would you describe your heartbeat while you communicated with the bird?"

The question was digressive, drawing attention to the questioner's area of expertise, and Abraham was annoyed. Nonetheless, he replied politely. The neurobiologist, apparently picking up on his irritation, jotted something on a graph. Abraham did a cursory breathing exercise, closing one nostril after the other, to restore calm.

Then the Inuit asked, "Do you recall the between-lives state?"

Abraham felt a sudden hot flush, as if he were caught in some personal, private act. The obsidian slits of the Inuit's eyes pried into the most vital area of his life. For the past year, and especially in recent weeks, Abraham had been obsessed with dreams that he felt sure were replays of a disembodied state. However, initiation committees did not accept dreams as valid memories.

Deciding to risk a fib, Abraham replied weakly, "Yes, I think I recall the in-between state."

"Speak up."

"Yes, Shaman."

"What do you recall?"

Abraham described his dreams of containment as in a bowl, from which he felt himself to be poured out like soup; of his intuition that other beings were about him in the void; of his attempts to keep contact with a being who was dear to him.

The American psychiatrist interrupted to ask if Abraham dreamed a lot and if his 'memories' might in fact be dreams. Why did the doctor question them, Abraham wondered. Was his description aberrant, uncharacteristic of the between-lives state?

"I do dream," Abraham said succinctly, "but not about the between state." This was a lie, but a small one. Still, the neurobiologist noted the galvanic response in Abraham's sweating palm.

"What do you dream of?" the psychiatrist persevered.

"Mostly courses of action I wish I'd taken."

"Ah yes: the substitution-compensation pattern. How are your flying dreams?"

"I spring up, don't flap or ..."

"Very good. I pass to the next examiner."

Abraham felt things were going rather quickly and smoothly. The Bengal swami went straight to an important point: "Do you recall training in the Powers from previous lives?"

"Yes."

"What level did you achieve? The last lap?"

Abraham blushed but produced an evasive answer: "It seems I remained in the first set."

"Why so?"

Abraham squirmed. "I was a slow learner, I guess." He was hedging.

"Verification?" the swami requested of the Algonquian, who closed his eyes to enter a fact-finding trance.

Meanwhile the examination continued. The neurobiologist raised his eyes from the scanners and asked, "Have you taken drugs in this lifetime?"

Were his readings worse than he imagined? "No sir," he said; "I have had only infra-systemic treatments, for minor pains."

"Have you ever been hypnotized?" A physician stared at him piercingly.

"Yes ma'am."

"For what purpose?"

"For anesthetic purposes, the removal of a cyst."

"That will do." The doctor turned to the next examiner, a representative of a new discipline — caste biologics, Abraham guessed.

"Do you know any Technists?"

"Yes. I grew up with Technist friends and neighbors."

"What do you think of their attitudes?"

"Potentially dangerous if carried through — if their theories could be put into action. But the use of technology is inherently cumbersome. It's a halfway measure. They have not progressed beyond the Age of Science, except in the quality of their inventions. Their philosophy is essentially that of pre-Wedding man."

The examiners smiled faintly. His youthful effusion obviously amused them as he had merely paraphrased what every Ahim believed. The neurobiologist was checking his encephalogram. Highly incoherent, Abraham imagined. Weak impulses. A poor show, no doubt.

The Dogon wizard asked suddenly, "Was a soothsayer consulted at your birth?" Abraham nodded and his heart leapt. A trap, he felt, was being devised. "What did this soothsayer tell you?"

"My name, occupations, failures, virtues, relationships."

"I see," the African expert said ironically without moving his lips. Abraham had contrived to convey nothing specific. "Tell me," the wizard pursued, "was this soothsayer accurate regarding your life so far?"

"Yes," Abraham admitted.

"So you have no reason to doubt the psychic's ability to predict your future in this lifetime."

"No."

"Now tell us what was foreseen for your later life."

Abraham's heart leapt again, sending graph needles flicking. He would have to tell the truth. All alarms were flaring. All except the Algonquian in his trance were watching the test equipment.

"She said," Abraham confessed, breathless with chagrin, "that I would be a warrior."

"Speak up," prompted the African.

"A warrior," Abraham repeated.

"But you say you are an Ahim."

"Yes, I am; and as an Ahim I am totally committed to the way of peace — to spiritual and psychic growth. I do not know what she meant. Perhaps it was a metaphor."

"Did she indicate that such was her meaning?"

"No," Abraham had to admit.

"What else did she predict?"

"She said, 'You will befriend a warrior race, but not for generous reasons.'"

"The warrior race has to be the Technists," the Dogon authority surmised, and all nodded. "Unless we are meant to think of a different planet."

The Algonquian came out of trance at this moment and the committee conducted him into another chamber to confer. The hawk feathers adorning his headdress fluttered as he walked. Abraham remained alone with a drink and his anxiety. Would they grill him further on the soothsayer's predictions for his anomalous future as a warrior? On his vague recollections of the in-between state? Would the Algonquian reveal why Abraham failed to master the Powers in his past existence?

Finally the group of sages returned, but did not subject Abraham to any more dreaded interrogations or revelations. They simply asked the final question — which was always the same — and he had prepared an answer. "Why do you now want to learn the Powers?" The Director voiced the query in his quiet way, searching Abraham's face with kind dark eyes.

Abraham gave the speech he had practiced: He was eager to grow; no other undertaking could capture his enthusiasm; only with Powers could he serve the community as he desired. All the usual clichés peppered his speech. But what other valid reasons could anyone ever give to request the Powers? Everyone must say pretty much the same thing, he imagined, even if it was a pile of micro lies. Powers were Powers. Everyone in his right mind — except a Technist, of course — valued them.

However, the examiners seemed to be listening for something beyond the usual prevarications. They scanned the test equipment, seeing from his galvanic response that he knew he was lying. They were not surprised apparently, just listening to see if he would get to the point after all. *What do they want to hear?* he wondered.

"What is your personal reason?" the Inuit probed with his glittering, impersonal gaze.

"I want, I want," Abraham floundered. The Inuit placed Abraham's speech organs under a veracity hold, making them more obedient to his deeper desires than to his superficial ones. Under its spell, his memory grew more accurate as well. Now, divested of the merely correct and altruistic, "I want to search for a beloved being," he confessed with a catatonic slur in his tongue. As the Inuit released his hold, the examining board hummed with comments.

"That is all," said the Director, and hustled Abraham out of the room. "We will call you in four days for the appropriate initiation rite."

5

IN THE TEMPLE OF SOL

THE TEMPLE OF THE SUN glinted, as if expectantly, winking as its many facets caught and magnified the rays of Sol. Inside, the atmosphere proved slightly hotter than outside, pleasant for the spectators to float in — and most did choose to lounge in the upper reaches of the faceted dome, spacing themselves to avoid crowding.

Guests arrived from afar, piping music loud and shrill, the raucous sounds belying the pipers' delicate forms. Dressed in gossamer, they fluted with joyful stridency through long phenamon tubes. Before the ceremony began, they orchestrated an orgy of sound and motion both on the ground and throughout the inverted cup of the temple dome.

The whole menden — a community of about a hundred beings — was gathered this day for the public Naming Ceremony. Many of them brought gifts, always something of their own making. Most are related through past lives but do not give much importance to the connections. As the cavalcade of former Earth beings swept over the mossy plain to the temple, creatures endemic to Xarbo emerged from their dwellings to marvel. Most of these species have long mobile tendrils that they can raise and puff up to shield them from the sudden night cold. Now the tendrils were at rest, sleekly hanging and trailing on the ground like vestments. The former humans shouted with delight to see the little karuners and palanthins. Slightly larger dandons, like Afghan hounds, greeted them with the sounds understood by all species on the planet.

As the naturally robed creatures watched, the throng of celebrants increased. The farther they progressed, the louder they trilled their music and the higher they sprang into the air. Bright bristling hair flashed like pyrotechnic bursts. Karuners, palanthins, and dandons followed the antics in amazement. The young men, especially, loved to exhibit special powers, or xenas Their sudden odd moves startled the others, who accepted the pranks with good humor, although ordinarily they would disapprove of exhibitionism.

The temple filled with celebrants, still piping full blast; the sounds echoed from its inner facets with ear-dinning shrillness. The piping diminished only when the honored one arrived. They scrutinized her for physical traits that might reveal something of who she had been on Earth. Former white humans had the most translucent flesh. African heritage manifested in spiraling twists of the hair. Former Asians retained epicanthic eyelid folds.

The young person whose name was to be revealed that day was marked, very faintly, with a rash of freckles on her upper limbs. They were already slightly iridescent and would be multi-colored like the stippling on a trout's flanks by the time she reached adolescence. As she entered the temple a space was cleared in the area directly under the dome for her with her mother and zildings. There they poised like hummingbirds while the crowd uttered joyous hoots.

The pipes subsided but the atmosphere simmered until the Clairvoyant sailed up to the little group around the honored small one. This psychic was clad in a tight-fitting dark robe to symbolize the mysteries to which she is privy. By tradition she should utter positive generalities about the youngster's future. Her solemn expression, however, hinted that she held no such intention. She waited until the dome was completely still, then spoke solemnly: "The young one before me, I feel bound to predict, will encounter an unforeseen influence from her past that will wrench her from her chosen path. I see much turmoil ahead for her. More precise I cannot be. Her zildings will struggle to guide her through many unexpected pitfalls. She is strong, but let there be no doubt: She will be sorely tested."

The Clairvoyant's words fell heavily in the silence that pervaded the dome. The young celebrant looked uneasily from one mentor to another, but none could clarify what might await her in the uncertain future. There was nothing to do but move on with the ceremony.

Shortly, Mother Zalda pronounced her daughter's name. She said it very softly to the zilding nearest to her, and the zilding passed it on to another without ceasing to repeat it, then on to everyone in the dome. Gradually the name gained volume as more participants uttered it, associating it as they did so with the girl's qualities. "Altherin, Altherin, Altherin," voices sighed through the temple with the soft sound of harps or bells where before the shrill pipes rang. The name curled its way throughout the temple, circulating and echoing and turning back on itself like a serpent of sound, a dragon of air made by Xarbian breath infused with good wishes. Afterward, everyone would remember her name and call her often by it, for by being named and named again she would develop the whole spectrum of qualities inherent in xaltherin: rainbow, harmony, and wholeness. Surely, well-wishers assured her, if anyone could outface difficulties, it would be one with such a name.

Eventually everyone drifted away, leaving their gifts piled in the center of the temple. After Mother Zalda left, only one zilding remained, a young female with rather large yavers, which flashed when she smiled like a mouth full of opals. She introduced herself: "I am Mother Melda. I will be your first teacher. I have registered your tone and can tell you something about yourself if you wish, while we walk outside."

"Oh yes," cried Altherin urgently, with a small frown uncharacteristic of her species.

"I am not a great Clairvoyant like the officiant who forecast your difficult future."

"What can you tell me? I am grateful for your help."

"My gift is to look into the past. This is usually a fruitless exercise — but hopefully it will yield insights to help you face coming conflicts."

"Please!"

"I see that you have lived many times before and have excelled in most of your undertakings. Generally, things come easily to you; you pick up new skills quickly, and you have often had beauty to your advantage. However, you grew suspicious of achievements that came too easily and therefore were timid to progress as far as you might have. Also, you have often waited for a loved one to catch up. Thus you became an expert in self-discipline, almost austere in others' eyes. Here on Xarbo, you refrain from breathing as deeply as you might of this elixir that is our air, this xaltherin. Do you think I am right?"

Altherin listened with bowed head and closed eyes, reflecting on all that Mother Melda said. "Yes; I think you have seen me truly," she said.

"And you are reflective, a natural self-analyzer. An unusual trait on Xarbo."

"Must I overcome this tendency?"

"In time you will." The young woman put a warm hand on the girl's dappled shoulders. "But do not try to do so by discipline. You must learn to trust instinct. Do not hold yourself back. The true way is not to mistrust reason, but to strengthen intuition."

"How can I do that, Mother Melda?"

The zilding smiled. Her charge had already made progress, asked an open question with no presuppositions. "That is a good question, Altherin. The way is to first learn what your instincts are. You can begin by finding out if you want to be a celibate — a sintor — or choose a mate. The tests for that depend on your immediate reactions, your senses and feelings. What do you think of the idea?"

"I know nothing about these tests. But I can tell from xarping that you are using your xenas to help me. I would be silly to object."

"Xarping, child? Now this betrays some tendency to take charge of matters beyond your scope. Beware of trying to control too much. Channel attention to the areas in which you need most to evolve. Remember that things go very fast on Xarbo."

Altherin felt the rebuke coursing through her veins like a tonic, stinging but also bolstering. Here was wisdom on which she could rely.

"Let's see how well you are doing in your exercises, Altherin. Let's see some xenas."

Altherin seized the cue and showed her zilding how well she could fly, with no false muscle-twitching or hopping, or even a grimace. She shot up effortlessly and sported among the brown mogdon leaves twenty meters off the ground. Then she sought out the blooms in their hideouts among the folded leathery leaves and plucked one from its stalk to bring down and present to her mentor.

"Very good, Altherin. Now tell me something you can 'see.' "

Altherin closed her eyes and shortly began to speak in a soft sluggish voice, describing haltingly but with attention to detail a menden that was located far beyond the horizon. She described the dwellings and their inhabitants, their idiosyncrasies and racial traces. She depicted the great forest that towered near it, and the little expedition that was heading out of the community for a day of adventure.

"You 'see' very well, Altherin, but do not trust your vision quite enough. Now show me whom you can contact."

Altherin closed her eyes and made faint guttural sounds that went out in all directions, traveling far in the clear atmosphere, and reached the ears of those for whom they were intended — two winged creatures who came to Altherin as if reporting for duty. The tiny minglin brushed her thistledown hair with its purple hairy wings, and the giant kragil circled slowly, as if not wanting to frighten her, but finally glided to a halt, its huge pinions titling, its toes like jaspers kicking up mossy spores. Altherin uttered a few reassuring sounds to her two visitors, looked at Melda questioningly and, with her consent, dismissed them.

As a final exercise, Altherin concentrated her attention on the moss-like growth under their feet and, although it had shown no signs of blooming, it quickly opened its tiny interstices and out popped minute flowers, covering the immediate area with a mat of white. Altherin was so delighted that for a moment she forgot the purpose of her demonstrations and rolled ecstatically on the fragrant fleece. Melda smiled widely, her yavers reflecting rainbow light.

"You have done very well, Altherin. Come here, dear. Now I must tell you something you are to remember. You must never give a demonstration of your xenas like this except for me or another zilding to measure your progress. You will not compare xenas with your companions, nor use them to satisfy curiosity about your abilities. Above all, you will not use them to tease or boast. But I know you would never do that. The xenas must be practiced every day as your instructors bid, but used only for actual needs."

"Yes, Mother Melda," Altherin promised gravely, and they hugged in the Earth-being way.

"Soon," said Melda, "you will begin some games with boys of your age, which I will supervise, to decide if you wish to be mated or a sintor. Prepare well. The games are taxing; you will need full alertness. All your senses will come into play, so learn well from all your teachers. Childhood will pass very fast here on Xarbo. If your progress is good, you will enter the games at an early age."

The small one thanked her mentor and turned quickly to go before the guide could detect the worry that creased her forehead.

6

THE TECHNIST

A S ABRAHAM LEFT the examining room he felt a bit lightheaded. The veracity hold that the Inuit had put on his larynx and mouth was still causing a slight numbness, while every impulse of thought pressed to be verbalized. He looked back at the antique building where the examination took place and thought: *Peculiar old pile. What Technist self-delusion to construct whole cities of concrete, steel, and glass! Droll to call these airless boxes efficient. But they're classics now, in their bleakness.*

Abraham decided to take the long route home through hanging gardens. As he reached a second level on an arching bridge bedecked with jasteria, he heard a buzz just over the edge of the bridge, as if a swarm of giant blue-bottle flies were descending on a feast.

"Ahim!" a voice called, vaguely recognizable although amplified. Abraham looked around to see if other Ahims were within earshot. It was the hour when most were at home practicing the Powers, and when Technists sometimes went afield in their machines — to jolt Ahims from their practices, it was suspected.

"Rollo the Technist," Abraham responded, conjuring what enthusiasm he could.

Rollo sidled his helimonopter to a position parallel with Abraham. *Only a Technist would talk while juddering in such a contraption*, Abraham almost blurted aloud with the truth-telling hold still affecting his speech organs.

"Where been?" Rollo blared over the *bla-blat* of his heli-blades.

Abraham avoided a direct answer. "Haven't seen you since Hawking Mall," he yelled above the roar.

"What a neighborhood, eh? Half the Ahims converted to Technists, half the Technists gone Ahim."

Abraham cringed to hear the commonplaces crackling over the loudspeaker. He turned to deviate from his old neighbor's trajectory, but the Technist veered to dog his steps, just clearing bridges with his blades, keeping a few meters above Abraham's right shoulder. Finally, the Technist landed his machine on a pedestal, slid down the chute, and bounced to a halt a few meters from Abraham. He was wearing old-fashioned plasti-fiber gloves although the evening was warm. Like most of his caste, he disliked unnecessary touching, yet he placed his gloved hand on Abraham's chest in the somewhat outworn gesture Ahims preserved for especially intimate friends. Such a greeting from a bare acquaintance, and with plasti-fiber gloves! Abraham's revulsion rose in his throat, pressuring to be expressed.

"Some gloves you have," he said carefully, neutrally.

Rollo did not respond to the ambiguity. He stood barring Abraham's way expectantly. His expression was typical of his kind when confronting Ahims: a peculiar combination of condescension and curiosity. Abraham wanted to say, *Take that silly smirk off your face. I am not going to spill any Ahim Power secrets. And don't look so superior either, because we do have secrets worth spilling.* But he did not say anything, and refrained also from pushing the smaller man aside. He recalled a counselor's telling him, "The best way to deal with Technists is to humor them a bit; then they will move on."

After all, this was an old playmate for whom Abraham retained some fondness. He said, "Well, Rollo, what have you been up to?"

"I service test equipment for Ahim initiation exams."

Abraham's mind shot back to the exam whose outcome he would not know for a few days. To Rollo he exclaimed jocularly, "Working with Ahims and not converted yet!"

"Say," said the other suddenly, "why don't you come over to my place? I've got a new focuser. I'd really like you to try it."

Abraham took a step backward in spite of himself. "You belong on Clone Island. You really do, Rollo."

"Forget the teasing and tell me honestly: Have you ever tried a focuser?" Abraham shook his head. "Ever seen one?" Again, a shake. "Aren't you even curious? How can you plumb the limits of knowledge and let a chance like this pass by?"

"Limits of knowledge": a catch-phrase among Ahims and central to their pursuit of Powers. Abraham smiled at the obvious bait. Seeing him smile and hesitate, the Technist persevered: "A focuser might just be a shortcut. Why not give it a try? You use galvanic tests, don't you? Encephalograms? Why not a bit of recreational technology? What will you do tonight?" Rollo persisted.

Abraham winced at this straight question and almost blurted the truth: *Replay my exams and worry about them.*

"Will you come with me or not?" This blunt approach suited Abraham better than the sly digs — and he did want to avoid fretting. Maybe it would do him good — and it might be illuminating or even humbling — to visit a Technist at this time of uncertain direction in his life. Maybe he would learn something new by seeing what a Technist does with a focuser.

"All right, Rollo, let's go," he agreed; then added, perhaps for his own assurance, "but I'll just watch."

The little Technist reminded Abraham of how to reach his home and accepted a boost up to his 'monopter. "See you there in ten minutes?"

"An hour," corrected Abraham.

"What," said the other in mock surprise, "you don't fly yet?"

"No."

"Not even levitate?"

"Just waiting for the training."

The Technist grinned smugly, shaking his head in mock pity. Abraham contained himself, but as Rollo buzzed off he thought: *You'll smile on the other side of your mouth when you find me sailing over you and through you.*

As Abraham walked beyond the center of the city and entered the Technist suburb, he began to see many helimonopters parked on the roofs, like giant dragonflies. An electronic hum pervaded the atmosphere, and sometimes the muffled sound of electronic music, which Technists had revived from the twentieth century. To close off the inner ear, mused Abraham, and with it the inner resources. In fact, Technists chose to view Ahim Powers as a return to primitive shamanic practices. If these should succeed, the balance of control would fall into Ahim hands.

Abraham glanced about with pleasure as he came up to Rollo's home. The entrance was a long archway of plants interlaced at the top so artfully that one could discern no support or evidence of pruning. Counterbalancing the symmetry of the arch, irregular stones paved the pathway and small shade-loving flowers poked their faces from between the cracks. It was a cool and fragrant tunnel that greeted guests.

"Well, well," Rollo boomed over his loudspeaker, in formal flyting style, "welcome to my well and wickiup. 'Tis true you traipse through the tunnel trail? I hoped to hear you hailing from high without heli."

"Soon you'll see me sail with psychic ciphers, eschewed by self-righteous scions of science."

"Veritably you verse. Yet venerable vestiges of verbal vehicles, victims of time, these flytings were first refurbished by our fathers as friendly fits to fire between us."

Rollo was referring to the ancient oral tradition called flyting in northern Europe but used also by Inuits as well as Italian and Spanish folk singers. Restored to common use by Technist sociologists, it is the ideal format for good-natured bantering, allowing both sides to exorcise hostility. Flyting is an extremely formalized argument requiring the use of alliteration. No one can make a fist while searching for same-sounds to start every word.

Rollo ushered Abraham into his sipping salon and offered a drink from a large built-in mixer with over a hundred choices. They sat on low meta-plastic nubs in shades of rust, which seemed to sprout like shiny mushrooms among thick foliage and flowers, while Abraham dictated half a dozen flavors and Rollo programmed their codes.

"Shall we relax our bombardments?" Rollo offered, rubbing his plasti-glass on Abraham's by way of toasting. Abraham nodded.

"Must say," he admitted, "you have a beautiful place here. Great garden."

"Thanks. I got some ideas from our old neighborhood. How old were you when you left Hawking?" Rollo leaned forward between spread knees.

Abraham sprawled back in the tangle of plants, sipping his drink, and reminisced with ease. The room was well aerated, insulated from electronic buzzes, and exuded an exquisite odor. He recalled how his family had moved out of the mixed-caste neighborhood called Hawking. "I must have been about ten." He smiled. "My parents didn't want me to become addicted to Technist gadgets." Rollo laughed pleasantly. *Really a good egg*, Abraham admitted to himself.

As courtesy demanded, the Technist made a counter-admission: "You may not have heard this before, but my grandfather was an Ahim."

"Really? And was he the only convert in your family?"

"Yes. He started as a historian. Not a highly technical field anyway."

"And what made him turn Ahim?"

"I heard it was for love of my grandmother — Althea, a lovely Ahim lady, they say. Of course I never knew her. She and Grandpa Adam died young. My father was only fifteen himself when Grandpa passed on."

Abraham felt an inexplicable agitation, and a quickened curiosity. In his excitement he scraped some dirt from a planter into his drink. He sat up. "Why did your father not remain Ahim? What made him de-convert?"

Rollo took the sullied drink from his visitor as he spoke: "Papa thinks his dad was not a real convert, that it was all for love of my Grandma Althea that Grandpa Adam tried for the Powers. Nothing came of it anyway. So Papa was skeptical about the Powers, says he wanted a more practical lifestyle for his own children."

It would be bad manners to persevere on such a touchy subject without the formality of flyting. Rollo fell silent as he pulled a portable anti-entropy device from a cubicle and set Abraham's drink under its grid. Abraham watched the dirt coagulate and fly to the top, where Rollo removed it with a simple spoon and launched a farcical discourse on the merits of technology: "Experiments with entropy entail extraordinary effects. Parcel into parts and purify; purgation then is possible." He laughed as he held up Abraham's drink, in which the six flavors were lined up in a spectrum, and took it to the mixer before handing it back.

"Kind you are," said Abraham, "to clean and reconstitute my cooler. But a caveat I would convey where molecular recombination is concerned. Manipulation of man-cells made monsters in the morning of genetic mechanics. Lacking caution, chemists concocted creatures not conversant with Consciousness, conscienceless clones: inhabitants of islands inimical to innocence."

"Consciousness knows if the clones will commit a comeback," parried Rollo jokingly. "As specialists, super-keen on single subjects, such servants should save us some sweat."

"Trying to tell me in truth that test-tube clones make truest Technists?"

Rollo took the thrust with good humor and laughed aloud. With deliberate gesture, he clapped Abraham on the arm but, unable to disguise his distaste for the physical contact, quickly withdrew his hand.

"I can't believe you'd object to a few automatons as servants, if it were allowed," said Rollo. "I remember you as a boy. You had a lot of tricks to make the rest of us work for you. You had us all running errands. You pretended to be inept and everyone stepped in to save you. Especially Technist boys; we rushed in with labor-saving devices, thinking we'd convert you if you saw how efficient we were. How gullible! You just reaped the benefits and went your way."

Abraham winced at the memory and had to credit his companion with insight. "I don't make a very good Ahim, I admit. I shouldn't be so greedy for immediate gratification."

Rollo dropped the topic and simply said, "Let me show you my setup here and then we can go to the play-tech room and have a session with the focuser."

Abraham agreed and followed his host through a relaxer room. With glee Rollo made him stand close to the wall and close his eyes. Abraham obeyed and felt himself being gently whisked off his feet to lie prone on a table. With a slight electronic whizz, a lever laid a steaming hot towel on his shoulders. He relaxed and let the flexo-massager work on his shoulder and thigh muscles. "It is programmed to feel out the tense spots," Rollo explained.

When the flexors retracted after fifteen minutes, Abraham peeled himself off the table, limp and grinning with pleasure. Rollo laughed, "I can't believe you want to take on those long-range Ahim goals. How can a sensualist like you postpone gratification?"

Abraham felt too good to argue. He just said, "And what do you do without an Ahim like me to amuse you?"

The two youths were laughing with camaraderie as they entered the holocast cubicle. A man in his prime was watching a newscast intently, impatiently waving a control wand to make the holographic image rotate. He obviously wanted to catch a certain angle before the image changed and was annoyed to be interrupted. Then amazement took over as he saw that Rollo was practically embracing the youth with him. "Perhaps you remember my father, Alther." The man nodded curtly and turned his attention again to the hologram. Under the mask of desire and disillusion, characteristic of Technists, in this one Abraham sensed something else that he could not quite identify: a sort of childish gleam that was vaguely familiar.

"How old is your father?" he asked Rollo when they were in the tunnel out of earshot of the holocast room.

"Thirty-five. He was nineteen when I was born."

Abraham was shocked, for both Rollo and Alther looked at least ten years older than they were. Rollo was actually four years Abraham's junior. *The Technist way*, he recalled, *takes a toll despite its innumerable labor-saving gadgets*. Abraham, however, could not regard Technists with the detached irony of his caste. He had grown up with them. He liked them. He felt sorry for Rollo with his impeccable hospitality and naive pride in gadgetry, his suspicion that Ahims covet them. Rollo was too polite to say so directly, and Abraham was too compassionate to disillusion him.

"Now let's go to the play-tech room," said Rollo, with a hint that even greater wonders would be revealed there.

7

ALTHERIN'S TRIALS

MOTHER MELDA, Altherin's most clairvoyant mentor, entered the youngster's dwelling through the roof, and egg mother Zalda departed before the roof material had a chance to reform.

"Today for the games you will wear this special garment," said Melda, and held out a smoothly fitting tunic and pants combination.

"But I'll look like a dandon in this," the debutante objected, "with these tendrils flapping around me!"

"The tendrils are special conductors. They will help you to sense the qualities and characters of the males who come near you during the games."

"So I will have more fun if I have these flaps?"

"Remember that, although you may enjoy the interactions, they are trials to help decide if you should be single — sintor — or seek a mate."

"But why do I have to wear this costume? Is it a ceremonial robe?"

"No. You wear the costume as an extension of your skin, just as the outdoors creatures use their long hairs to better test their environs. Except that the costume will not keep you warm. So don't forget to come in at night."

Mollified, Altherin laughed in delight at the prospect of cavorting with new companions and pretending to be another kind of creature. It appealed to her as a hilarious play with her in an amusing role. She held Melda's hand as the two levitated out of the dwelling. They headed quickly for a nearby garden where the trials were to take place.

When Melda signaled that they had arrived at the testing grounds, Altherin landed by her side. "First," explained the zilding, "we will merely look on so you can see how the games are conducted. I will explain what is involved. When you know enough, you will leave me and join the other youths. They are all dinzils of mine; in other words, I am their zilding too."

Altherin saw that six or seven male figures and as many females, all dressed in creature costumes, moved deliberately around the garden, engaged in a ritual dance of acquaintance. The male characters moved up to each female in turn with a slight swooping motion that caused the tendrils of their costumes to sway toward her. Then they stepped apart and both stayed musing for a few moments.

"They are savoring the feel of each partner," Melda explained. "Soon I will call them over and ask for their impressions." Altherin watched as the dance continued and each female was approached by the same male at least two or three times. Then Melda made a signal and they all came to sit at her feet. "What do you have to say about Zorath, Grilda?"

"He is strong like a phenamon branch," replied the slim costumed figure, and everyone tittered — except young Zorath, who looked half pleased and partly embarrassed.

"And Growald?" she again addressed the frail Grilda.

"He is secretive, like moss that closes as the sun goes down."

"And Zorath, what have you to say about big Belina?"

"She is quick and nimble. She sometimes seems to fumble, but her mind is all synapse, all alertness; it shifts like a flitterben on the wing."

"Very good. Now I want you to continue the dance and include Altherin here. She too is my dinzil. When I call you again I will ask for your deepest impressions. After that you may choose partners with whom to spend time alone, if you wish. But remember that this is not required. You are young; you have many dances ahead of you. Some of you will discover that you are meant to be sintor. So enjoy, relax, and get to know each other fully."

Altherin soon picked up the light swaying rhythm of the dance, which remained grounded, for the land was a good conductor for interpersonal communications. She could feel a current conveying the qualities of each partner through the bottom of her feet. A rather stolid personality would slap her flatly on the soles as when she landed quickly after flying. A nervous boy seemed almost to sting her with vibrations of high frequency. As she became accustomed to the motions, she began to take in more and subtler impressions. Not only the ground was conducting waves of information; also the tendrils of the costume vibrated with diverse messages. The youth who at first seemed stolid produced a very pleasurable effect through the coat of tendrils she was wearing; he could caress the whole pelt at once with calm attention. But there was no time to linger with an individual. The purpose of the dance was acquaintance and comparison. She must come to recognize the variety of ways in which males express themselves and decide if she was inclined to become more intimate with any of them.

In fact, one youth stood out from all the others. Each time he drew near, he did not seem to cast an impression her way but rather drew her out of herself. She could feel her own strong and delicate essence flowing toward him and could sense his appreciation of it. She was pleased and flattered to see what a powerful sensation she produced in this somewhat older youth. Later, when Melda interrogated her pupils, Altherin expressed her reactions to him with much enthusiasm. "Like a zilding," she stammered, "if ... if a zilding could be so young."

"And you, Waldin, what do you say about Altherin?"

"She makes me feel warm and strong. With her I am myself, but more so. I feel at home with her."

"Do you want to spend time Alone Together?"

The two young ones eyed each other gravely. Waldin agreed almost immediately. Altherin was not sure what Being Alone Together involved, but her instinct was to go towards those who appreciated or needed her. She was courageous and adventurous. She agreed.

"Waldin has spent time alone with partners before, so he knows the instructions. I will not repeat them, but let him teach you. Remember that you may break off the progress at any point. But you must come to me and report what has happened. Above all, do not progress beyond where your instincts direct you."

The two withdrew to a little grove. Two other couples were moving off in separate directions. Most of the group did not form couples, and the disbanded individuals returned to their homes. Altherin and Waldin walked silently for a while. Then he began the instruction. "There are five stages to Being Alone Together," he said. "It is important that if one of us feels bored or uncomfortable that we say so, and then we stop and part without bad feelings." Altherin felt a thrill of anticipation shivering like the first rays of Sol on her torso. "The first three stages are exchanges," he continued. "Do you want to hear them all first, or just one at a time as we go along?"

"Which is better?"

"I took them one at a time when I started. That way you aren't thinking ahead."

"All right. Tell me one at a time."

"First stage is exchange of gifts. We should make something that tells what we see in the other."

Altherin was delighted with the prospect. She used her innate intuition to xarp Waldin for a few minutes and configured what her gift should be. She chose a fallen mogdon branch to work with. Using xenas, she quickly made its molecules obedient to her designs: an object sculptured so all surfaces were smooth and rounded, a form slightly concave, emblem of receptivity, yet green and strong for youth and virility. She liked her companion. Even if she did not go through all the stages with him, she felt sure that she would find a mate and not be sintor, and it was all coming so easily.

Waldin had not completed his gift when she finished hers, so she stretched out on the mossy ground to wait for him. She closed her eyes and listened to the muffled sounds of foraging karuners and the distant harsh notes of a kragil. She did not hear Waldin as he approached. He had made a colorful toy for her by reconstituting a dry leaf and animating it with his powers so it flew about at his will like a colorful flitterben. He made it brush the little droplets at the ends of her hair. When she opened her eyes she saw the light shining through it and for a moment thought she was seeing a new species that was truly alive. She gave the shrill Xarbian whoop of glee and was about to hug Waldin in the Earth-being way, but he forestalled her. "Holding is for a later stage," he said. But she could see he was happy that his gift gave her pleasure.

"The next stage," he said, "is word-exchange. The best way to start is to tell each other why we chose the gifts we did."

Altherin gave him her sculpture and told him what it symbolized. He turned it about in his hands and said he was glad she saw him as receptive yet manly. He told her why he made the gaily flying toy: "You are beautiful and full of motion. You are very changeable, a bit nervous, as if you are afraid to stop and breathe deeply — so you flutter from one thing to another."

Altherin was pleased that he understood her so well from such short contact, although his vision of her was not altogether flattering. On the one hand, she felt that she need not try to hide anything from him; on the other hand, a little doubt crept in concerning his courtship. She cherished the idea of a partner who admired her wholly, and Waldin had sensed her deficiencies.

The word-exchange continued with the two telling each other simple, heartfelt things: what they liked, disliked; their happiest moment; their greatest fear.

"I like the phenamon leaves," said Altherin, "when they are folded so tightly you can just barely see the flowers bundled up inside. I like that feeling of secrecy and fullness hidden away inside the strong leaves."

"Oh, I like them best when they have matured and float down off the trees like great beings with wings spread out; and against the light you can see every vein and every secret revealed."

"I hate the night when Mother is at rest and I must be quiet but I cannot sleep and I imagine the dreadful cold and my skin creeps with thinking of it and I know the giant winged kragil is hunting the little karuner. Although I can hear nothing from inside the walls, I know that outside there is a savage Xarbo consuming itself — one member consuming another. And I know we were like that too one time when we lived on Earth and ate its animals and plants. Sometimes I dream a bad dream, that I have to go to live on Earth again because I fail to reach Completion."

Waldin touched her arm sympathetically. He gently rubbed the light freckling of her shoulders, and a few iridescent scales shone on his hands.

"Your skin smells like pollen," said Waldin.

"Why did you touch me?"

"The next stage is touch exchange. Do you want to go on?"

Altherin had appreciated the sympathy of his touch. If touching meant giving of comfort, she wanted it. However, she sensed that it involved more, which she was probably not prepared for. More what? She had no way of knowing but had picked up a hint of a need that he felt and she didn't, a need that he might press on her and she would not be able to fulfill. Yet she did not want to reject a person who wanted her. So she said "yes" with half a heart.

Soon the young male's hands were gliding everywhere over her smooth iridescent skin and sweeping back her hair so it sprang and quivered like quills. Altherin could sense that the touch of her body had a unique effect on his metabolism, which was soaring, although he was not engaged in strenuous movements. It puzzled and unnerved her, aware that the effect was produced by her although she did not intend it. She tried touching him on his shoulders and around the face. She did not care much for the sensation, but he became ecstatic at the slightest touch of her fingertips.

"Beautiful Altherin," he breathed, "soon we will reach the final phase of Being Alone Together. No girl has come to me as fully as you have. I cannot begin to say what you now cause me to feel. But you must share it or you would not be still here."

Altherin was about to break away and admit that she did not share his feeling, but suddenly it was too late. Now Waldin was rapt in a trance, and rising from the position by her side. She had heard about the frenzy of courtship dances and tittered about it with other girls who spied on lovers. But nothing had prepared her for the intensity of the sight.

Waldin, who earlier that day seemed so calm and almost passive, was suddenly in a pitch of Xarbian frenzy, emitting involuntary cries of great shrillness. His whole body seemed crammed with an emotion that carried him about of its own volition. His passion escaped him in shouts and shrieks, and pitched his body into a whirling dance, both on the ground and above it. Altherin found the dance graceful despite its frenetic stops and starts, but felt ashamed to be watching as a spectator. Panic gripped her. She had no right to be there and witness his passion without sharing it. She had wronged him, had failed her test. She should have pulled away at the first inkling of a doubt. Now she did not know what she should do. If there was one more stage after this, it must be still more intense, and more demanding of her. She quivered with fear and guilt. Waldin was oblivious to her condition, involved confidently in his trance and spinning ecstatically toward the final stage of Being Alone Together.

She quivered uncontrollably and felt a pressure behind her eyes. No tears formed, for Xarbians never weep, but she remembered vaguely a similar experience from benighted lifetimes on Earth. With wobbling legs and stinging eyes, she fled from the grove, leaving her companion twirling in the air, ignorant in his joy, spinning under the leathery folded leaves that drooped as if to mantle him in their wings and hide his shame.

Altherin ran, unseeing. The unaccustomed dry sobs weakened and exhausted her. She tried to levitate and go to hide herself in the giant leaves overhead but discovered that in her distraught state she was incapable of engaging the necessary xena except to hop jerkily up and down. The landings jarred her so much that she abandoned the efforts and crawled into a crevice, perhaps the home of a dandon, where she hid her face in her arms, shuddering until she dozed off.

She awoke to the sensation of someone xarping her — a person who cared for her. Who was it? Perhaps Mother Zalda or Mother Melda was trying to awaken her telepathically. She jumped up quickly and saw that Sol was reddening the horizon's rim. She could not see its orb for the phenamons, but knew that it must be very low. Panic gripped her once more. She knew things happen very fast on Xarbo, but wondered: *Must I die for my mistake? Is it that serious?*

Altherin ran and hopped as fast as she could toward the menden, but her unstable state of mind made her run off course and lose her way in groves and gardens with no sign of dwellings; she could sense the call that xarped her as a faint signal that she could not locate. It blurred and spread and seemed to surround her. It was full of solicitude and encouragement, but she could not localize it.

Perhaps it is the final blessing that will send me into my next life, she thought in desperation. And as she ran she imagined how it would be to die and pass on to the in-between state and have to choose some other place in which to live. She rebelled at the thought of exile from Xarbo, knowing that she would not have another chance to take form on this planet. *It is unfair,* she thought, for she had not committed her folly in malice. *I don't want to die,* she groaned inwardly as she came to a clearing and the last red sliver of Sol sank behind a distant grove and the chill came down out of the empty sky.

8

FOCUSING

"SO, YOU'VE NEVER used a focuser?" Rollo asked, amazed. "Actually it's considered taboo for us Ahims. I'm not sure why. What is it, exactly?"

"You might think of it as a device to give you instant enlightenment, an apparatus that creates coherent brainwaves. Through sympathetic response, the brain transitions into super-coherence, which permits focusing or extreme powers of concentration. You see microscopically; or in multiplicity, like a spider; or empathetically; or any way you want."

With a flourish the young Technist pressed on a drawer front, causing an instrument to be propelled forward as if offered on a platter. Watching for his friend's reaction, Rollo grabbed the gadget, a simple circlet of hard translucent plastifiber in which minuscule metallic chips were embedded. These flashed subtly, apparently activated by his touch. As Rollo encircled his head with the flashing crown, he turned to Abraham with bright eyes: "Have you ever seen a plant think? Observed cells deciding to divide?"

Then he stared at his friend with penetrating intensity and remarked, "Your eyeballs are contracted due to wariness. Your skin is pinched in patches, colder where tensions keep blood from entering some capillaries."

"Sounds like infra-red camera work," Abraham essayed.

"Yep. The focuser is a multi-tasker. You don't need cameras, microscopes, infra-organism imaging. You capture it all with one device."

"But it tampers with your faculties."

"Yep. Enhances them, that is. Want to see some molecules? I've got some tongue scrapings here."

Abraham hesitated but thought: *Seeing like a microscope can't be too dangerous.*

Rollo pressed another drawer front, extracted another plastifiber ring, and adjusted it on his friend's head. Abraham waited tensely. At first nothing seemed to happen. "I guess my brain is too incoherent for a focuser to fix," he remarked, preparing to take off the apparatus, rather relieved. But Rollo pressed an almost imperceptible button at the rear of the ring and suddenly power coursed through Abraham's brain. "Whoa," he cried. "My head's taking off like a helimonopter! What did you do?"

"Just ramped it up to 'extra surge' to blast through your resistance."

Overwhelmed, Abraham forgot to peer into the vial containing molecules in suspension. He was caught up in observing his own synapses, which were snapping perfectly, without effort, like hits at the electronic arcade. Then he noted other functions working in harmony with the nerve connections: blood bringing in chemicals, his breath feeding air to the blood, his heart conducting the whole cycle. He lost all sense of being an observer. He was the heartbeat, the chemical exchange, the firings between dendrites. Momentarily apprehension intruded, made him stand back and question what he was doing. Then again he became engrossed in his functions. *I'm losing myself again, just heartbeat now. But wait, what if I fail to focus? What then? Or if I focus unclearly, jumble the beats, or go too slow or too fast?*

Panic spread like corrosive acid in Abraham's divided mind. He could almost feel his fear infecting the nerves, like an outbreak of herpes zoster burning the circuits. Worst of all, although he knew he normally did not control his autonomic functions, now he identified with them so closely he had the illusion of managing them. He began to hyperventilate, obsessed with the task of focusing, lest a lapse in concentration should result in a malfunction in heart, lung, or brain. Tension phased into spasms, spasms into convulsions.

Seeing Abraham judder, Rollo snatched the focuser off his friend's head. "You're short-circuiting!" he yelled. "What were you thinking?" Angry and fearful, he ran to an intercom outlet to summon his father.

"What's up, Rollo?" Alther asked as he rushed in. "You interrupted me in the middle of re-programming some equipment."

"I wanted Abraham to sample Technist efficiency. I just put a focuser on him and he went haywire. Don't know what he was trying to do. Didn't even look at the vial of molecules I showed him. His eyes rolled up and now he's lying there like a ..."

"I see him. Looks sort of familiar. Who is this boy?"

"Used to be a neighbor."

"Looks more like family."

Alther plucked a first aid kit off the wall and selected a finger-shaped object, which he pointed at Abraham's temple. It was a brainwave coordinator, engineered for just such emergencies. Alther jolted Abraham with a small voltage from the instrument and the young man slowly came to, shaking his head as if to dislodge an irritant.

"Where were you?" Rollo demanded.

"Not sure," Abraham mumbled. "Hard to say. Maybe the in-between state."

"What's that?" Rollo was alarmed.

Alther interjected, "It's the continued state of consciousness that Ahims believe they experience after the body dies."

"Holy Heisenberg! You mean I almost killed him?"

"I doubt it. But these Ahims are engrossed with the psyche. They catalogue every state of consciousness."

"How do you know so much about them?" Rollo felt Abraham's pulse, peered under his eyelids, while questioning his father.

Alther replied, recollecting, "Your grandfather Adam was like that, always talking to my mother Althea about how he felt, as if he was responsible for it — or wanted her to approve of it."

As Abraham lay in quasi comatose repose, he registered Alther's voice at a subliminal level, where it struck him as unaccountably intimate. The words 'in-between state' crackled in his hyper-stimulated brain like a spark in a smoky room. And the term induced a vivid sense of pursuit: a longed-for figure, a sensation of longing, in a place where no forms existed. He marveled that he could have a memory of a situation without sense impressions. Yet the sense of that 'place' was more real than anything he had ever experienced. It was the place of pure passions. For an instant he glimpsed the object of his desires: Althea, a presence at once regal and welcoming. Hearing her name pronounced had brought back a blur of endearing images, of lithe arms reaching out to him, of soft hair swirling.

With these perceptions, Abraham fell into a deep sleep. Rollo and Alther put him to bed and left him with piped-in fragrances to soothe his slumbers. In fact, Abraham did not dream but awoke with a sense of foreboding and regret. He was perplexed by his sortie into the in-between state and his vague recognition of a beloved individual whom he sought. From Alther's remarks he could deduce who she was. It was bizarre that she should be Rollo's grandmother, and that he must have been her husband, Adam. He had no recollection of that family life except for some vague recognition of Alther — their son! Now he knew why Ahim counselors discouraged delving into one's previous lives. It was most confusing. In the present incarnation, he had no blood tie to Alther and Rollo, but they were closer now than any of his family: joined to him through his connection to Althea. Despite the panic attack and probable damage done by the focuser, he had made a step toward understanding his current purpose: to gain Powers that might allow him to connect with his beloved Althea.

Yes, the Technist appliances had some virtues. The focuser enhanced his perception. Actually, too much. It made him tune in to the doings of nerves, veins, heart and lungs: functions best left autonomic, unconscious. Now he knew why synthetic devices such as focusers were dangerous. More than ever he yearned to be initiated into the true, safe Ahim practices. He needed them. No woman could capture his interest. He was virgin in thought and body. Only that elusive beloved one of his past life could draw him. The only way to find her again was to acquire the Powers. But how, he wondered, would he convince his examiners to initiate him? Could he bolster his bruised psyche enough that they could not uncover his caper with the focuser? He had only a few hours to clear his mind with meditation and decide how truthful he should be during the most important test of his life.

9

NIGHT OF XARBO

Altherin crouched shivering in the suddenly chilly and darkening space. All homes would be moleculocked by now. If she were a Completion, she might have a special skill, a xena, to create shelter on the spot. But if she were a fully developed Completion, she would not have brought on this emergency that necessitated a shelter. It was useless to speculate on theoretical situations. She was who she was, and futile wishing would get her nowhere.

Altherin was about to prepare her mind for death when she remembered one of Mother Zalda's first teachings. "Never stay out after Sol goes down," she warned, "but in case you find yourself in crisis, I will teach you a call that will make the outside creatures take pity on you. They will come to your rescue. They will stop foraging to save your life. But only once can you use this xena. They will not come a second time."

She had to perform the xena immediately, Altherin knew. But she had to perform a mind-calming exercise before she could accurately recollect the sound that would bring the creatures to her. She hoped they were near, within the range of her call. As she calmed her mind, her own temperature dropped and she felt the cold somewhat less. Then, when all was icy silence inside her, she fished for the little cry that she must bring up and out to send for her rescuers. She dipped for it delicately, as with a little silver hook, not wanting to distort or lose it before she could utter it at the proper frequency to be effective. When she caught it, she recognized it at once. Deftly she drew it from the silence and let it pulse in her cheeks as she had seen her mother do when teaching it. Altherin felt deep gratitude to Zalda for this xena as she let her cheeks pulsate with the sound, which she could not hear, for it was lower than the frequency audible to former Earth beings.

A karuner was the first to come. He wobbled toward her with his feathery purple tendrils already half-raised against the cold. She cried out when she saw him, for she had never seen such a creature puffed up and did not recognize him. But then she realized with relief what he was and let him nestle on her lap to warm her vital organs, and she curled herself around him as she continued to send out the soundless cry for help. Soon her back was protected by a dandon, large and lanky by day but now dense and thick as a bear with his tendrils sprouted out around him. Palanthins, chubby in their conical furry quills, hung from her arms. Other tiny species that she did not recognize clung to her toes and knees like tufts. Thus swaddled, Altherin fell from exhaustion into a deep and tranquil sleep.

When she awoke next morning, her furry mantle had melted away into the woods and she found herself sprawled on the tough, firm moss touched by the slanting rays of Sol, already clear of the horizon. With powers restored, she flew home as fast as she could.

She found all her zildings gathered there with Mother Zalda. She wondered if these mentors had formed a search party the day before or if they had come together to pass judgment on her when she returned. Of course they had already xarped her failure with Waldin, but they would ask for her version of what happened. They had been dressed for some ritual, perhaps an aid to her return, but were now disrobing to signify that the encounter with her was not to be a ceremony — not a joyous occasion.

When all stood unclothed together, they first checked Altherin's condition. When they saw she was unharmed, they asked what stage she had reached with Waldin. She told them, and then the thought gripped her: What can have happened to him?

She asked, and a male zilding — Father Grandar — answered: "You will discover his fate when you have learned to care enough to xarp it for yourself."

"Must I die for my transgression? What will become of me? I would have died in the woods if I had not remembered mother's one-time call."

"The effect is always appropriate to the cause. You did not kill. Why should you fear for your life?"

"I never erred before, never incurred the Law of Commensuration."

"This sort of heedlessness is typical of youth, yet unworthy of you, Altherin," Mother Melda said. "Now tell us what happened after I left you with Waldin. What instruction did he give you?"She nodded as Altherin recollected the stages that Waldin taught her. Apparently he had been faithful to the teaching. "Now tell us why you went into the exchange of touches when, as you say, you did not feel entirely confident about it."

"I wanted to please. I wanted to give. I saw that Waldin liked being touched."

"What was the first thing I taught you?" Mother Zalda asked crossly, disillusioned.

"Do not patronize, do not condescend. Be heart-open."

"And you presumed to please a boy older than you, who has much more experience and who is more advanced in the xenas!"

Altherin hung her head dejectedly.

"Do you know how you 'pleased' him? What do you think he felt when he reached the climax of his courtship dance and found himself alone?"

Altherin shuddered. She imagined the feeling must be desolate. She had no experience as yet of frustration, but she could sense the grip of some unknown grief closing in on her, enveloping her with a solitude more painful than the panic produced by night cold. She knew she would have to suffer the same pain that she had inflicted.

"We as your zildings will see to the Commensuration," Mother Melda said. "You must understand why we do it: so you will see clearly the results of your actions and pity the victim of your folly by suffering his fate. The Law is inexorable and you must suffer this sooner or later. Now we will appoint one of our numbers to serve you your due consequences. Remember that they are your just desserts and imply no malice on the zilding's part."

Altherin was shocked to learn that a zilding, one of those who so far had represented only comfort and encouragement, would be the instrument of her penance. She looked up to see if she could guess who it would be. And instantly she knew: It would be Father Grandar, a zilding whom she had seen only a few times but who stood in her eyes as the epitome of manliness. Handsome, with deep and brilliant coloring, Grandar was in his prime. His muscles still rippled under the iridescent skin, although his face was lined with signs not so much of Xarbian mirth as of deep thought — perhaps even of transgressions atoned for with pain and succeeded by a brooding self-assuredness. He was the most powerful and mysterious being known to Altherin.

"Father Grandar will take you to live with him and lead you through the stages of Commensuration."

The tall zilding did not speak but nodded in signal, and she followed him through the roof of her mother's house. His shoulders flashed red as the sun hit them, the skin scalloped like the jeweled feathers on the throat of a half-remembered bird. Altherin followed him home in awe, her admiration mixed with foreboding.

10

INITIATION

A BRAHAM KNEW THAT CLARITY of mind was most important in initiation procedures, yet he kept careening into conjectures: Should he divulge the identity of the being whom he pursued between lives? If he did so, could he hope that his examiners might direct him to her current location? What had the Algonquian uncovered in trance about why Abraham failed to reach Completion in his previous life? Would they detect the effects of the focuser? Abraham's mind revolved in these digressive thoughts during the pre-Initiation lectures.

"From life to life we swing," the swami was saying, "like acrobats clutching at trapezes as they fall within our reach." Abraham's mind snapped to attention. *What do the trapezes represent? Lifetimes? Yes, that must be it.* The swami continued: "Between each grasping there is a letting go, an agony, a leap of faith. And so it is with all great crises within a life. All familiar things fall from our grasp and we can only hope that new ones will swing within our reach, that we will not drop into an abyss."

The abyss! Abraham knew it well. Each night he dreamed of a bodiless state in which the being who was his only stability slipped from his grasp and he was left alone, unwilling to accept bereavement — clutching, gasping after help that melted away into a mysterious buzz, a sound without sense, a Xzzz. Abraham repeatedly sweated and threshed over this sound, trying to complete it, never succeeding. What if he were denied Initiation and never gained the capacity to seek his beloved? His Althea? What would he do then? Fulfill the soothsayer's prediction and join an alien army? Abraham felt cold fear lodge in his throat.

"... from the ancient word Ahimsa." Another guide was explaining the origins of the term Ahim. "Formerly merely a moral precept of doing no harm, the expression has gained new relevance today. It refers above all to an ecological principle, in which the doer of harm knows himself to be the long-range victim of his own ill-doing. So the Ahim is pre-eminently the far-sighted one who prepares himself for unknown tasks. The world is always changing, but by being on the spot, one can respond appropriately. Thus the Ahim is also one who cultivates himself first, and then his garden."

Abraham irrelevantly flashed on Rollo's exquisite garden courtyard and sipping room and on the skill in botany for which Technists were famed.

"We do not reject technology out of hand but seek to go beyond it," the guide continued. "You are mature in appearance, but the invisible channels within you are weak and disconnected."

At first Abraham thought these words were part of the formal introduction to Ahim values. Then he realized they referred to him personally.

The neurobiologist scrutinized him. "Have you taken drugs since your examination?"

Abraham was jolted from his reveries. "Why?" he asked stupidly in his surprise.

"Answer."

"No, doctor."

"You appear distracted, and your skin is pale. Something has happened since your exam four days ago."

The group of guides and examiners was silent now, looking at Abraham. He thought: *They don't have a galvanic patch on me.*

Perhaps I can brazen this out. They can't make me go through another exam; it's double jeopardy or something.

But the neurobiologist was pulling a contraption out of a satchel. A kriyagraphic camera! He aimed it at Abraham and made several exposures, getting close-ups of head, heart, and bowels. The cylinders were picked up by a smirking Technist, who promised to have them downloaded within minutes from a nearby laboratory, ready for a life-system reading. Meanwhile, instruction continued.

"Listen carefully, for once the initiation rite begins there is no stopping for questions. The in-between state will be induced in you. Your thought processes will be short-circuited via a series of complex or unanswerable questions that you must try, nonetheless, to answer — not aloud but in your mind. This is called the de-thinking process. It will end abruptly in a trance, in which you will re-experience death and the in-between state, and will be 'reborn' with all circuits temporarily clear. Then you will be given your new name and a new mother, who will guide you in what powers, if any, you are to receive. Do you understand?"

Abraham nodded, although his head felt fuzzy and none of the information stayed in focus. Then the Technist came back with the kriya images ready for the reader.

"All right, Abraham," said the neurobiologist finally, switching off the reader, "tell us what you've done. Your life-force is putrid green and fear flames emanate from your midriff. Your cerebral output looks like scrambled eggs, your heart barely registers. What have you been up to since we saw you last?"

Abraham quavered to the core. He had lost the last vestiges of control over his destiny. Nothing remained but to make a full confession and trust the guides to give him what he needed. He made a last-ditch attempt at bravado with a bold question: "Do you know what a focuser is?"

"You tell us what you think it is."

"It's a device the Technists use to give them instant, temporary enlightenment."

"And you are familiar with this gadget by first-hand experience?"

"I didn't plan to, but I ran into a Technist friend and he talked me into trying it. I want the Powers so much, and it seemed the focuser would give me a foretaste."

"It is dangerous precisely for that reason. It tampers with the faculties that we must nurture with all delicacy." This from the physician.

"Yes, ma'am, I know. But the situation was novel and my friend's experiences seemed genuine and ... well, very impressive."

"To put your head in a focuser is like putting a flower in an oven." The swami who earlier had spoken of "acrobats" and "abyss" perused Abraham pityingly.

The little group of sages looked on with alarm as Abraham described his sudden jolt into hyper-clarity, his intermittent identification with functions of heart, brain, and lungs; his panic on imagining that he was responsible for the functions, but incompetent. "Luckily my friend was there. I guess a focuser is not so bad if you know how to operate it."

"Perhaps — if you have no intention to cultivate long-term Powers. Stimulation by such machines overburdens the faculties that you need for their cultivation."

"Then I've ruined my chances forever?"

"Never forever. Much depends on how extensive the damage to your nervous system proves to be."

"Then I may still be initiated? Please! I know I made a big mistake but I learned from it. I am totally committed to the true Ahim way. If I'm not initiated I don't know what I'll do!"

"Pleading will not influence the decision here. We will act for your best interests, regardless of what you imagine them to be. We have a trance report to consider. Then the de-thinking process will begin."

The Algonquian stepped forward and tendered a recording he made while in trance. It told all that he discovered about Abraham's failure to reach Completion in his previous lives. A short, barking voice, unrecognizable as the Algonquian's own, snapped out bits of information as if it were snipping bytes out of a text: "Motivation distorted. Desire to impress. Self-sabotage to retain dependence."

The voice faded and the group adjourned to decide Abraham's fate. All the information was in. He had been unable to falsify even a minor detail. He was revealed as a weakling prone to Technist temptations. He awaited the de-thinking process glumly resigned, a different person from the one who had come to the examining place a few days before, hoping that with a few small lies he could get a higher initiation than he deserved. Now he feared that he would not be initiated at all. Perhaps he would be denied all Powers, and have to spend this lifetime learning humility or compassion or honesty: something so fundamental that he would lose sight of his final aim altogether. *So be it,* he thought, and the time for de-thinking was on him.

The assembly of sages stood in a circle around Abraham. As they fired questions at him, he had to pivot to face the questioner. The brusque turns added to his sense of imbalance. He was given only a moment to try to answer each question in his mind, although that was a patent impossibility.

"What does the Wedding of Science and Religion mean to you?" Abraham began to make all the usual associations for this juncture in Ahim history: Wedding of Physics and Metaphysics, Mysticism and Realism, Religion and Technology, Idealism and Realism ... Then he realized that he was thinking just words without knowing what they meant, and another question hit him: "What is the sound of one hand clapping?" Abraham drew a complete blank on this question and began to laugh, but his laughter was cut short by another volley: "Where does the voice go when it falls silent?" He felt himself sink inward, into a semi-trance, identified with the quieted voice. He felt lulled but was drawn to attention by more questions: "What was your first impression on being born this time?" Still in a semi-trance, Abraham recalled how, in infancy, he registered the mood of this planet where he had once more taken on flesh, a planet where conflicts are latent, where uncertainty reigns, where great good lies in potential while how to realize it presents a perennial puzzle.

"Your last recollections of your previous life?"

Oh, Abraham gasped inwardly. He had a sharp pang-like memory of his sudden demise while he wondered yearningly: *Did she wait? Will I find her? How will I know her?*

"Tell me a truth stranger than fiction," one of the shamans was prodding him. But Abraham had floated on memory into the in-between state. In a whirlwind, he relived his tenuous bodiless reuniting with the Althea entity, and then the doldrums where he remained alone while she eluded him — and finally, his surrender to a second-rate rebirth.

The guides brought him out of his trance, calling him by his new name: "Adam, Adam."

"Adam you will be called, for you have made no progress since your last life. You are fixated on a relationship established in that period. We have found your pursuit of that relationship to be evolutionary, however. As Adam, you will resume the quest of your desires. Although you are weak for the undertaking, you may begin instruction in the basic Powers, to be administered over five years on a probationary basis. Your Second Mother is here to take you with her and give you the teaching."

11

GRANDAR'S BED

ALTHERIN AWOKE EACH DAY in the unfamiliar bed and wondered what she was doing there. Then she remembered how she had let young Waldin fly into a state of unfounded ecstasy because of her, and how she had to experience his humiliation and frustration by the Law of Commensuration. Her nights now roiled with turmoil, then sleep hit deep and dull. In the morning, she looked about the sumptuous room and tried to place the objects she saw there: the weaving tinted with brown mogdon bark and purple tingleberry juice, the large cushions with satiny contours. They all seemed familiar. Then slowly she would remember that the previous evening she had lain on the weaving or draped herself over the cushions and their colors and patterns became more and more alive and beautiful to her as Grandar stroked her shoulders.

At first she thought she would have to please Grandar, gratify his desires, and so compensate for her failure to fulfill young Waldin's. "You enhance my strength," Grandar murmured, "and renew my blood to youthful vigor." His scarlet shoulder scales seemed to glow like coals in the twilight. He was very highly colored for a Xarbian and emanated a power that held Altherin in awe. She was flattered that he desired her.

The first night she flitted about his house, letting him see her body from all angles, absorbing his admiration. His gaze filled her with lightness, she felt buoyed up. She danced in the air above him just beyond his fingertips, letting his desire rise to the pursuit. She could feel heat shooting out from his hands, luring her.

When bedtime came, Altherin's ecstasy mixed with a tremor of misgiving. Could she contain the full effect of Being Alone Together with him? If she had to suffer for what she did to Waldin, then there must be something painful or dismaying about the experience she was about to undergo.

Grandar did not seem threatening. She watched his face for a trace of cruelty but found none. His powerful, spare features kindled with an almost drowsy pleasure. His passion for her tinged his inner Xarbian light with a ruddy glow. Her inner light shone rosy too. As they lay down together he made no menacing gesture. He merely stroked her dandelion hair, over and over, and let it bounce and spring to his touch. Soon Altherin thrilled to electric currents traveling from the roots of her hair and over her face and shoulders. When at length Grandar touched her shoulders the tingling bolts spread into sheets deluging her whole body. She began to move against him to please and seduce him, and he accepted her advances with soft encouraging sounds.

Long into the night — and into each successive night — the caressing and seducing continued. Altherin felt passion piping in her shrilly as a Xarbian flute, strong and unbridled as only Xarbian passion can flare. Alternately it buoyed her, then weighted her with turbulence and heat. Sighs shook her chest and left her breathless, gasping. She became frantic, tried desperately and blindly to lead Grandar to a further step of interaction. Blindly, because she was not sure what more could be done together, but she felt a profound lack growing in the recesses of her vitals, threatening to tear them apart as mogdon roots do a rock that they have penetrated.

For many days, Altherin felt a languor drugging her mind and body both night and day. This drug seemed to be a distillation of Grandar that had invaded her. She was imbued with him, thinking only how she might please him — always conscious, as she moved, of how he looked at her or might look at her. He was never truly absent, yet when they reunited after even a short separation, joy bounded in her and made her leap high. Levitating thus, she even struck her head on the ceiling at times, so forgetful of all else was she when Grandar was present.

As time went on and her urges to blend with Grandar were repeatedly stymied, her frustration grew and stretched like a kragil spreading its bony wings. She felt like crying out from the pangs, and her pain induced an anger toward Grandar. The shrill passion converted into hate and resentment.

But the languor had been so delicious that she did not want to give it up, so she fought to keep the anger down. Now when Grandar reached out to touch her, sometimes she flinched and turned away with loathing, and if he touched her anyway she felt an irritation, as if a dry phenamon leaf had scraped over her skin. But then when the irritability passed, she was even more receptive to him than before. As desire flooded in, the contrast with the passing bitterness made it all the sweeter and her heart opened and gaped with longing to be accepted by him to the fullest.

Grandar, while responding to her, kept a degree of independence. He never yielded fully to her, yet betrayed no struggle for self-control. His was a mysterious equanimity. Sometimes Altherin wondered if it were not precisely this self-sufficiency of his that made him so irresistible. If he were to sail madly into a courtship dance, perhaps she would reject him, but he never lost his calm.

Altherin began to hold imaginary conversations, rehearsing pleas to Grandar to satisfy her or release her, use his wisdom to restore her peace. But she knew that what he was doing to her was prescribed for her own Commensuration. She would have to endure it.

If the exasperations and conflicts had been restricted to her time in bed with Grandar, she might have had some leverage over the situation. At least she would know when to anticipate her martyrdom and could reconcile herself to certain hours of turmoil. But the feelings he engendered spilled over into her days. While engaged in other acts and with other people, she found her mind revolving around him and the sensations he set in motion. Waves of longing beset her while she practiced the xenas with her tutor, and she was incapable of following instructions. A mogdon tree could have toppled onto her and she would have been powerless to bound out of its way. Also, when fits of anger toward Grandar swept in, nothing else could penetrate her awareness. She was the plaything of her own passions, like a plant that opens by day and closes at night. Grandar was her Sol, warming her by his nearness, freezing her with his withdrawal.

Then, just when she thought she would crack with the strain, her dilemma unexpectedly began to resolve itself. By shifting between extremes, Altherin found that a bit of the cold stayed when the heat returned, and when cold rage overtook her a small trace of warm receptivity still lingered. As days passed, gradually anger tempered desire and desire assuaged anger, until she found herself responding in a new way to Grandar's touch. She did not wince but felt no sensual pleasure. Gradually a friendly attitude replaced the insatiable hunger, an acceptance of a fellow being bound to her through the Law of Commensuration. They gradually dropped their roles of warden and culprit, of awesome zilding and eager dinzel. They were accomplishing their fated task and she was gaining freedom from his influence.

One day she said, "I am suffering less from our Being Alone Together."

And he replied, "You are right. This is as it should be. Cool layers of evening are settling on our bed."

"I almost miss the strong feelings of before."

"Yes, that is natural. It is because the pains are imprinted in your system. They awake memories. That is inevitable under the Law of Commensuration. However, in time you will be purified of these imprints. Then you will be completely free."

"Now what must I do?"

"Allow this coolness to settle in you. You have been tempered in the play of opposing forces." In fact, Altherin could sense greater strength and flexibility in the very fibers of her being. "You will gain much headway in the xenas now," Grandar predicted. "The energies that were bound to our bed will spring up into one-pointed concentration like a flame that shoots to the skies."

What Grandar predicted proved true. Gradually Altherin mastered the xenas with less and less effort. In the long run, Grandar's touch gave her liberty instead of bondage; her world was a place of renewed possibilities. Before, she had been a child without a will, following her zildings' instructions. Now that she had experienced desires and fears and revulsions, she knew her own potential for good and evil. Evil had come so close to devouring her sanity — in the night woods and in Grandar's bed — that she embraced her liberty with a zeal to use her energies for benefit. The Law of Commensuration would quickly correct her if she acted to harm.

A space within Altherin was freed of turbid feelings and prepared to hold greater, impersonal desires. Eventually she could scarcely remember her unruly passions, yet she was still vital with a verve to master the xenas and explore her destiny. Her body, only, was like a locked house. No motion of heat or cold could come from or to it.

"Father Grandar," she said one morning, "I will be a sintor." The words came out without her thinking, the spontaneous outcome of the changes within her. There was no point to arguing for or against it. She was a celibate. It seemed now her indisputable nature. It would be foolish to pretend to seek a mate, against the grain altogether. Grandar nodded. His eyes were rainbow bright with the aura of Completion.

"Now," he said, "you will remain with me until your powers are perfected. You gain much strength for undertaking them through energies you absorb by lying with me in tranquility. When you are ready, another zilding will take you into his custody. He will be your traveling companion. You will tour the galaxies and visit the place where beings similar to us dwell: Earth where we have all lived before, the planet of the Zeklings who visited Earth long ago, the exile Island of the Clones, and the strange and wonderful Oracle Island."

12

SECOND MOTHER

ABRAHAM — NOW ADAM — blinked, dazed by his sudden thrust into a state of innocence. He drank in the initiation guides' words as an infant does milk, nourishing because they seemed so just and compassionate and appropriate to his situation. The guides had acknowledged the rightness of his quest for Althea! "We have found your pursuit of that relationship to be evolutionary. You will resume the quest of your desires." He turned to his Second Mother with a feeling of gratitude and utter trust. Little childlike tears sprouted from the corners of his eyes and tickled his face.

However, Adam soon found that he was not to be coddled like a child. Far from it. To acquire the Powers needed for his quest, he had first to master some basics. His new Mother prescribed a regimen of martial arts. "Wake up." Tap. "Wake up." Tap, tap. Stinging blows from her hand chops rained on Adam's buttocks, interspersed with orders to awaken. With a voice like water, his new Mother still could startle him to the marrow. He leapt to his feet without taking stock of where he was or why he should bound. And just in time. The woman was diving with hands outstretched for a throttle hold. Seeing her gesture, Adam winced, and she seemed to sense the moment of weakness. Without rising from her crouched position, she twisted and caught him with a stabbing slice at the shins. Adam hopped out of her reach, howling.

"Wakefulness first," she admonished, "and all else after."

"Yes," Adam agreed, rubbing his shin and using the pain to build psychic momentum for a counter-attack. He launched himself, hands foremost aiming a punt. But she sensed his intention and sidestepped while he fell sprawling.

"Never attempt an uncontrolled body-hurl against a Tai-Zen Panther. You see this saffron headband?" Mother tapped her forehead with a gnarled finger like an old plum twig. "I won this by letting young fellows like you hurl themselves to destruction. You are lucky I'm responsible for your next five years or your folly would lead you to disaster."

Adam felt his heart flatten like a chastened dog. His shoulders slouched. He wanted to crawl back into bed and never see this witch of a teacher again. He felt sure his initiation guides had made a mistake in relegating him to this woody, pitiless woman with her violent ancient techniques. As usual, she had succeeded in putting him in a resentful, petulant mood.

"Just tell me why you have to insist on your superiority," Adam hissed. "I know you have your saffron headband. I know I am no match for you. So why do you ambush me? I didn't whack at your butt."

She laughed her artless watery laugh, so aggravatingly free of personal rancor. "It's part of your EDT, don't you know? You'll never gain the Powers you want unless you pass your Ego Demoralizer Training. And you don't need to be sarcastic."

"Oh, really? There must be an easier way."

"There are many easier ways."

"And why do you have to be such an old-fashioned purist?" Adam asked, inspecting the scrapes and bruises he had collected since moving in with his Second Mother.

"The Tai-Zen-Yogic traditions were revived and modernized as far back as the Renaissance of World Cultures. They are not obsolete by any means, but are proven methods for quick awakening. You have only five years of probation. You tend to fall into complacency.

You must learn to be alert but not aggressive — humble but not passive. Yogic practices were added to your regimen for a different reason. Perhaps you can tell me what it is?"

"I wouldn't know," said Adam, sulking.

"Try, child."

"Same reasons, I suppose. The disgusting diet keeps me hungry; hunger triggers alertness, perhaps an urge to find prey. The postures, equally disgusting, must be for the humility thing."

"Your guesses are intelligent but tainted with resentment. Apply more learning and less feeling."

"They must have to do with that cursed focuser."

"Yes. What did I tell you about it the first day?"

"Your sermon: 'Perception without compassion can lead to revulsion and catatonic retreat.' "

"Yes. Compassion is the feeling that accompanies expansion. To focus down a narrow channel can make you fear and loathe what you perceive. A focus on yourself can lead to catatonic suicide — as it almost did in your case when you used the focuser."

"I get the idea."

"But we have strayed from the question. You must practice postures and diet to heal the fine nerves blasted by the overload on your system. Not to mention your tendency to try to control every situation. We have to break you down and rebuild you."

"I see," said Adam dejectedly.

"I know you think I am cruel, but be assured I am precisely the teacher for you — an Eclectic who can work on you both physically and psychologically. So you see, I am not a purist — rather the opposite. But we Eclectics prefer action to talk. This is your last chance to ask questions."

"Is this all I'll be getting for five years? More fasting, standing on my head, and flapping my elbows to ward off attacks?"

"You'll be glad to hear the answer is no. Soon I'll give you methods to release your energies in new ways. But you cannot know about them ahead of time. Will you trust me from now on?"

Adam decided to give his teacher a vote of confidence. He did his exercises as prescribed. Most difficult was response to the unexpected 'panther' attacks. Sometimes his Mother knocked his meager bowlful of dinner from his hands with a flick of her big toe and, when he tried to recover it, impelled by both anger and hunger, she continued to flick it beyond his reach. At times he lunged at her vengefully but soon learned that the more vehement his reaction was, the more he fell under her control. Gradually he learned to hold back his instincts and used his energies slyly and cautiously, conserving them for the right moment to retrieve a bowl or deviate a blow. After a few successes, he asked if he was acquiring a little bit of Power.

She threw back her head and laughed her watery, guttural laugh. "You haven't reached zero point yet, son. Don't try to figure out your status. It will only discourage you and hinder progress."

She continued to attack and provoke and humiliate him, always testing his patience beyond its capacity. And after a few months she added another species of provocation. She would crawl into bed with him and with one deft stroke arouse him so that he threw himself toward her, surfing a wave of lust. She would roll out of reach in a flash and stand naked and mocking. When he tried to capture her, she let him come close but always eluded him. Frustration gave way to fury, but she ordered him to desist on pain of 'panther' punishment. Once he disobeyed, determined to catch and humiliate her. But she fulfilled her threats and defended herself mercilessly with hand slices to his biceps and blows to his hamstrings until his arms and legs were helpless. He realized he had made a big mistake, weakening himself by his insistence. At last he came to expect and to live with even the sexual harassment.

13

ISLANDS IN THE SKY

"'ISLANDS,'" FATHER GRINDIL EXPLAINED, "are planets conducive to existence as we know it. The term is an ancient one, still in use on Earth, where it designates plots of land in the midst of an ocean."

"What is an ocean?" Altherin wondered. Everything that her third zilding told her sounded like a music-tale, full of wonderful unfamiliar words and images.

"'Ocean' is part of the vocabulary developed on Earth to refer to certain large bodies of water. Now you will ask what 'water' is." He looked at his dinzil with candid brow-less eyes, his gossamer eyelashes sparkling. He laid a gentle hand on Altherin's speckled shoulder and pointed with the other to the crystal depths of the sky.

"Think of the air," he said. "Think of how delicious and refreshing it is when you inhale deeply and you feel it nourish your brain and your viscera. Water is a clear, sparkling kind of air that Earth-beings drink in with their mouths instead of their nostrils. It supports life, but it is liquid like blood. And the ocean is a large amount of water very much like blood, for it is permeated with dissolved minerals, particularly sodium."

"I seem to remember."

"Yes, you might very well remember details of your previous existence. But it is not worth the effort. You will receive guidance in purposeful recollection before you reach Completion. But that is for another time and another zilding."

"You are the most beautiful zilding." Altherin hugged him in the Earth fashion. "Can you tell me just a little about your previous existences? Who have you been on Earth, Father Grindil?"

"I'll tell you just a little. Then we must get back to our studies. As for being beautiful — every successive zilding seems more attractive than the previous one. That is how we hold your attention!" Altherin laughed the loud, quick Xarbian laugh and her yavers shone in the brilliant light of Sol.

"Once I was a man of the Mongol race, which originated in the continent of Asia."

"Continent?"

"Yes, as in 'self-contained.' Earth's surface is mostly water and the self-contained units of land are divided by it. But I was born far from the native place of my race, which is noted for its patience and precision. As a young man I was an inventor of machines."

"Machines?"

"Clever conglomerates of minerals and other elements of highly specialized characters that can be used to give the illusion of specific xenas if operated in prescribed ways."

"It is hard for me to picture them."

"Think of flying a festival chariot. Only Earth chariots fly themselves; they are machines. Think of enduring a night without moleculation. Without the xena to organize the molecules of our dwellings, how would you endure the cold? On Earth, contrivances generate heat. Xenas there are in a primitive state of development, so all locomotion, communication, temperature control, etcetera are complicated and call for constant new inventions."

"Doesn't that lead to speculative experiment?"

"Indeed. No Xarbian wants to repeat the trial and error processes endured in prior existences. All consumption of energy entails a cost. It is the Law of Commensuration on the physical plane. And it is impossible to calculate the full cost of an invention when you want certain effects and prefer not to count side effects or raw materials consumed."

"And you were a creator of these inventions?"

"Actually I worked on fuel for vehicles and temperature control units."

"Fuels?"

"Fuels produce energy by molecular or nuclear shifts. I spent hours improving induction of nuclear energy, which had fallen into disuse due to fears of commensuration. In fact there had been spectacular failures — explosions and catastrophic chain reactions. Leaders in both science and religion united to exact a ban on further experimentation."

"What is religion?"

"Beliefs and ceremonies surrounding the Source of xenas. In the past there were confrontations between adherents of science and of religion, but in time there was a Wedding of the two. In practice, Earth-beings remain divided between those who seek xenas, which they simply call Powers, and those who pursue experiment and science."

"And you were one of these."

"Only for a while, in the excitement when the ban on nuclear experiment was lifted, but later I walked out. I underwent what would be known as a reversal on Xarbo."

"What made you change?"

"I began to study the Powers mentioned in the lore of all religions. These Powers had been practiced by a few who had 'psychic abilities' or held 'animistic beliefs,' and many doubted their authenticity. I was one of the first to break down barriers and reveal how xenas could be accessible to anyone, the learning systematized rather than left to chance. My training in science proved helpful. I just had to shift my attention from external resources to internal resources that develop the Powers. Of course, as such xenas increase, one begins to intuit the Summit, the Source. I was one of the pioneers in the integration of science and religion. That is how I earned my right to be born from a Xarbian pearl."

Altherin regarded her zilding with admiration. What adventures he had been through! She wondered, too, who she had been on Earth and how she had earned her right to inhabit a pearl — someone destined to reach Completion: self-contained like a 'continent.' "What does 'pearl' really mean?" she asked.

"Now we are deviating too far from the task at hand," Grindil warned her. "Let us not go further into academic knowledge. Pearls are products of water and of turmoil. Later you will learn more about them."

Altherin imagined that her training with Grindil would consist of ever-accelerated practice in flight. She had made great strides in this ability while living with Grandar. She had circled Xarbo many times, visited distant mendens, mastered their dialects, and xarped variations in their customs. She expected Grindil would teach her how to fly beyond the orbit of Xarbo, and that this would require a long apprenticeship. She knew there was no atmosphere between galaxies. There must be some means of suspending breath. Completions, of course, could do that.

"Stop speculating." Grindil xarped her. "What I have to teach you now is very important. It is the true basis for travel."

Altherin stared at him with iris eyes. He disappeared, then immediately reappeared.

"Since childhood you have passed through the walls of your home," said Grindil. "You have there the xena needed for travel to far galaxies. When you pass through a wall you instinctively make a thought-print of yourself and 'remember' to materialize yourself on the other side. You have done this spontaneously time and again. Now you must note exactly what you do in this process, for it will take you anywhere you want to go."

"You mean I will have to prolong the bodiless state long enough to go to far places?"

"Speculation again! No, 'prolong' is not relevant. Transfer is instantaneous. You will not be flying, which is movement through space, and therefore time. With thought-prints you travel with the speed of thought, which is infinite. You transfer yourself in zero time. You already do this in penetrating walls. You need now a new concept of destination and a clearer one of printing."

Altherin was electrified. She was on the verge of an enormous voyage. Before Sol set, would she have transported herself thousands of Xarbo-girths away?

"But you must pay attention." Grindil drew her back once more from daydreams. "To travel requires a tremendous reversal. You must drop expectations entirely. You expected to fly to other planets; is that so?"

"Yes, Father."

"But instead you will leap to them. Now listen. Every time you pass through a wall, you dematerialize. In the interim you exist as a thought-print; that is a code in consciousness of a specific entity — you. What you probably have not noticed is that the print emerges from a brief dip in pure consciousness. All-containing, all-nourishing, it encompasses every potential as xaltherin does the full spectrum of light and sound. To travel, you need only to set a destination before 'breathing' in pure consciousness. I will teach you the setting technique."

"What if I get stuck in the thought-print and don't materialize?" Altherin felt a tremor, imagining herself a frail code lost in the vastness.

"Do not worry, little one. As long as the girl Altherin is in life, her code will manifest itself physically as well as non-physically. It is one of the great wonders bestowed on us. We need only learn some control in choosing when and where to be physical. The Summit has taken care of the rest."

The first location Grindil taught her to visualize was planet Earth. Memories from past existences made it the easiest of all places for her to cognize vicariously. As Grindil conjured Earth's orientation among other celestial bodies, and then the details of its surface, Altherin had only to xarp accurately his mental pictures. She saw Earth first as a mote reflecting light from its Sol, a vague and distant twinkle. In the interim dense clusters of other suns, planets, and moons, all gave or received the gift of light. Grindil focused on certain guideposts between Xarbo and Earth. They constituted a sort of tubular map. Altherin's voyage would be through that tube, which in perspective looked like a cone stretching and bending far into the distance, a cornucopia with Earth at the small end like a speck of pollen.

"What do you see?" Grindil interrogated her after each phase of the envisioning.

As Altherin described the heavenly bodies en route, she created her map, until she viewed Earth as a whole, as it might appear from a fellow planet, then from its own singular moon.

"What do you see now?"

"A speckled sphere. It glistens like skin."

"And now?" Grindil prompted, as they visualized Earth from within its own atmosphere.

"A dense substance in the air, like webs, but they float. Underneath they make shadows. There is much texture. Many wrinkles, colors from red to green and smooth expanses of blue."

"Now I will show you the exact place of your materialization on Earth. If you can pick it up you are ready to go. What do you see?"

"A flowing substance. It must be 'water.' A liquid like blood that flows without a skin. And some sort of mogdon grows tall beside it. On the horizon I see a menden. It is more complex in structure than our mendens. It has passageways in the sky between structures and the air is thick and opaque — maybe with disintegrated waters. How will we breathe?"

"Do not worry. We will not materialize on the grossest physical plane where breathing is necessary. We will assume our own rate of manifestation here on Xarbo, which is subtler — and below the threshold of visibility on Earth. No one there will see us, and we will be exempt from the physical laws that prevail on Earth. You have followed my maps and pictures well. Now we will review them thoroughly. Tomorrow we depart."

14

THE SPIRAL UNWINDS

ONE MORNING, WHEN MOTHER had delivered a particularly provocative stroke and Adam barely refrained from lunging at her, she turned a hypnotic gaze on him and said, "Now you are ready to begin the real learning. Listen carefully." Adam gasped with surprise, for he had come to believe that self-defense and self-control were themselves the objects of his lessons.

"What you have undergone," she explained, "is a period of purification and stimulation. We will start to do something with the stimulated energy. I have made your energies surface in various forms: as anger, lust, pride, and hunger. Now you will see how all these urges have a single root. When any of these instincts pressure you, focus on them. Instead of grasping at me, or your food, or something else, you must notice the impulse itself and trace it back to its source. That way, you will re-absorb the aroused energy. With practice, you will recapture it closer and closer to its point of emergence. Then you will cognize the root of your powers."

She taught him techniques to acquire a neutral attitude in the face of provocation, to master anger, sex, and hunger in the Ahim way. Gradually he learned to view pain and frustration as impulses detached from stimulus, and enjoyed the miraculous relief of doing so neutrally — without desire to eliminate his drives, control them, or act on them.

When he had mastered the art of neutral attention, he discovered something new. Beyond every sensation lay another feeling that gave rise to it, subtler and more powerful but less vehement. Once he acquired an equanimous attitude, Adam sank effortlessly into cool currents, each more enlivening and pleasant than the previous one.

Thus the gambit of his training took an unexpectedly pleasurable turn. He began to smile at his teacher, and she smiled back. She gave him his Ariadne's thread to navigate the labyrinth of his being and recuperate the clarity and power that lay at his core. When he deviated, flying off the handle or indulging in sexual tumescence, she set him back on course: "Quick," she said; "this is the energy you need for the Powers. Trace it to its source!"

Soon Adam realized that it mattered little how his energies expressed themselves. All intense emotions and sensations, regardless of content, could be reconverted into their basic constituent, which was fuel for the feats he hoped to perform. As he traced every impulse back to its origin, Adam began to sense an entity quivering somewhere below and behind his viscera. It radiated vibrant magnetism like a coiled rattlesnake potent with striking power. Adam asked his Mother if his perception was accurate.

"Yes. You have noticed your sacro-helix. It is a spiral like an electromagnetic coil that can impart energy of unimaginable magnitude if you know how to tap and direct it. Well done, Adam. Now you must learn to uncoil the helix cautiously and use it for constructive ends."

Adam's Mother began to use unexpected new techniques. He had thought that sexual and martial provocations were close to unbearable, but now she tested him more severely, to give him immediate access to the sacro-helix. The more intense the emotion, the straighter and clearer the path to its source. She would hold a pointed fingernail to his jugular vein, a known Tai-

Zen method for a quick kill. Adam had to flip from her grasp with all his might, fearful for his life. Only a tremendous surge of adrenaline gave him strength for such exertion. He stood up panting, feeling still the knife-like wound of her nail.

Then, "Quick," she would say, "access the source. Sit down in the coiled toils of the helix. Let it buoy you." Adam felt light, filled with amazing power. Still it was vague, a fine vapor penetrating every cell and capillary.

At night Mother came to Adam's bed and pressed her firm, ageless body to his so that he throbbed with sexual impulses and almost burst with yearning that rose like sap in a young trunk. Now she let him penetrate her, but he had to lie still and let the ecstatic sensations travel at will until they pervaded his whole body. Then she whispered to him, "Find where the sensations come from. It is not from me, although that is your illusion." And Adam refrained from indulging fully in the sexual act to contemplate the fountain within himself from which all the thrills and waves of desire issued. And again, it was always that little coil in his lower abdomen that sent out the impulses.

"Why can't we be mates and have children?" Adam whispered once.

"Ha, ha," laughed the woman with a silvery sound that made his flesh ripple; "they all ask the same thing. The Siren sings as in the oldest epics and the adventurer wants to stop his journey and tarry with her."

Slowly and carefully she disengaged herself from Adam's embrace and sat on the edge of his bed. "Don't you remember why you came to me? Have you forgotten your initiation? Have you changed your mind? What do you want now, Adam: Powers, or a safe life with wife and family? You must know that I will never marry, but we could find you a suitable wife to whom to transfer your desires. And you could choose a Technist occupation that does not require any Powers. What do you want, Adam?"

"I want to pursue my Althea," Adam said, remembering his purpose in being initiated. "Why do you make me forget her, Mother?"

"It is only natural. What is before our senses is most real. Such is the limitation of the grosser faculties. But soon you will be gaining finer abilities and your goal will become more vivid."

When Adam at last learned to channel his sacro-helical energy, he was shocked at the result. In addition to the expected enhancement of hearing and eyesight, he gained the power to focus attention on past events. He discovered this one day when Mother backed him into a corner and once again it seemed he barely escaped with his life. The crisis reminded him of something in the distant past. Adjusting his attention, he was startled to find himself in an earlier existence. He was thrust up against a metallic wall, cornered by an enemy with a weapon that emitted a rending beam. He had not escaped. His opponent destroyed him. The laser blade ripped his chest and his spirit fled in horror, watching the mutilated body drop behind it. Adam flinched to remember the catastrophe.

"You remember something, don't you?" Mother asked.

"Yes. A bad thing."

"But through a good and necessary skill. Memory is the most accessible faculty. Before you learn more active abilities, you must lay groundwork in memory. If you seek a beloved being, you must recollect why she is important to you. Then you can begin a search."

Adam had to agree. Shortly, random gushes of information flooded his memory. During his life with Althea, he was a historian. He worked with Technists in their narrow, one-pointed style. Reams of data flooded him, for he had to follow Technist methods to observe recurring patterns and forecast a future free of past mistakes. Ahims, of course, knew the pitfalls in this method — but Adam had played the Technist game. Now he regressed, mumbling a jumble of historical sequences: the Age of Experimentation with natural and synthetic fuel sources, genetic engineering phasing from agriculture and animal husbandry into human eugenics, and the early probes into outer space. He recalled in fragments the decline of written ciphers and the rise of holography, the polemics about cloning and space travel. He riffled through the epoch when an avant-garde announced the Wedding of Science and Religion, and the epoch when Technists — dedicated to the former — and Ahims — taking impetus from the latter — vied for preeminence. And he remembered how in his last life he favored the Ahim way yet continued to dream of typical Technist achievements: conquests in space and immediate gratification of trivial personal desires.

Mother, observing the strain induced by these issues from his past, changed his regimen. Instead of stimulating and provoking him, she taught breathing exercises and other techniques to calm and restore his system. Adam was flabbergasted to learn that the two years of teasing and tormenting had all served simply to direct his attention to the helix. Now that he had access, he could pose a question to this spiral of energy as to a genie. He had only to formulate a wish, cognize the helix, then he could surf back and forth among lifetimes, conjuring his various identities.

"Now," announced Mother, "we come to a more difficult type of memory exercise. You must recall your beloved and understand her role in your development. This is difficult because these memories can create turmoil."

Adam learned how to conjure an image of his Althea — her appearance and mannerisms. At first all he could see were spots dancing in his eyes, but eventually the spots came into focus and he saw they were freckles on the woman's arms. Then he saw the same reddish freckles on an upper lip, and he saw how the lip smiled, and finally how the taffy-brown eyes smiled too. His Mother had him repeat the beloved's name as if it were a mantra. Thus elements of personality could be cognized. "Althea, Althea," he mumbled inwardly and a barrage of images struck him suddenly, some visual and others purely intuitive. He saw the leap of her hair in the summer breeze, the strong brown crook of her wrist holding onto their son — whom he had never much loved, partly from jealousy, partly from distaste at seeing his own willfulness mirrored.

Then began a series of more subtle, intuitive perceptions. He sensed Althea's strong, optimistic, cheerful, and disinterested character. She bolstered him, even in memory, tenuous as the connection was. She injected him with the tonic zeal to evolve. Because of her, he realized, he had turned his back on Technist temptations and opted for the Ahim way — although not without lapses in his resolve.

He tried to follow her plea to gain the power to join her. But his intention was tainted with pride. Although with her he had been a faithful and considerate mate, within him lurked a primitive urge to solicit surrender. After her death, it was possible that she might be waiting still to lead him, and a small sullen part of him held with mastiff tenacity to the never-granted wish to master her.

"I never knew I wanted to dominate Althea!" Adam exclaimed to his Mother.

"I suspected as much, or you would not have jumped at me so fiercely in the early stages of your training." Mother cast a sardonic glance at him. "Do you know that the will to conquer is a deterrent in reaching your goal?"

Adam sighed. Too often he stumbled over weaknesses that undermined his heart's desires. Nonetheless, he was allowed to proceed to the next phase of training. Now he would begin to have intimations of his beloved's present state. He must learn to visualize where and what she was before he could cultivate even elementary powers to reach her.

At first Adam picked up a repeated signal, an image of something like a crystal ball. It stayed in focus for three or four seconds, then disappeared. He lost contact with the helix and clairvoyance dissipated. After repeated glimpses, he deduced that the 'crystal ball' was a planet. He must be viewing her place of residence from a great distance. The refractions and reflections of prismatic colors must characterize the atmosphere of her new home.

"All I can see is this pretty sphere flashing colors," Adam complained.

"Try to perceive the name of the place," Mother advised. "The name will carry with it more details."

Adam came to regard his sacro-helix as something of an oracle, dwelling like a Sybil in a cavern of his own body and relaying messages of past and future with miraculous accuracy from some mysterious all-knowing source. He took Mother's advice and asked his helix what name belonged to the crystalline planet. The helix seemed to quiver like a snake and the sound that it hissed vibrated through his whole system before it condensed in his eardrums and he could vocalize it as syllables. It began like a gargle, a rough "ghh," which mutated when other syllables followed: a wide "ahh," a trilling rattle of "r," a sharply exhaled "bohh." "Gharrboh," Adam essayed. But the helix seemed to wriggle and hiss at him, transmitting the word repeatedly until he corrected himself. "Xarbo," he gasped at length, and fainted under the complex of associations that the word triggered.

In subsequent sessions, Adam pieced together his experiences of the in-between state, when his beloved had left him suddenly for a destination called Xarbo, leaving no trace or echo or clue to what sort of place it was. Then he knew he had been reborn and entered a long phase of forgetting and was just now awaking from its numbing effects. Now, after much fumbling and groping, at last he found his goal again. He must determine where Xarbo was, what it was like, and who among its inhabitants his beloved might be.

Now began a period of fitful visions of delightful and frightening apparitions, of strange animals with purple fur, of enormous plants and microscopic ones, of ear-splitting sounds and ominous nocturnal silences. He struggled to focus on beings more like himself in hopes of finding among them the one he sought. But his powers were pushed beyond their limits. Mother called a halt. He was overtaxing himself. She ordered recreation. Together they went out to hear epics chanted, listening by the hour to recitations of exploits from the time of distant forebears, the heroes among Inuits and Australians, Greeks and Egyptians — and then United Earth peoples: old astronauts and pioneers of space colonies; the adventurer who sought his love on Clone Island, where she had been sent by mistake or intrigue.

Adam felt chords of sympathy quiver in his breast as he heard the poignant songs of the great heroes of all ages. Technist and Ahim alike could weep and rejoice in their exploits. But Adam's mind kept wandering to his own quest, which was suspended in a slump of mental exhaustion. All the desire and aggression that had been aroused and directed toward his Second Mother was now transferred onto his beloved and the veil that hid her from him. He fumed at himself for failing to rend the veil, and thus worsened his weakening condition. At the peak of impatience, he could do nothing until his resources were replenished. His helix had lost its vibrancy. He was stymied on the brink of true power, acutely aware that his time of probation was drawing to a close.

15

ALTHERIN ON EARTH

T O PREPARE HERSELF FOR TRAVEL, Altherin had to practice all the calming exercises she knew. At first she was too excited to pass through her house walls. When she joined Grindil, he saw she was pulsating and changing color, so he knew she needed further calming.

"I will tell you more about what to expect, little one. This should give you greater confidence. After we land by the flowing water, you will see many beautiful varieties of plants, more than we have on Xarbo, and Earth plants love water. Later we will move on to a menden and pass through the dwellings at will.

"You will find that, although all the races whose traces exist on Xarbo live on Earth, they are divided more pronouncedly in two types. One is a large race generally a head taller than most Xarbians. Their bodies are lean and strong. They live in small scattered mendens in simple structures, not unlike those of Xarbo. They can communicate mentally, but crudely, and cultivate many of the other xenas we know — although, as yet, those in Completion are rare, and highly revered.

"The menden that we envisioned yesterday belongs to the second group. They are smaller and weaker, for they have placed their dependence on external sources of power. Still, there is much intermarriage and conversion from one group to the other. Thus you will see intermediate types, and you will see the big ones visiting the cities of the small ones to borrow their devices or sit on pedestals to practice the xenas. Since the so-called Wedding of Science and Religion, cooperation has been highly valued — at least in theory."

"I want to see these Earth beings for myself. I am ready."

"Let's be sure you remember how to proceed."

"First I review the tubular map and other images of the destination that you gave me. I xarp them clearly without interruptions. Then I go into thought-print and automatically materialize at the location visualized."

"Good. Do it. I will be with you all the way."

The trail to Earth came easily to Altherin. She envisioned the constellations en route in sequence, then finally the earthly solar system and, at last, the riverine location Grindil had conveyed. Then she abandoned all thought and image, as she did when leaving her home each morning. But now she materialized, not under Xarbo's Sol but Earth's. The clear liquid flowed in a channel cut in Earth's crust and made a sound as of many karuners murmuring. The great plants like mogdons were different from their Xarbian counterparts. Instead of wing-like leaves drooping in clusters, they had minute leaves or sharp little tines. She could hear them, closer to the ground than any Xarbian foliage, fluttering frantically, and even large branches swayed. She crouched in terror, thinking these strange vegetal beings were gaining momentum to swoop.

"Steady, child." Grindil was beside her. "There is movement in the air that causes these mogdons to sway. It is produced by differences in temperature, which set up a flow. You do not feel it as we remain exempt from the grosser physical effects here. Still, you will be able to see and hear many strange things."

Altherin was delighted by the tangle of plants that reached to her knees. Flowers were huge and lush. They would not have withstood the sudden night chills of Xarbo.

"Come," said Grindil. "We must visit the menden." He pointed out a three-story structure on the horizon. "That will be our first aim. Prepare your thought-print to stop there."

The building was a typical multi-use Technist creation with an electronic arcade and other games and refreshment dispensers on the lower level, laboratories on the central plane, and high priority view dwellings on the upper floor. Interspersed among doors and windows were platforms, some occupied by helimonopters. Altherin and Grindil entered the midsection, where they found themselves in the laboratory of a neurobiologist. Bolstered in a seat to keep him upright despite weak posture, the scientist wheeled himself along a counter by pressing his foot to a pedal at the base of his chair.

"This Technist is an expert in body functions," Grindil explained. Altherin suppressed a giggle, then remembered that she could be neither seen nor heard. "He measures changes that indicate one is ill or lying or weakened or strengthened by particular influences. Even the other group — the Ahims — use such services for their initiation exams. Among these Technists, experimentation is still considered a positive behavior — and some of their data can be useful for positive outcomes. There is simply a toll to pay. The most obvious of course is the deterioration of the scientist's own body while he sits at his counter for many hours. Ironically, he neglects his body while studying physical functions. This is a self-contradictory people, but quite likeable in many respects.

"You might be surprised at the ingenious experiments they would subject your yavers to, for instance. They would measure how many units of pressure your 'teeth' could exert per square centimeter, then by trial and error find out that the pressure is irrelevant. Without access to xaltherin they could never deduce that yavers serve to assimilate our Xarbian air. Yet they feel obligated, as scientists, to put forth theories. For instance, since yavers sparkle so conspicuously, they might speculate that they are signaling devices. They cannot xarp beyond the range of their gross senses and machines, but are eager to be of service.

"But these are trivial details. Enough of the scientist. You must gain a broad view of this planet before we leave. You have many other islands to visit."

They peered down through the ceiling of the electronic arcade and watched while people amused themselves by trying to hit moving targets with little electron guns. "Technists especially," Grindil pointed out, "are highly competitive and dissipate much nervousness in such games."

Altherin was about to object to such waste of energy when she was distracted by a woman pressing a button on a wall panel, releasing a pellet into her hand. Altherin recoiled when the woman put the pellet in her mouth.

"No; she is not polluting her mouth," Grindil laughed. "Here there is no xaltherin and no yavers to absorb it. Earth-beings nourish themselves through a 'digestive system' that grinds up and chemically dissolves nutrients. A favorite quick 'meal' here is a pellet called a Vita-roll, or 'life-pill' if you will. Actually, these beings are much involved in giving pleasure to their digestive systems through a variety of flavors, textures, and densities."

"Flavors?"

"Like hues or colors in nourishment. Materials are collected and processed in central factories and piped into homes and arcades like this through a labyrinth of underground tubes."

"Earth must be riddled with them!"

"Yes indeed. And there are other systems that conduct images and sound vibrations undetected through the air to be accessed by special tuners and amplifiers and made visible and audible."

"Do these people have time left for purposeful activity?"

"The Ahims, yes. They work on developing xenas, as I mentioned. We will visit them later. While here, let's check out a Technist dwelling."

They penetrated to the top story through its floor and found themselves in a sipping salon fashionably furnished with ferns, dripping waters, and a miniature jungle of orchids in a glass cubicle under a skylight. The invisible visitors sat on mossy seats that reminded them of their native planet. Altherin flushed, embarrassed to watch the two dwellers press buttons and sip from a cup. She was spying on intimate pleasures.

"Let us look at another form of recreation," Grindil nudged her. They thought themselves into the play-tech room, where they found a lone man. He wore only a breech-clout and held a contraption. Altherin wondered if the garment served ceremonial purposes. "No. It serves to cover the area of procreation. Such parts are considered immodest on Earth." Altherin marveled at the contradiction of people who would pollute their mouths in public, for pleasure, and yet not allow others to see all parts of their bodies.

The Technist set his gadget on a pedestal and backed away, holding a remote control device. He made several self-portraits that he projected to reveal shoots of color emanating from the body's outline. After drinking a certain liquid, the man took another series of aurographs, which he again projected and scrutinized. The colored emanations had changed. "Wheww," he said, impressed with himself and the liquid stimulant.

Sensing that it would be a waste of time to analyze this form of recreation, Altherin looked to Grindil. He nodded and together they emerged onto a heli-platform that commanded a view of the city. Nearby on a platform sat an Ahim — not much larger than the Technists, but erect and firm, with superior muscle tone.

"We will follow this man to his home," said Grindil. "You will have a slightly different mode of transport, a 'ride' as we call it. You will set your aim on a moving target and let him take you where he goes. Just envision this man when he moves as a ribbon of images in the air. You will become part of his ribbon and your thought-print will make you materialize where he stops."

The air was thick with helimonopters as the Ahim picked his way on foot across high bridges decked with plants and out to the city's perimeter. Beyond the pales of Technist territory, he practiced his power to fly and made little leaps as high as the bottom tree branches. When he reached his community, he entered a structure made of earth with panels of plastiglass, simply but ingeniously designed for some purpose Altherin could not figure out.

"The panels are an old system to accumulate the heat of the sun during the day. The heat is preserved in water and stored for night warmth and washing."

"Washing?"

"On Earth there are residues in the air that cling to the skin, which itself exudes sticky substances. Technists use anti-entropy machines for much of the cleaning, but they are costly in many ways — some not yet counted. The Ahims prefer old and tested systems as stopgap measures until the xenas are perfected."

The man's mate met him in their vestibule. On close view Altherin could see they had coarse pores and a generally gross appearance compared with Xarbians. A crisis was apparently afoot for they rushed out and walked swiftly through the small menden and entered another dwelling. There, lying on mosses in a skylit room, lay a woman with distended abdomen. Altherin looked questioningly at her zilding.

"The woman's egg has matured in her and she is about to reproduce. Our guide and his wife are experts — something like pre-natal zildings — who will help the little one come into the world."

Altherin was electrified with amazement. Eggs matured within the mother! Then the baby itself must be there in that pearl-like belly! The team of experts worked now with the mother, administering massages and instructions, sets of breathing exercises and balanced pressure to regulate the emergence of the child. When Altherin saw the little face appear swathed in blood, with eyes clenched and no body as yet visible, the sight was too grotesque for her to assimilate. She lost consciousness and dropped at Grindil's feet.

16

THE SANITARIUM

ADAM RESTED ON A BED of dense mosses bred especially to conduct the Earth's healing powers. The transparent walls of his dome tent polarized light and insulated from heat. He could see birds as they swam through the air. Due to polarization he did not see the sheen on feathers or the glistening of pine needles. His neural specialist had him lie on his back so the Earth could recharge the subtle energies of his sacro-helix, which had lost its vibratory propensities due to overstimulation.

Forbidden indulgence in personal memories, Adam amused himself by reviewing the history of healing. His ailment, in the 21st century by the old calendar, would have been diagnosed differently depending on the society in which he lived. Some ancient Africans and Pacific Islanders would perform exorcisms, attributing his illness to a malignant invader. Traditional Asians would consult ancient systems to regulate energy flow. Old-fashioned southern Europeans would blame the liver as the origin of his troubles and pipe tonics into him. In other locations his malady would be termed a nervous breakdown; he would rest in bed, perhaps prodded to recall why he had 'wanted' to fall ill, and be plied with chemicals. Eventually specialists discovered that exposure to other sufferers, and to electronic devices, was harmful to neural patients. Only gradually, after the Wedding of Science and Religion, did some traditional methods return to augment technology.

Now Adam had half a dozen experts to help him, headed by the sanitarium supervisor, an achiever of Completion, as all heads of Ahim institutions must be. His hand-picked staff included a Navajo Night Chanter, an Endocrinal Masseur, a Tantric Dakini, a Zen dietician, and a Technist neurobiologist famous for his invention — a machine that could monitor even the faintest helix emanations through a combination of electronics and acupuncture. Once a week Adam had to lie on his belly while tiny needles were inserted at the base of his spine and a scanner recorded the sporadic output of the malfunctioning nerve center.

Adam was located near a grassy flat where a group of advanced practitioners of Ahim powers did their daily physical and mental exercises. Emanations from these practices were especially beneficial to damaged nerves. Lying belly-down for his acuscan, Adam's eyes grazed grass-tips extending like a little forest, visited by butterflies and the shining lintz beetles that had hatched in a spaceship returning from a watery planet. Not hard-shelled like Earth scarabaei, the lintz possessed soft translucent bodies filled with phosphoric fluid.

"If I had my way," confided the Technist acuscanner, "I would juice some of these beetles. We have observed increased brainwave coherence in birds and reptiles that feed on them. I bet my bottom blipper those bugs would be tonic to brain-damaged patients."

"But," Adam objected, "animal experimentation is illegal. Even Technists observe the Fundamentals of Coexistence."

"Yes, yes, of course. But whoever signed the agreement didn't foresee how such blanket prohibitions could set back medicine. Besides, are creatures from another planet really animals?"

Sensing that the conversation was phasing into contention, Adam adopted the alliterative flyting mode: "Such cavils conjure catch-words from citers of written ciphers — the lawyers of yore looking for loopholes."

The neurobiologist on the acuscanner followed suit, thus admitting the subject had potential for animosity also on his part. "For the purpose of preserving a person's life, the low life of the lintz is little price to pay."

"The limit is never 'one little lintz.' Remember the race of radium-ridden rats. Experiment is essay and error. Some errors even are never erased. Earth equilibrium may end in empty entropy if one species is sacrificed to save some other."

"You sound like a historian!" The neurobiologist lapsed into flat prose.

"I was one," Adam admitted, "in a previous life." With a smidgeon of covert malice, he watched the comical, confused expression on the acuscanner's face. Technists did not officially recognize reincarnation, insisting that there was no proof of it and that none of them recalled an in-between state or previous lives. Clearly, the doctor was curious about Adam's knowledge of history but could not delve further without admitting his informant came by it in a previous lifetime. Reluctantly he left Adam, first carefully removing the needles from his sacral area and assuring him that the scan showed good progress. The encounter ended on a professional note, a stand-off with no agreement but diplomacy intact.

As Adam watched the volunteers exercising each morning on the grassy plot, he was reminded of the tremendous setback he had suffered in pursuing the Powers. The atrophy of his sacro-helix prevented his completing phase one of the project that would culminate — he hoped — in interspatial transit. In fact, few had ever mastered the art of suspending body functions necessary for inter-galactic travel. Without that Power, his project was hopeless. He despaired of a renewal of the five-year trial period, since the first probationary time had proven too rigorous for him.

In fact, after convening briefly, his initiation guides set strict conditions on his discharge from the sanitarium. He had to discontinue all instruction in Powers and take two years of reprieve from all but the most basic exercises in breathing, postures, and diet. As he left the clinic, Adam smiled bitterly over the term 'reprieve.' His only purpose in this life was to rejoin his beloved and he was forced to sit idle now. He might have to resort to Technist Rejuvenation Injections. Would Althea be aging in her current life at the same rate he was? And who knew how many lifetimes it would take him to rejoin her! He had sacrificed so much to get to the point of cognizing her present location. How ironic, if he had to wait for another incarnation and relocate her! No, he must get to Xarbo. But how in the Great Galaxies was he to do it?

17

ORACLE ISLAND

G RINDIL HAD TO USE all his resourcefulness to revive Altherin in the heavy Earth atmosphere. No xena existed to handle such an unforeseen occurrence as fainting at the sight of a birth in progress. He gave her brainwave transfusions, but could not risk depleting himself. Finally, they limped back to Xarbo, where Altherin took some time to recover before being briefed on her next destination. The place, Grindil announced, would be Oracle Island.

"What is an Oracle?" Altherin was quick to ask.

"It is one who speaks the truth. One who lives where past, present, and future coexist. The term on Earth is related to the word for mouth. But the Oracles whom you will meet, and perhaps consult, have no mouths."

"How will they speak to us?"

"Through xarping, of course."

"Can we xarp with entities anywhere, of any type?"

"No, dinzil. We can xarp any entity with weaker intuition than ours. Only equal or higher entities can xarp us, and the higher ones have the option to accept or resist our xarping."

"Are these Oracles higher than we are?"

"In some ways, yes. They have the greater span of knowledge. They have the perspective to foresee results of any action. But they have no ability to act, so they cannot realize any of their own predictions."

"Do they live in a place like Earth?"

"Like the swamps there. Oracle Island is a great shallow sea of water mixed with chemicals, some of them common to Earth and others rare or unheard-of. The only natives of this planet, except certain mollusks and minute aquatic creatures, are insects."

"Insect Oracles?"

"No," laughed Grindil.

"Then who are the Oracles?" Altherin was all amazement, eager to learn.

"They are human brains. Their presence on that planet is fortuitous to the most fantastic degree. One might imagine that the Summit ordained it."

"Do you mean physical brains, Father, or minds?"

"An intelligent question, Altherin. Strangely enough, I mean quite literally physical brains."

"But how could brains get there? You mean someone thought-printed her brain and nothing else? A mistake? A bad take-off? A crash landing?"

Grindil chuckled. "Now you are wandering into idle speculations. You could never guess how they got to where they are. They came housed in human skulls and carried by human bodies in the usual way. They belonged to certain 'astronauts' of early spaceship travel. When the ship foundered on Oracle Island, they must have jumped from it and were killed, probably battered against the shells of giant mollusks, life forms that flourish there."

"But if they were killed, how can their brains still be there?"

"The minerals that abound in Oracle Island waters are so nourishing to human cerebral tissue that the brains survived after everything else decayed. The skulls, no doubt, cracked and the liquid flooded in to bathe the brains in an elixir that not only kept them alive but enhanced their development. As you will see, the brains are now immense, scores of Earth-years after the crash."

"How big are they?"

"You could barely cover one if you sprawled on it. Of course that might destroy it. It's a delicate organism."

"What about the mollusks?"

Grindil described the giant oysters of Oracle Island and explained how pearls are created. "You see," he concluded, "the Xarbian eggs or 'pearls' birth those who were like irritating sand on Earth but made a reversal and evolved to act constructively."

"When do we go to Oracle Island?" asked Altherin impatiently.

"We'll go as soon as you can visualize the destination clearly."

The next few days were devoted to training in goal-visualization, the same xenas that Altherin had practiced before her journey to Earth. At first she saw a murky globe with wraiths of vapors obscuring the planet's surface. She had to learn a special technique to penetrate atmosphere and gradually gained a clear picture of the globe's surface, covered entirely by liquid with gently rippling tides pulled by a team of moons. She glimpsed phosphorescent bubbles everywhere, some of them surfacing to burst and shed a yellowish glow in the haze.

"It is fortunate for the Oracles that haze covers the planet at all times. A few direct rays of its Sol would overheat them."

Soon Altherin picked out forms of enormous shells half-submerged in the shifting smoke of the waters. Currents white as milk alternated with crystal clear ones. Immersed forms appeared fitfully and in parts.

"Now look for the brains," Grindil instructed. "Once you can distinguish them. we will visit."

It took Altherin two Xarbian weeks to pick up sight of the Oracles. They were flattened beyond recognition as brains. Free of the skull, they had spread in breadth and appeared as enormous jelly-fish, floating sinuously on the gentle tides. Altherin arrived among them instantaneously once she envisioned them clearly. Here, she could materialize and found herself fully physical, bathed to her waist in the shallow waters, which felt like warm, thick air that moved. It was an uncanny sensation, for on Xarbo there is no water and the air is completely still.

Then Grindil spoke and directed her attention to the Oracles.

"I remember," he said, "the first time I came to this island with my own zilding, Mother Cosbic. I could not believe that these naked, gelatinous beings could know the far-flung secrets of the universe. They were so vulnerable, you see, and I, like so many male youths, associated power with toughness."

"Did your zilding scold you?"

"No," laughed Grindil, "she did not even straighten my mind, just prodded me to question an Oracle."

"What did you ask it?" Altherin cast a sidelong glance at the convoluted pinkish-gray mass undulating on the striated waves.

"I chose to test it. I asked that it xarp me an image of my own menden and my family."

"And did it?"

"Listen, child." Grindil placed an affectionate hand on Altherin's speckled shoulder. "As the images of those familiar things flooded into my mind's eye, I had no way in the world to judge whether the oracle transmitted them or if I created them from memory. Mother Cosbic shook with laughter. She knew what I had tried to do. You cannot test an Oracle."

Altherin looked with apprehension at the strange creatures floating near her knees and quivering in the currents. There were three of them, recognizable as brains but less convoluted than brains confined to skulls. The rounded segments were opalescent, like the 'pearls' in Xarbian nurseries.

"Go on, ask a question," Grindil prodded, instructing her in their proper ceremonial name: Life of Living Waters.

At first Altherin could not prepare her mind to xarp for she was rather afraid of the gently swaying liquid that lapped around her waist and tugged her off balance if she closed her eyes. For a while she could think of nothing to ask.

Finally, she stilled her mind and let her body sway lightly in the current. She called on the Oracle closest to her: "Life of Living Waters, tell me by what sign I will recognize my life task."

At first no answer came forth. No words or images appeared on the clear expanse of her xarping mind. Then she began to cognize something new, an experience she had never entertained. At first there was but a ripple or swell on the pool of her mind, a delicate disturbance. Then she realized that the Oracle was transmitting the feeling she would have when she recognized her destiny, the emotion that would confirm she had found her life undertaking. Soon the feeling burst from the mental realm to pervade her whole body. Her viscera seemed to expand and writhe with tickling sensations. Around her heart, especially, the feelings proliferated like ramifying cracks. Or — and here the Oracle transmitted a metaphor to help her understand — she seemed to unfold in a new way, as if she were a wrinkled and fully folded mogdon leaf that spread and unfurled to reveal the blossoms hidden in its bosom.

"Do you understand, child?" Grindil saw her gasp with delight. "Do you have more questions before we leave this island?"

Altherin xarped again. She cleared her mind and heart of all input and sent out a second query. She asked the Oracle to grant her an image of the situation that would arouse the sensation she had just now enjoyed.

The sudden, clear image of a strange male jolted her. It was evident he was not a Xarbian, for his skin was opaque and uniformly colored, his hair flat and dense, appearing to Xarbian eyes as a dark moss coating his skull. At first she recoiled in disgust. But then, remembering the training of her zildings, she neutralized her xenophobic tendencies and allowed for a reversal. Then she could perceive the entity objectively. She saw that the face before her was filled with longing and hope. It was seeking earnestly, and she sensed that she had to help this male fulfill his destiny. She felt a tug in her chest cavity where she had just entertained the stirrings of her own fate. She guessed that this alien was connected to her in ways as yet unknown.

Altherin was overwhelmed with the weight of her own ignorance, of how much must surely take place within her before she could accept a link with this strange creature. Shudders of revulsion and cordiality alternated in her flesh, causing the waters around her to ripple as she lost stability.

Grindil, who had monitored Altherin's xarping, steadied her with a sympathetic hand. He knew she had chosen a celibate life. He had prepared her to meet candidates for her compassion, but not her passion.

18

SEX SPA

ADAM KNEW THAT ANXIETY was a major deterrent to helical reconstitution. As weeks passed, he did his breathing exercises faithfully, but still, worry crept in. As diversion, he prescribed for himself harmless trips into Technist territory. After all, he was excluded from the main area of Ahim dedication, which was the Powers — so what was left to him? Of course he knew better than to fool around with focusers or other dangerous gadgets or chemicals. But he did visit Rollo and watch holocasts of epics, news items, and documentaries. Historical ones still held his interest, he was surprised to learn, although he knew that history was of no practical value, along with most academic disciplines, since virtually no one put into practice the lessons learned.

He snapped aurographs of Rollo, who experimented with various recreational chemicals — and felt a bit ashamed for this, knowing that Rollo was ruining his chances to learn Powers and become an Ahim, should he wish to change. Still, one did not impose one's views; it was one of the Fundamentals of Coexistence between

Ahims and Technists. Only through playful flyting could polemics be aired. No one ever won an argument, but flyting helped preserve peace through the Atomic Crisis, the Ecological Crisis, and the Currency Crisis.

Intolerance lay always just below the surface. For instance, Ahim purists would eat no synthetic food, and Technists snickered about how such purists managed to live in zones conducive to crop cultivation. They teased in flyting that Ahims allowed environment to condition them — and Ahims retorted that this was more moral than conditioning the environment. Diplomatically but smugly, they claimed they would free themselves from all conditions and limits: subsist without food, water, or air; be oblivious to extremes of temperature; fly free of Earth's attraction. The Powers were their trump. They could concede to minor tricks, even partake of Technist chemistry and engineering, as long as they progressed toward ultimate wins.

Adam, with freedom curtailed, was vulnerable to Technist temptations. Friends and family warned him discreetly to use caution. He knew he was courting, if not disaster, at least the risk that his life would take a radical turn. But his commitment to join Althea could not be derailed. He counted on that to keep him on track. Technist amusements could divert him from anxieties, but not from his life's goal. This he kept always secret from Technist friends, for they would be skeptical of such a grandiose plan. Their projects were short-range and outward-directed — to engineering better food-delivery, inventing amusing gadgets, breeding more magnificent plants — but they seldom questioned the effect of their activity on their inner state. They could be outrageous hedonists — their sexual gadgetry was notorious — yet paid for their pleasures with martyrdom in sterile plasti-cubes. From their viewpoint, Ahims' dearth of technology was a worse form of self-denial, Ahim rewards meager — a bit of hopping vaunted as flying. More spectacular achievements occurred, but at random, not repeatable by experiment. However, some minor Ahim powers induced growth in plants, controlled weather, and calmed recalcitrant animals. Technists accepted these as actual technologies.

"Adam?" asked Rollo one evening after they both had created some original flavors in the Technist's sipping salon. "How would you like to work at Honiary?"

Adam laughed. He could not picture himself performing work in the usual Technists' sense of fitting parts, tracing circuitry, or performing their other onerous chores. "I don't think so, Rollo," he replied neutrally, politely hiding amusement.

"I can tell you don't really enjoy the games we play. They bore you. I think I know why."

"Tell me."

"You don't have a project, Adam. 'All play and no project makes a sulky son,' our grandparents said."

Adam was moved. "You are a good friend, Rollo. You care. And you are right in principle. Completely right."

"Then you'll try for the post at Honiary? I asked if they would let you test, just in case."

"I can't do a Technist job, Rollo. It would drive me crazier than I was before the sanitarium. This position may be fine, but not for ..."

"Listen, Adam: They want an Ahim. You don't understand; it's an Ahim job!"

Adam listened to the job description. It required someone with a smattering of Powers and at least potential for communicating with other species. Adam recalled his childhood argument with a blue jay. Honiary was a honey producer strapped by the limits on species control and eager to experiment with ways to divest bees peaceably of their product. Communication with insects was unheard-of even among Ahims, although adepts could speak with birds and mammals. Honiary conjectured that, although Ahims probably had no motive for talking with bees, they might have the capacity. The company wanted a young unformed Ahim who had not committed himself to a life project but had access to, and was willing to use, communication Powers.

Adam spoke to his guides and gained permission for this low intensity activity and the right to specialize in communication for the specified purpose only. He lined up a tutor and tested for the job. He was hired.

From the Ahim tutor Adam learned ancient rituals of consent that had been used to make game submit to the hunter. Adam remembered vaguely having used such techniques in past lives. His tutor was an Australian, who admitted that the rites he taught had never been used on bees, but only on animals to be killed for meat. It would be up to Adam to adapt the methods to Honiary's purposes.

Adam soon found that Rollo was right: He felt much better for having a project, even one not central to his life's aim. He felt a surge of gratitude toward his Technist friend. And with gratitude came greater receptivity. He joined in Rollo's recreations with more zeal, no longer able to view them with ironic detachment. When he made a major breakthrough for Honiary — seduced bees into abandoning their hive in a sort of hypnotic trance — Rollo persuaded him to celebrate with a session at a Technist spa.

Adam's breakthrough was not of the sort he would himself desire, for the bees did not literally consent to give up their honey — if, indeed, bees are capable of consent. He assumed they are, since they can be so adamant at refusal. In any event, he agreed to celebrate at a major pleasure center, where Rollo would show him the ropes.

Adam was only mildly enthused about the prospect of sharing in Technists' pleasures. Knowing their aversion to physical contact, he expected a highly depersonalized situation. And he was quite right. The spa was devoid of human occupants, as far as he could see. He and Rollo separated at the entrance. A Tunnel of Love had been reserved for each of them. Rollo waved good-bye with a sly grin.

Adam found himself on a conveyor belt that took him down his private 'tunnel' and exposed him to repeated applications of hot, moist towels to all parts of his body by silent mechanical hands. At the end of the tunnel was a 'libido computer,' an infamous masterpiece of Technist engineering. Adam sat in the little alcove of the machine, which Rollo had described affectionately as the 'joy dispensary.' Adam felt minute vibrations in all parts of his body as the computer 'read' him: his metabolism, the intensity and frequency of his libidinal pulses. It would assign him to the most delicious and automatically prolonged sexual experiences of which he was personally capable. He saw a needle rising on a scale of ten to a hundred and imagined this must be an indicator of his sex drive. His, he suspected, was a powerful one. He fantasized pushing the pleasure devices beyond their capacities, provoking a scandal on the evening holocasts: "Renegade Ahim blows the works," they would trumpet.

Adam did not have much time for reverie, for the conveyor soon deposited him onto a bed of grasses that tickled him in a way he liked without knowing quite why; they produced a sensation somewhere between hilarity and prurience. Then the conveyor carried him off to a foam bath. He was at just the right point of arousal to appreciate the gentle massage.

The light erotic sensations intensified in the polymorphous polygon — a space shaped like a sarcophagus to outline the body, but in the softest of materials. Adam lay still for a moment, thinking this was a recess between sessions. Then the current came on and he felt an excruciatingly pleasurable tingling in every organ. And he felt it particularly in his sacro-helix.

Yes, his helix clearly was being stimulated. Was — yes — reactivated. He could not doubt the fact. It was vibrating in tune with the polymorphous polygon's circuits. Waves of unbearable bliss pulsated from the helix through his whole body to his head. He realized too late that it might be destroying some of his finer circuits. He made a tremendous effort to tear himself out of the polygon. Surges of unprecedented pleasure held him captive. His own libido, augmented by the appliance, riveted him in place as a high voltage current would, even as he tried to escape, pushing hands and feet, his least affected parts, over the edge of the titillating trap.

No sooner had he gained a little ground than the vibrating sarcophagus swiveled and wheeled him smoothly on runners back into the tunnel. This, Rollo had warned him, was the ultimate. His head would now be firmly held in place while electrodes shot a stimulus directly into the libidinal centers in his brain. There he would wallow in virtual pleasure until he pressed an ejection button or collapsed into unconsciousness. Adam looked about frantically for the button. He saw it, but too late to abort the program.

The electrodes sent their first pulsations into his brain. At the same time a wave generated by his own helix coincided with it. The intensity of the combined stimuli sent his body jerking in erotic convulsions. He had no control whatsoever over his limbs. Pulses of sheer physical joy spilled over from the erogenous zones to flood his whole system, making it dance with abandon as if possessed by a goddess of love — an invisible female power whose form eluded him but whose effects were most manifest. Mixed with pleasure was an overbearing sense of awe, an almost nauseating fear of what his traitorous body was doing despite his puny attempts to control it.

Gradually the jolts became less compelling and Adam was able to press the ejection button. The wave patterns of electrodes and helix had finally interfered negatively and neutralized each other. He landed, dazed and exhausted, in the vestibule by which he had first approached the Tunnel of Love.

19

ECTOPLANET

"ALTHERIN," GRINDIL CALLED her gently from her shocked entrancement with the alien entity predicted to figure in her destiny. "For now," he continued when he had her attention, "forget the future and I will help you visualize a strange and amusing place. You won't be able to visit it for reasons that will soon be apparent. But you will find a virtual visit both entertaining and educative. It is called Ectoplanet. I want you to xarp with me now and tell me what you see. Are you with me?"

Altherin felt the powerful mind of her mentor sustaining and guiding her. Gratefully she let herself be distracted from her vision of the person who, inexplicably, was to figure in her future. Gradually she began to share Grindil's view of the mysterious Ectoplanet. Once she was involved in witnessing events on that distant place, Grindil took mental leave and xarped back to the Oracles. He approached the great mind that had revealed to Altherin fragments of her destiny. He addressed it in thought: "Life of the Living Waters, I come to you not as a Completion wishing to share in your thought-free ecstasy but as a humble seeker of information, like any dinzil. As you know, I am a guide, responsible for the young person who just now questioned you. Grant me knowledge of the circumstances in which she will meet the male of her vision."

As Grindil absorbed alarming hints about Altherin's future acquaintance, she was mercifully oblivious, completely taken with the bewildering world to which Grindil had sent her. At first, Ectoplanet appeared not much different from Oracle Island. It seemed hazy and swirled with forms half-revealed, half-concealed. On closer examination she saw that there was no mist here, except the ectoplasm of which the forms themselves were made. Nothing here had substance, and no sooner did a form appear than it changed into another, perhaps unrelated. Some apparitions lasted longer than others, but none for more than a minute. They all seemed too weak to sustain themselves and crumbled, yielding without resistance to their successors.

Some of the forms she saw were familiar: Earth humans of the two varieties, both large and puny — these usually in association with some of their inventions; they pressed buttons, poured chemicals, piloted vehicles with the curious look of aplomb they adopted when operating their gadgets. There were also other Earth creatures, and the flowing uniformly colorless earthly water. Many scenes involved grotesque courtship dances. Men encountered females lying in seductive positions and closed in with erotic gestures and alien methods of Being Alone Together, but then both partners would change form or dissipate altogether.

The courtship dances and maneuvering of machines seemed to predominate and to last longer than other visions. But fleetingly Altherin could make out other amazing images, seemingly composed of random fragments from earthly situations. She saw men and women with exaggerated sexual parts. She saw dwellings of the smaller earthlings fly through the air, their inhabitants lying in an ecstasy induced by chemicals. She saw monstrous shapes covered with shingles like Xarbian scales hardened into an armor to resist pellets a thousand times harder than the kragil's jasper toes. Gullets opened and gobbets of flesh were crammed in, wringing with blood. Fingers caressed and clawed and strangled and pressed buttons and made ritual gestures. Colors diminished and heightened. And realistic scenes were transposed into surreal ones, shapes exaggerated and hues vibrant.

Although much of what she viewed was born obviously of sentiments either horrific or beatific, Altherin was untouched by them and merely witnessed the fleeting images as chaotic curiosities. She wondered how such a world came about, so she fled back to Grindil to ask.

"Father, Father," she tried to penetrate his mind. He was deep in xarping and at first she could not get through. When he opened his eyes his gaze was vacant, still not focusing on her, but she prevailed on him, repeating her questions until he came around.

"Yes, what you saw is a strange place indeed, and unique in the universe. Ectoplanet is made of ectoplasm, a subtle substance that is sensitive to mental vibrations. This stuff is held together in high concentration by the force field of the planet. It is so located that thoughts from Earth bombard it continually. What impressed you most?"

"The way things change so fast."

"Of course. In fact, they change with the rapidity of thoughts. All the ideas, hopes, and fantasies that are not realized on Earth escape its atmosphere at a vibratory rate to which the ectoplasm responds. The 'plasm is molded immediately in the form of the thought. Once the thought decays, which is very quickly, the corresponding form dissolves. What you saw is the substance of which dreams are made."

"What about Xarbian dreams? Do they materialize somewhere too?"

"Yes, all thoughts take on a body sooner or later. But Xarbian thoughts, although fewer, are much more powerful and coherent than earthly ones. There is little speculation or day-dreaming on Xarbo. Night dreams are usually hints of future destinies or warnings of actions to avoid. Xarbian thoughts, if they are to take shape, do so sooner or later on Xarbo or in the locations of destined duties. They serve more obvious purposes than the random firings that beset earthly brains. Things happen so fast on Xarbo because our ideas materialize more quickly and forcefully there and we see where they lead. Not so on Earth. No one there knows that thoughts take shape on Ectoplanet. They are like irresponsible fathers who do not know they have created offspring. You will learn about the shortcomings of other beings and choose how to be of help. Right?" He tweaked her encouragingly under the chin.

"I guess so, Father," Altherin replied a bit wearily. "Do we go home to Xarbo now?"

"I'm afraid not, dinzil. I have decided it is better that you extend your tour of the planets before we go home. There is much that you must see to prepare you for your destiny. Let me tell you about a few places. Then you can choose which one you want to visit next."

Altherin cheered up with the prospect of deciding her own itinerary and listened attentively as Grindil described Clone Island; Zekling planet; and Cannibal Planet, whose inhabitants destroy each other without truce.

20

LAUNCH

After the sex spa incident, when Adam's sacro-helix was unintentionally reactivated, his moods fluctuated radically. He underwent surges of energy that flattened out suddenly so he could barely drag himself from his chair. He watched holocasts or pressed mixer buttons for hours without initiative to even pass judgment on what he viewed or tasted. His feelings and desires rose and fell restlessly and jerkily. He became a nest of fantasies, desires, and visions. Elements of his true life project — images of Althea and his in-between state — mingled with wild fantasies. He envisioned himself in positions of immense power, commanding others to fulfill his slightest whim. He became a sink of secret vice.

Adam feared to tell his guides or mentors that his sacro-helix had been reanimated in most dubious circumstances. Through ignorance, he took a huge risk that he had been incapable even of foreseeing. His advisors had told him in no uncertain terms to stay clear of Technist games and pursuits in general. They made a blanket prohibition and he ignored it. He had no excuses. But now that he was becoming a maniac for power and sex, he realized he had to confess what he had done and ask for help — not only for his own sake but for the sake of those whom he might exploit if his condition worsened.

"You say the machine sent impulses directly to the pleasure centers of your brain?" His Second Mother was, surprisingly, compassionate. All his mentors showed forbearance. The damage was done. There was no point in berating him. Their kindness was frightening. There was no doubt: They pitied him, were treating him as an impaired person. He imagined that they would send him to a sanitarium. He would become an invalid shunted from one clinic to another as he suffered relapses beyond repair.

He was surprised when, after conferring, his guides told him that he was to resume training in Powers associated with the helix. Since it was activated, they explained, its force must be channeled. The random visions and sporadic bursts of undirected energy were injurious, but if he came regularly for instruction, he could harness the power that was driving and bedeviling him. It was not a question of his deserving the Powers or not. They had been awakened. His potential must not be wasted now that it was spilling forth.

So Adam again began exercises to channel the helical impulses. He traced his maniacal desires back to their source and reacquired the energy that threatened to escape him. Painstakingly he learned to control every wisp of power that emanated from the base of his spine. Instead of being jerked at the flailing end of the lash, he became the hand that held it. And he learned again how to consult the helix as his private soothsayer.

Meanwhile, he continued his work at Honiary, a position that won him respect in Technist circles. Rollo was proud to be his acquaintance and to have referred him to the job. The young Technist never pressed Adam to divulge intimate matters, even when he saw the devastating effects of the Tunnel of Love. He apologized for leading him astray. At first Adam rejected his old friend: "I wish I'd never met you. I could have died in the push-pull of your 'love' machine."

Rollo kept a discreet distance but frequently recommended Adam for promotion at Honiary. He sent herbal teas and diet supplements with brief notes: "Hope these help your condition."

Finally Adam relented; he was getting the help he needed for recovery. It would be petty to retain a grudge. They resumed their friendship, solicitous for each other's welfare and eager to offer help from their respective areas of expertise.

Adam was at Rollo's house when the first news of a new planet burst over the holocasts. Astronomers constructed a hologram simulating the planet, and the newscaster carried it with her during the announcement as a globe that she rotated in her hand, pointing out the relative smoothness of its surface, devoid of mountains and polar caps or, in fact, any manifestations of water. No mist, she said, surrounded this sphere as it did other planets that foster life. "It is assumed," she conveyed, "that the planet is rich in underground springs. There may even be caverns filled with some sort of fossil fuels. Of course, this is speculation."

Space travel, the factions had agreed years earlier, was not worth the powder. The old space colonies and Clone Island of exiles had been left to their own devices, to develop or wither as they would. However, exploration for the sake of founding new colonies was abandoned as uneconomical and probably unethical — if one were to extend the Fundamentals of Coexistence to outer space. Which Ahims did without question. Technists were resigned to the policy only on economical persuasion.

Then suddenly news came over the holocasts that a Technist scientist probing the galaxies with kriya-radar, allegedly for recreational purposes, had received pulses from the direction of a distant solar system. He called in colleagues with more precise equipment. They ascertained the provenance of the signals to be a particular planet. Kriya-radar, sensitive to the emanations peculiar to life forms, could measure quite accurately and at immense distances the quantity of organically produced energy radiating from a particular location. The newly found planet identified itself as a host for life little different from that known on Earth, and also a treasure trove of highly concentrated organic substances. Technists saw this place as a possible storehouse of fuels usable on Earth. Ahims, who did not consider advancement of technology desirable and who were more concerned with eco-ethics, were vehemently opposed to the idea of exploiting the planet.

Nonetheless, Technists began to organize an expedition. To retain a semblance of diplomacy and a tincture of legality, the project leaders argued that the planet must certainly be a derivative from an Earth colony — perhaps created by Clones —

and therefore fair game. Its emanations were very much like those of life on Earth.

Adam snickered at first. Technists, despite their fetish for scientific objectivity, were prone to wishful thinking. Their pipe dreams often took the form of pseudo-scientific speculation. He viewed the plan to explore the new planet with skepticism. However, after several months of work with his Second Mother and several other helix experts, he gained the courage to revisit the question that obsessed him before his earlier breakdown: *Where is Xarbo?* He had cognized the name of the place where his beloved was reborn, only to have further pursuit snatched from his grasp. At first the momentous possibility of gaining an answer excited him too much. He tried for several days to frame his question, which had to arise from a quiet state if an answer were indeed available. Finally, "Where is Xarbo?" he whispered silently down his veins and nerves to the sage center at the base of his spine.

Immediately something stirred in the depths of his image-making mind. An impulse shot to his brain, a code with the answer! At first he saw merely a spinning. It could have been any planet, or a ball on a seal's nose. He tried to focus on salient features: mountains, craters, canals, cloud patterns. Nothing came. The ball seemed hollow, insubstantial. Something was wrong. It was not a real planet at all.

He was about to give up in disappointment when he glimpsed a hand holding the globe. It was the hand of the newscaster whom he had seen on a holocast! He was looking at the simulated hologram of the newly discovered planet over which world-wide uproar was raging. This must be Xarbo! This must be where Althea had resumed a form! Overwhelmed by the evidence, Adam fainted.

As soon as he recovered he rushed to Rollo's house and asked his friend to turn on the holocaster. As he suspected, the expedition to the newly discovered planet was almost ready to launch. The leaders, however, were unwilling to venture into unknown territory without at least one Ahim on the crew. The ostensible reason was to retain diplomatic relations between the two Earth factions; Ahim objections to the project threatened to topple the longstanding but unstable peace arrangement. Other motives were less explicit. For instance, if anything went wrong — or even if all went well — Ahims should take some of the blame or credit. However, the more important reason for including an Ahim, as Adam could guess from his experiences with Honiary, was to profit from Ahim Powers. Technists would not give official credence to such abilities, but they would not attempt anything as important as this expedition without the Ahims' supposed abilities to communicate with alien species, to subsist with minimal supplies, to draw on emergency resources within themselves. Technists could not quite imagine what skills the rival faction was capable of, but they were smart enough to seek an Ahim who might practice them.

Adam asked Rollo how the expedition leaders would find an Ahim willing to join them.

"Ahim applicants will abound." Rollo bridled at the imagined challenge. "Not many savvy Ahims surf to satellites of stars under their own steam. Who is picked for this pilgrimage will be a pioneer in planetary paths."

"Take two breaths, Rollo," Adam chuckled. "Just tell me how the search is being conducted."

Rollo relaxed his barrage of flyting and explained how information banks were being plundered for the bios of Ahims in Technist employment. The aim was to find someone not too committed to Ahim ideals and goals to consider an offer, and yet adept in enough Powers to be useful. As he explained all this, Rollo began to have sparks of insight. "You could be the one! Adam, you could go! And will you, some time," he added, excitement emboldening him, "tell me why you changed your name?"

"Yes, I will — but you have to help me fit that Ahim slot on the expedition."

Rollo agreed eagerly, pulled strings in his areas of influence, and succeeded in procuring an interview for Adam. However, the grilling was worse than expected. Again, as at his initiation interviews, Adam was keeping the motive for his application secret. Not only would his yearning to rejoin Althea on Xarbo come across as self-centered and irrelevant to expedition goals, but he might be judged an extremist among Ahims, a wild-eyed zealot ready to self-destruct in order to reincarnate on the planet where his beloved supposedly resided.

"What is your interest in joining this launch?" the committee insisted.

"I enjoy deploying my faculties at large," Adam improvised. "At Honiary I can communicate with bees. I find this fulfilling and wish to enlarge my sphere to another planet and other more exotic species."

"You realize that your galvanic responses are high as you make this response. This usually indicates falsehood."

Desperately Adam tendered an alternative: "It can also indicate simply high emotion. My great enthusiasm for this project!"

Finally they accepted his application and Adam found himself en route to Xarbo — or what he presumed to be Xarbo — much faster than he had hoped, considering the many setbacks he had suffered. It seemed too good to be true. Would he be disappointed? Would the glistening planet of the hologram prove to be actually the home of Althea reincarnated?

21

LANDING

WHEN ADAM LANDED on Xarbo after rematerialization, his doubts were momentarily allayed by the euphoria induced by Xarbian air. The rainbow-hued substance was later to prove both a blessing and a curse to the raiders from Earth. But at first it seemed a marvelous elixir, which heightened all the senses and sharpened mental faculties.

Adam and his Technist accomplices encountered their first surprise as soon as they set foot on the planet. Their feet simply would not stick to the surface, apparently due to a low gravitational force. Each step sent them scooting twenty centimeters above the ground, effortlessly as if on air skis. However, when they saw Xarbians maneuvering through the higher reaches, they assumed at first that such higher flying was promoted by a subtle technology. They finally accepted Adam's opinion that Xarbians had perfected the skill of levitation that Ahims were still cultivating on Earth.

It seemed that Xarbians must also have either acquired an uncanny fearlessness or else they had a secret weapon, for they showed no dismay when the strangers landed. They neither fled in awe nor approached with curiosity or menace. Those who saw the landing flew off quietly, no doubt to inform leaders. This behavior convinced the Technists that they were dealing with a well-armed, highly logical people, possibly devoid of emotions, likely possessed of high technical development. As they explored the planet cautiously, they continued to seek signs of technology and were amazed to find so few of them.

The dwellings had the appearance of great refinement, an intangible quality that could derive only from the use of sophisticated materials and methods of construction. Yet there was no evidence of factories, no roads even, and no traffic going to and from the villages. As explorations continued, the expedition leaders had a sinking feeling, for they had committed an inordinate amount of time and fuel to the undertaking on the gamble that fuels would be plentiful on the planet. However, although Xarbo harbored humanoid inhabitants, there appeared to be no industry, manufacture, or mining. If fuels lay hidden under the surface, it would be up to the explorers to ferret them out — not a practical pursuit if all equipment and expertise had to be imported from Earth. And that appeared to be the situation, for Xarbians proved to be neither miners nor engineers. In fact, they did not seem to be farmers either. No work of any kind was in evidence.

A further complication cropped up when the explorers tried to light a fire. Tired of preserved rations, the travelers hunted and killed a Xarbian animal the size of a large dog. Its red blood promised edibility. Hastily, they tried to cook a portion for testing. The first to attempt to light a fire singed her nose and a shoot of flame parted her hair. Her companions laughed nervously, but their amusement soon turned to bewilderment as several of them tried the same operation and failed in the same way. The flame roared up a few feet and dissipated. The air would not support burning, although it obviously was oxygenated, for they could breathe it. It seemed heat was conducted so efficiently that fire spent itself as soon as it was lit. The hunters abandoned their prey, speculating that the Xarbians must indeed be primitive if they could not cook their meat. Others, persuaded by Adam, dared to imagine that the locals might be advanced in ways as yet not perceived by the newcomers.

"Adam," Rollo apologized, "I have persuaded you to come on a tail-of-the-comet chase — mainly because I had signed up. There is nothing here. I hope you won't get into trouble with your teachers, or guides, or whatever you call them."

"Trouble? Oh," Adam smiled nonchalantly, "I am not worried. Really."

"Still, you must feel let down. You could have made a name for yourself extracting secrets from these people, but they're just a bunch of naked primitives."

"I am genuinely glad to be here. You have no reason to regret encouraging me to come."

Rollo shrugged. Sometimes his Ahim friend seemed motivated by private incentives directed at purely personal rewards. When he finally learned what drew Adam to Xarbo he was flabbergasted.

22

MIRACLES

"**G**REAT GOD OF THE GALAXIES," exclaimed the Technist leader with easy blasphemy, for he believed in no gods. "All alert. All alert. Arms at ready. I don't know what this is, but stand by for top emergency."

The band of fifty adventurers who had manned the spaceship to Xarbo scrambled into formation to confront sudden danger. They faced a small army of approaching Xarbians dressed in what they imagined were uniforms and sounding high-pitched instruments, which they took for trumpets of war. The screeching was almost unbearable to earthly ears. Lieutenants, fearing a sonar weapon, ordered insertion of earplugs. The locals carried no flags or other insignia but they bore little wagons, which floated at the end of tethers like balloons and contained objects that the Technists could not make out.

Adam, too, observed all this from the rear ranks. What he saw reminded him of a scene from an ancient epic. He, like his companions, carried a hand weapon at ready. They were outnumbered by two to one but, as the band of natives grew closer, raising no dust from the firm mosses, they could discern no weapons nor untoward motions. The Technist leader warned them not to fire in panic. He stepped forward to meet the Xarbians with a flat hand raised in a gesture that meant 'peace' and 'please stop where you are.'

The locals seemed to understand; they halted and imitated the gesture in unison. The effect en masse was rather military-like. Adam recollected records of certain Earth armies before world unification. However, the salute was simply a reproduction of the visitors' own gesture of greeting. Now the natives seemed to present their own greeting, more complex and ritualized. They lowered the little wagons on their tethers as their guests watched cautiously. The head of the group, a female of average height, shoulder-high to a Technist and only chest-high to Adam, stepped forward and spoke words that the travelers took for a speech. They could not understand the language, of course, and attributed to imagination the coincidence of some Xarbian sounds with Earth words: Sol, pearl, isle, oracle — pronounced in the French way.

The wagons contained garments and ornaments, each rich and unique, and the group offered these to the guests after the brief speech, which seemed peaceful in tone. The Technist leader, however, cautioned against touching the objects in case they were contaminated. It was scarcely believable that a defenseless society could have the courage to meet a sophisticated, armed invader without show of fear or resistance.

The gifts lay at the feet of the intended recipients. There was an awkward moment. The Technist leader decided to try a leap in the dark and asked a question in several Earth languages: "What do you eat?" He thought it a neutral enough question. And a practical one. The spaceship's supplies would be exhausted in a few weeks and it would be worthwhile knowing if they could be restocked.

The Xarbian leader seemed to understand as she stared at the Technist's repeated gesture of inserting something in his mouth. Instead of proffering the hoped-for answer, she expressed alarm and disgust. Another of the foremost Xarbians whispered to her and together they began to gesture in apparent reply. They extended their arms as if scooping air or swimming, bringing their hands back to their faces. The Technists shared guesses as to what the gestures meant: Were there fish somewhere on this planet?

Did they themselves fly up, swimming through the air like birds, perhaps to hunt edible winged creatures?

The Xarbians sensed that interpretations were off base and made repulsing moves as if to push back the errors. They continued their airy gestures, encompassing greater space, dancing almost as if to embrace more air. Then they bared their teeth, which were strangely translucent, crystalline, like quartz in the older natives and almost diamond bright in the younger ones. Soon the whole troupe was grinning broadly, clearly making a point of displaying their extraordinary teeth.

"Yes, we know you must eat," said the head Technist in exasperation, "but what?"

The pantomime continued for a few minutes, but to no avail. The voyagers tried another line of communication. They stated baldly, "We have come in search of fuel."

Only one of the Xarbians seemed to understand, an elder with vaguely Asiatic features who nodded as if remembering the word from a distant past and repeated it with drawn-out pronunciation. Then he shook his head and made a palms-down gesture with an air of finality.

"He must mean there is no fuel here," interpreted a psycho-neurologist. "I wonder if a galvanic resistor would register lies among these creatures."

The leader cast him a warning glance and asked the elder, "How do you construct your buildings?" Through pantomime, he made his question understood almost instantaneously and the Xarbian sage replied through a dramatic demonstration of xenas.

The would-be miners gasped as the ground a few meters away began to bulge and rise like a loaf of bread in the oven or a nascent volcanic mountain. They felt their hair rise and their palms perspire when the bulge took on form, as if modeled by invisible hands, and structured itself into one of the ovoid dwellings like those they spotted earlier. One Xarbian in particular was focusing on the structure with arms crossed. When, after a few minutes, the process was complete, this male invited them to approach. They clustered around the building, loath at first to touch it as if it might be hot. Once their fears subsided, they were curious to see the inside, but could find no doors.

"How do you get into it?" asked an engineer. The Xarbian could not have heard the question; his back was turned and some musical instruments were still shrilling. Nonetheless, as if in response, he walked straight through the hard, opaque walls of the newly materialized edifice. Then he reappeared instantaneously in their midst with only a fleeting rupture to the walls and no apparent detriment to his body.

Waves of panic fluttered through the group from Earth, inducing spasms of queasiness. Three miracles in rapid succession had belted them. It was obvious that their hosts could walk through solid matter, disappear and reappear at will, and some could read the Earth beings' minds. How else could they interpret questions that were not only couched in an alien language but also sometimes out of earshot?

After the encounter, the travelers met to discuss what they had observed. The general feeling was one of frustration as well as bewilderment. None of their urgent questions had been answered. They still did not know what they might eat on Xarbo, nor what fuels if any existed there. It seemed the locals did not need the substances on which the visitors depended. Reluctantly, they turned to Adam for help: "Will you meet with these creatures and try to get more details on what they're up to? Can you monitor their minds the way they monitor ours?"

"I will do what I can. But no, I cannot monitor their minds."

"You have tuned in to other species on Earth."

"Yes. Higher intelligences can access lower ones at will. But not vice versa."

"You mean these naked natives are higher than we are?"

"To all appearances, yes. Possibly they have a way of permitting lesser intelligences to tune in on them. I will need to be alone for some days of preparation to approach them."

Adam set up a dome tent at some distance from the space vessel. He would not need nourishment during his period of mental preparation. For this his mates were grateful. Once alone, he ruminated on his situation. How could he settle down to his telepathic exercises and ignore his own great reason for being on Xarbo? On the other hand, he could not sneak off alone on the strange planet, not knowing what dangers lurked, or what his companions would do if they caught him. Still, there was no disciplining his mind to the assigned task while it was excited at the prospect of reunion with Althea. How would he recognize her as a Xarbian? What if she had developed a new set of relationships that excluded him — or had forgotten him altogether?

Summoning all his courage, Adam put aside his qualms. He would have to find a means to seek out Althea while upholding his obligations to the expedition. Suddenly, it was obvious. He must discover Althea's new identity and then prepare his mind to ask the required questions of her, telepathically. He had flashbacks to when his wife gave him counsel over their dining pedestal at home. Nostalgia and longing swept over him as he remembered the tall, self-possessed woman who had married him and hopefully waited for him after their lifetime together ended. He remembered with tenderness her roseate earthiness, her beauty as of a long-stemmed burgundy iris. She had been earthy, but her spirit was a bright beacon.

Adam trembled at the thought of reunion. How would he know her? Would he have the old feelings when he saw her clad in the translucently clear Xarbian flesh, the untouchable delicacy of rainbow-hued skin, short of stature but lively as a sprite? And how would she react to him, heavy still with the taint of Earth, hairy, porous, gross of bone? Worst of all, he was freighted with self-doubt.

Adam made a supreme effort to cast off self-defeating thoughts. He got down to the business at hand. First, some physical postures to smooth out the taut and nervous muscles. Then some breathing exercises to regulate metabolism. His mind began to settle. At last he was capable of consultation with his helix. He had to have precise knowledge of Althea's appearance and whereabouts.

The first image that came in reply to his query was a flowing stream with bubbles floating on it. He wondered for a moment if Althea had drowned in a strange river. But no, he was made to focus more closely on the bubbles. The flowing had ceased. The iridescent circles flattened. The apparent fluid was not water but clear flesh. On it rainbow-hued speckles reflected light. This was Althea's hallmark — and apparently her birthmark on Xarbo: her freckles! Adam almost leapt out of his skin with excitement and had to coax himself back down, for only in quiet could he learn all that he had to know.

Now he glimpsed a form beneath the speckled skin: the figure of a young woman shaped as all Xarbians are, very like an Earth human but with a concave abdomen and a stiff but delicate corolla of hair, like a ripe dandelion. Adam scrutinized the face eagerly, and his vision centered on it in close-up, catching it in its actual situation. The young woman was talking earnestly, then listening to a voice of invisible provenance. Was she talking to a parent? A lover? Adam was afraid to ask. He searched the features for signs of his dear one. Yes, Althea used to toss her head in just such a way when she was impatient. Her nostrils distended a little in just this way when she heard important news and wanted to take it all in, almost as if she tried to inhale the information. Adam could see Althea within this personality, although the Xarbian girl was younger — about half Althea's age when she died. *She should be just my age*, Adam conjectured. *Although she might be older, by Xarbian time. Perhaps aging is less evident on this planet.*

Adam asked his helix for directions to reach his beloved: first a picture of her dwelling — which looked like all the other local houses to an untrained eye. The community too was indistinguishable from others. Then the helix seemed to spin within him before more images came, and it directed him to some landmarks: a meadow where purple hairy birds congregated; a small grove of enormous trees; a faceted dome clearly a communal building, perhaps for government or religion. He felt he could follow the markers en route to his destination, and hoped he would remember also how to return to his tent if need be.

At last Adam asked his internal mentor for Althea's new name. Would she still be essentially Althea? Perhaps this being with a different name would have nothing to do with him. Wouldn't she have a destiny of her own in these alien circumstances? To know her new name would introduce him somehow to her milieu of new friends, her strange parents, her mentors in undreamed-of skills, and — who knows? — an alien lover. Adam choked on the knot in his throat as if he anticipated inability to pronounce Althea's current name. To utter it would be an invasion of her new world. To call her would be to awaken her from a reality she chose to enter distant from him.

If she had wanted to be with him, she would have waited and not gone off to the fascinating Xarbo when she saw him fall short of it. She would have lived her new life on Earth, accessible to him, sharing earthly ups and downs. Adam felt resentment. Doubts, anger, and self-pity crowded his system, producing a turbulence through which he could not mentally navigate. His mind was too unstable to grasp further information. He had to abandon his quest for Althea's name — or any further knowledge. He would have to make do with the vision of her appearance and the directions to her dwelling.

An unexpected emergency almost ended his quest. As the Xarbian sun lowered itself over the horizon he realized that all heat was leaving the atmosphere. He ran to the spaceship just in time to take shelter before night set in. Next day he returned to his bivouac to resume calming exercises and cultivation of telepathy.

Three days later, when Adam emerged from his tent after composing his mind, he was still not sure what to do. Automatically he scanned the horizon for the faceted dome he had envisioned, and walked until he found a community. The natives were strangely calm on seeing a stranger among them. He stopped one of the passers-by and sketched on a wall an image of the faceted structure. With typical Xarbian alacrity, the stranger did not bother with schematic directions. He called for a rather large floating wagon and motioned for Adam to jump in. Soon they were racing through the brilliant light-refracting air, Adam in the wagon towed by the self-appointed guide. It was amazing how they did not create any draft as they sped. Adam calculated that they were moving at fifty to a hundred kilometers per hour, judging by reference to the ground, but he felt no wind in his face, no buffeting pressure. His hair did not fly in the air.

The two passed over a fertile area with strange birds foraging in it. Adam saw that, although the vegetation was lush, there was no ground water visible. They sailed by enormous trees whose half-folded leaves sheltered flowers or fruit; Adam was not sure which. Then he saw the dome and a hundred fingers clutched at his stomach. Since the dome of his vision existed, no doubt the woman did too. Awe thrilled him as he admired the brilliant facets on the structure; he associated them with the person he sought. Her teeth and eyes and stiff fine hair flashed with equal brilliance.

Adam thanked his guide with a light embrace and felt encouraged that it was reciprocated. These were not unemotional geniuses as his Technist companions conjectured. They were kind and cordial. Now bolstered as he walked the firm low moss between the temple and the town, Adam saw that the community must number under two hundred. It would not be difficult to locate the face from his dreams. Word had obviously travelled to this place that the Earth people had landed not far away. No one stared. Some greeted him with a slight nod. He approached one of these and again drew a sketch on a wall, of a Xarbian woman with circles on her shoulders to represent speckles. The stranger was surprised, but clearly recognized the person represented. He pointed Adam down a path between buildings and drew a diagram to represent the two bifurcations that he must take to reach his destination.

Althea's home! Adam trembled, his veins swelling with life excited to alertness by the prospect of love. *Is this how epic heroes felt when they reached their dear homes after long travails? The epics never told of these emotions. The hero's breast is firm but mine is not,* thought Adam. *I have fared far but I quake like a child awaking in the dark. How will I approach her? What if she does not remember me? What if she rejects me? How will I win my way into her graces? Will I be able to engage in telepathy?*

Adam almost dropped the metallic rock he had grabbed up to help him keep grounded despite the minimal pull of gravity. He was relieved to see that her dwelling had openings, unlike the model with which the Xarbians surprised his companions. He stepped up to what he guessed to be a door, a tightly fitted slim piece of glittering material that looked like mica and was similarly semi-transparent. He saw movement of heads within. A woman opened the door. She was old, Adam guessed from the lack of sheen on her skin scales, and when her lips parted in surprise her teeth were not blindingly brilliant.

Behind her, he glimpsed a delicate straight stem of a body about as high as his chest, the shoulders mottled with multi-colored spots that became iridescent as she moved. Overwhelmed by sight of the longed-for figure, Adam stepped over the threshold impulsively without waiting for invitation. All strangeness and doubt fell away from him. Although the Xarbian woman resembled Althea only in a few special traits, there was no doubt in his heart that this was she. She exerted exactly the same influence that Althea had, the sense of a gentle bulwark, an unimposing wisdom, passion held in check by reflection. Unspoken promises of a haven, of guidance, emanated from this as yet incomplete being. He dropped his ballast as he entered the house and shot up half a meter to bound toward her.

The two women looked up at him incredulously. Then with shrieks like the music he had heard from the Xarbian flutes, their teeth flashed, their dandelion hair bobbed, their bodies danced and capered. It was Adam's first exposure to Xarbian laughter.

After the hilarity died down, the older woman flew to him with a scarf of sorts and tethered him like a wagon to a fixture near the floor. The house was extremely simple, Adam noted as he swayed slightly upward at his post. The structure seemed to be made from the hard, highly metallic soil of the planet, but there was none of the crudeness or roughness of similar structures on Earth. The material was not porous. It could have been cast aluminum, but the color was pinkish. Perhaps copper, Adam thought, but it apparently did not conduct heat although the walls were only a few centimeters thick. There was no furniture. Sitting and lying places were sculpted into the walls, the floor arranged on several levels. Adam took all this in as a sort of mental reprieve before tackling the all-important mission of breaking the communication barrier with his long-sought beloved.

She had approached him and stood within a meter now, staring at him as he tried to maneuver his feet onto the floor. He managed to wedge his feet under a low ledge and faced her. Yes, there were the rainbow freckles on her shoulders — the distinguishing carry-over trait from her lifetime as Althea. Impulsively he hugged her. If anything could, his embrace should awaken memories of him and their life together. She responded instinctively, delicately — not with Althea's old hearty hug, the strong encompassing band of earthly arms. Like all Xarbians, this girl was ethereal, yet vital in a high electric way.

He gazed questioningly into her face. She had not recognized him as her earthly husband, he was convinced, but stared at him in astonishment. She had not been shocked by his gentle embrace, but seemed to know him in a way he could not grasp — almost as if he were a threat of which she had been forewarned, perhaps a threat glimpsed in a soothsayer's vision. He was foreknown but not altogether acknowledged. She expected him but did not welcome him. She was alert and cautious. He held her at arms' length to scrutinize her and let her examine him, and she appeared uneasy. His looks did not please her, he could see. She felt his scrutiny to be impertinent. She was not his. He would have to win her.

23

TICKLING OF THE HEART

ALTHERIN WAS CONFUSED. Her insecurities had re-awakened and been mobilized against her. Since she had glimpsed the alien of the Oracle's vision, she was in constant crisis, requiring concerted help from all her zildings as well as Mother Zalda. She was afraid for her sanity. What if this stranger aroused in her the obsessive sensations that had beset her in Grandar's bed? That her destiny should be delivered in the form of a male seemed a violation of her decision to be celibate and of all her efforts to choose a life project. And what a strange abhorrent male it was! Totally unlike the magnificent Grandar or the tender receptive Waldin, this Earth being was grossly crude, his skin deformed by tiny forests of dead brush. His breath smelled of stale digestions, emanations from a bodily system unknown among her kind. It reminded her of the fearful Cannibal Island, just visited. He epitomized everything unclean and uncouth.

It took all of Altherin's ability in reversal to keep from fainting at the prospect of further meetings with her fated mate, or accomplice, or whatever he was meant to be. She had to work long

137

at her exercises to control the xenophobic instincts. Mother Melda gave her extended instructions in the techniques, reminding her that the male himself must have some xenophobic qualms and that on Earth there were no known means to control these instincts except for some rules of diplomacy and formulas of ritualized speech. Deep-rooted hostilities, Melda explained, still lay tangled in the human breast, not even admitted as innate but attributed instead to intellectual error or 'prejudice.'

While Altherin tried to master her turbulent emotions, she had Adam housed in a specially made structure. Her friends and relatives ferried down mogdon fruits to sustain him and began to teach him rudiments of Xarbian language. He seemed eager to learn and even tried to imitate the high, airy piping gusts of sound with which Xarbians pronounced their words. More importantly, she received advanced instructions from her fifth zilding, Mother Rozden, in how to allow a lesser intelligence to xarp her. Still. she had to fight her tendency to lock herself off protectively, like a dwelling at night.

Time was pressing. How long the Earth visitors could remain was dubious. After three days, a preliminary ceremony of Being Alone Together was arranged for Altherin and Adam. Mother Melda brought the two into a grove. She gave them ceremonial garments with sensory tendrils to aid them in becoming acquainted. She did not remind Altherin of what had happened at her last ceremony of this kind. It was unnecessary. Besides, the girl's destiny was more complex and difficult than Melda alone could grasp. She left her with a compassionate pat on the arm.

When Altherin saw her partner approach appareled as a dandon she could not suppress a shriek of laughter. She bounded in the air, turned somersaults, flitted around him — not derisively, for derision is foreign to the Xarbian emotional spectrum, but with innocent revelry. She saw his look of dismay, his fear of some hostility on her part. She quelled her merriment, but the outburst of humor had disposed her to view him as less of a threat than before. Now his dismay awoke her compassion. She touched his face, pitying the coarse prickling facial landscape for its patent ugliness.

Obviously overwhelmed by the sudden unexpected tenderness, her companion began to sprout waters from his eyes. Weeping is unknown on Xarbo and Altherin imagined it to be a token of communion, equivalent to a Xarbian sigh. She received the hot drops of his eye water in her hands, gingerly. And her acceptance of it aroused him to more emissions, accompanied by shudders and spasms.

She touched the tendrils of her costume to his and xarped the jagged emotions that produced his weeping. They created a sympathetic turmoil in her breast, a commingling of pity and fear: a sensation like that of xarping a palanthin, the trembling senses of an animal caught in the toils of mortality and ignorant of destiny. The sensation reminded her, too, of the pangs she felt when witnessing the birth of the blood-swathed Earth baby. And again she felt that she would faint.

She lay down on the mossy ground to regain composure. Her companion must be made to understand. She practiced the technique that would allow him to xarp her. When she heard him gasp, she knew he had succeeded. She saw that he looked to her as an extraordinary being, stronger and more accomplished than he. He was bewildered by her vulnerability. She let him xarp the fact that on Xarbo both joy and grief are more intense than on Earth. She let him experience in full the bodily dread that his physical aspects — and especially his weeping — inspired in her.

Suddenly he changed. She saw it first in his facial expression. The waters ceased to flow. She xarped him. He had rallied when he saw her dilemma. He was calling on all his resources to calm his own mind and spare her the sympathetic shudders that his turmoil caused. She was amazed that such an apparently primitive being could be so sensitive. Again, waves of compassion filled her. And again his tears flowed uncontrollably. Yet, once he realized how his crude sentiments disturbed her, he showed surprising powers of self-mastery.

As Altherin cognized this unexpected rallying power of her earthly counterpart, she began to have strange, vague inklings. Somewhere she had shelved a memory that showed this being as weak and dependent. Somewhere this face had looked at her pleadingly. Vaguely she sensed that they were to undergo a reversal together.

I knew you in another life, she confided, opening the xarping byways for him to receive and respond.

I leaned on you, I know, Adam replied.

I seem to remember. I liked that in a perverse way. But I also pitied you.

Earth festers with contradictory feelings, long clung to.

But changes can happen very fast here on Xarbo.

Instinctively Altherin realized that she must hold back the body-choking spasms of pity induced by this strange yet familiar outsider. She must check her tendency to relinquish her own wishes in order to meet another's passing needs or whims. She must beware of condescension or outright contempt. As yet, her proper role in this relationship was not clear, but she sensed a new direction had to be taken. Where it led would be revealed in time.

Surely the Earth person had been sent to tempt and try her. With typical Xarbian zest, Altherin accepted the challenge. Perhaps her encounter with this half-remembered alien would develop into mutual opportunity. She had wronged him by assuming he brought only degradation. Perhaps with him she would understand, and right the wrong she had committed with Waldin.

As these thoughts ramified in her mind, her body felt a corresponding ripple, as if roots were quickly penetrating and opening fresh channels in her chest cavity. The sudden motion produced a tickling sensation, as if her heart were secreting trickles like the eye-waters of her companion. She was stilled with wonder at the unexpected effects this human being induced in her. And she remembered vaguely that, somewhere, she had felt this tickling before.

Altherin let her companion share the sensation that was expanding around her heart. He took a deep breath of xaltherin as he tuned in to the awesome tingling. She closed her eyes to share it more fully, and recollected with a jolt that she had experienced this elation first on Oracle Island when she asked the Life of the Living Waters to give her an omen by which to recognize her fated path.

The Earth being was looking piercingly into her eyes, as if searching for something that should be swimming there. She xarped that he was trying to find a sign of recognition from the past life. She gave him the gesture of negation, to indicate that recapture of the past is not a fruitful pursuit.

For a moment it seemed he would weep again, from grief. But he rallied quickly and shot a question at her with unexpected clarity. She was shocked, could not believe what he was asking, annoyed at his boorishness. How could he, when she was so open, trusting in his good will?

He had asked for her present name. Did he not know that Xarbians never utter their own names, nor xarp them to another, even in the most intimate circumstances? That it is a simple matter to learn another's name from acquaintances? That there is no need therefore to ask that one give away the most heart-close gift?

Altherin tossed her dandelion head in frustration, resisting the question as if it were a barb in her flesh, as if she would cast off this inconsiderate request for unnecessary sacrifice. Embarrassed to refuse a request, she shrugged impatiently and her fine hair flopped to her shoulders and upright again. Seeing her discomfort, Adam at first looked bewildered. Then a great wave of joy spread over his face and through his limbs. Altherin was astounded. She conveyed an inquiry to him. He touched her shoulder gently, where, beneath the animal costume, lay her freckles. *I know you now for sure,* he intimated passionately: *I would recognize that head toss anywhere.* Seeing that she did not share his sentiment, he apologized: *I know you said it's not good to be attached to the past. But it was only through memories that I remained faithful in my quest to find you.*

Altherin was moved but had no reciprocal commitment to confess. Instead, she explained her repugnance for his question, conveying how Xarbians hold their own names as sacred gifts and receptacles of personal power. She tried to give him some concept of the power of sound as it resonates in the Xarbian yeldom.

He in turn told her how the familiar toss of the head, which just now moved him to joy in remembrance, had always been a sign of his trespassing. *I promise that in this lifetime I will not insist on having my way as I did before with you. With Althea.*

His humility struck Altherin as ambiguous, but she put the intuition aside to deal with later. Again she tried to draw him out, to discover why he made his way to her on Xarbo: *What does your mind ask of me?*

Adam was suddenly jolted from his dream of personal fulfillment and reminded of his mission on behalf of his expedition. He had resolved to convey earthly concerns to his chosen Xarbian guide. *What do you eat? Do you have fuels? Why is your language cognate in part with Earth languages?* He blurted the pragmatic inquiries as if he had been programmed.

Altherin was taken aback by the suddenly impersonal turn of communication. It rang false to her yeldom. Is this what her companion wanted most eagerly to know after a lifetime of searching for her? As a Xarbian, she had no concept of a mission that might require putting aside personal evolution in the interests of a communal enterprise.

With suspicions aroused by his sudden change of tone, Altherin nonetheless answered his questions clearly and succinctly. She produced an infra-vision of yavers exposed to xaltherin, breaking it into the elements that Xarbians could assimilate. He was made to see how from the clear atmosphere a liquid was distilled to speed through a circulatory system, not red and indigo like blood vessels but uniformly clear of color like aqueducts in the unsullied flesh. The nutrients, he could intuit, were quite different from those needed by Earth beings. Xarbians have no bones as such, require no calcium or iron. He xarped a question about the mogdon fruit. Did Xarbians not eat of that tree? Altherin was mildly repulsed. She showed him an image of native birds pecking at the fruit.

"Only animals eat on this planet!" he exclaimed aloud as he thought it.

"Anima!" she trilled in recognition.

Anima, animal, animation... . Why are our languages alike? he inquired mentally.

All Xarbians have lived on Earth in previous lives. Perhaps all Earth languages have left traces here.

Adam asked his last question aloud, testing to see if the word might be one of those salvaged from Earth: "Do you have fuels?"

Altherin knew the word was vaguely familiar. She searched her memories. Yes, it had been explained by Father Grindil. He had told her about the substances adapted on Earth to permit travel without thought prints, about the vehicles like air carriages that required kinetic means of locomotion. Just how these things functioned was very vague to Altherin and seemed imponderably cumbersome and complicated. But she remembered without doubt that the required substances had been called 'fuels' and that Father Grindil used to create them before he walked out of the place of their manufacture.

She told Adam emphatically that Xarbo had no fuels. He flashed back: *How could kriya-radar show so much energy if there is no technology here?*

Kriya! Altherin echoed. *Xaltherin is kriya! Sol is kriya! Kriya is everywhere — in mogdons, mosses, all creatures.* She leapt around the grove, repeating the word, indicating that life is everywhere on Xarbo. She tried to communicate to Adam the vibratory rate of life close to its most intimate pulse. He tried to follow her, but recoiled as if stung. He could not withstand the high frequency generated on this planet beyond the level of appearances. He would have to remain on a superficial level of physical acquaintance with her and her habitat. At least for now.

24

HAVOC

W HEN ADAM RETURNED to the spaceship, he witnessed a beehive of activity accompanied by excited buzzing.

"What's happening?"

No one would stop long enough to answer. Feverish preparations of some sort were under way. Finally someone advised him to ask the linguist.

"Where have you been?" The linguist threw Adam's question back in his teeth.

"It's a long story; I'll explain later. What is all this excitement about?" Adam insisted.

"We got tired of waiting for you ... (Adam interpreted: they got scared and restless in unfamiliar surroundings) ... and decided to try something for ourselves. (Adam interpreted: typical Technists, can't keep from meddling). I was sent out to try communication with the natives here — in a plain, commonsense way, without any of these so-called powers or fasting and musing in a tent."

The overt hostility shocked Adam. He knew that Technists were contemptuous of spiritual practices. Flyting with its elaborate alliteration would normally soften such expressions. But the little linguist was snapping at Adam rabidly. Under the strain of the fluky expedition, carefully wrought tissues of civilization were breaking down. *A short jaunt outside the pales of society, and already we abandon our safeguards for peace,* thought Adam. *The situation must be desperate.*

Adam tried to keep a neutral tone: "What did you do? How did you attempt to communicate?"

"Quite simply," snarled the other with laser-bright eyes, "I programmed my linguistic computer to record all Xarbian words with cognates in Earth languages. I set the recording device in a wall where the locals pass frequently. After a few days I had a list of a hundred-odd words obviously derived from our languages. Using those words and derivatives thereof, I carefully constructed the questions we wanted answered."

It occurred to Adam that he could easily become a scapegoat for the collective panic that gripped the explorers. The linguist was not the only one governed by eye-flashing fear and tongue-lashing anger. As casually as possible in the tense atmosphere, Adam asked, "What questions did you ask?"

Exasperation twitched the linguist's flabby flesh, his breath coming now in forced blasts. Adam conjectured that the man's metabolism was rising to a point where he could not assimilate the rarefied xaltherin. Adam offered a calming breathing technique, but the other refused. Asphyxiation was setting in, Adam could see, with the skin turning blue, the eyes bulging. Finally, the small man fled into the spaceship, to an inhaler tube, leaving Adam alone amidst the bustle.

It was with immense relief that Adam spotted Rollo. His friend, however, did not seem pleased to see him. "Adam," he pronounced uneasily, avoiding eye contact, "a bad thing has happened. I don't understand just how."

"Tell me something, for the love of living." Adam grasped his friend's arm. Rollo winced and Adam released it.

"You know how we Technists think — and how much depends on this expedition. If we go back empty-handed, we will be subject to penalty. We squandered so many resources to get here."

"What happened?" Adam was beginning to smother as his own metabolism soared with anxiety.

"A group — the captain, dietician, fuels engineer, and linguist — made a sortie. The linguist had devised a scheme for making our questions clear. They asked the local leaders point blank, 'What do you eat?' And they came back as flippant as you please: 'We eat air.' Then they asked, 'Why are our languages related to yours?' And the natives said, 'We have all lived on Earth before.' Whatever that means."

"Reincarnation. Transmigration of consciousness. Multiple lives." Adam's anxiety soared as he noted the extent of Technist ignorance and incredulity. "What else did they ask?" he probed with a sense of impending doom.

"Finally, they tried: 'Where are your fuels?' The energy detectors have been going crazy here, so we are positive there's high technical activity going on somewhere, maybe underground. It's a fact as plain as a dial face. So we insisted on knowing where to find the fuels. And they refused to answer. They lied baldly: 'We have no fuels.' Then we figured if that was a lie, probably everything else they told us was too. These creatures are tranquil-looking devils. They come with gifts and peaceful appearances, but they are trying to starve us. They mock us with an appearance of goodwill. It's the most cynical, cruel ..."

"But Rollo, you know the Ahim way can account for all they have told you. They aren't lying. I saw how they nourish themselves. And they were on Earth in earlier lives, which accounts for linguistic coincidences."

Rollo stared at Adam in embarrassed silence. Obviously he thought his friend was deluded but did not know how to disillusion him: a typical Ahim-Technist impasse. Disbelief was a protective mechanism for Technists. If they gave credence to what the Xarbians told them, it would not only render this expedition useless, but also confirm everything Ahims had been proposing for years: that technology per se was but a stopgap measure until the intrinsic powers of humans were sufficiently cultivated.

No wonder, thought Adam, *that at this crisis there is so much resentment ready to pounce on me. If I say 'I told you so' I may be a dead man.* "Rollo, tell me just one thing: Is there a plan to kill me?"

The short youth took a step backward. "Whatever makes you think such a thing?"

"All this activity, the hostility, everyone ignoring me."

"Not you, Adam!"

Not me? Why not? Of course. My paranoia was getting the better of me. They can't kill me, the token Ahim on the trip. It would be like declaring a world war. "Who then?" he asked with an ache in his empty gut.

"Oh Adam," cried his friend, "things escalated very fast. Perhaps because so much is riding on this expedition. It must not fail. The captain is furious. He threatened the natives, had the linguist warn that weapons would be used against them."

"What did they say?"

"At first they wouldn't understand 'weapons.' So we killed one of the local animals to demonstrate."

Another fundamental rule of space travel gone down the drain, thought Adam in despair. "Then what?"

"They looked shocked, displeased. But not scared. They said something about their law."

"And what did our people do?"

"The captain laughed in their face. He said that clearly they could not enforce their laws if they had no technology. If they brought out weapons, they'd tilt their hand, prove they were lying. It seems we had them cornered."

"So what did you do then?"

"We figured their technology isn't concentrated in weaponry or they would have been at our throats already, but we didn't want to act too precipitously. We held a council and decided to send a party to give an ultimatum: Either they answer our questions — our needs — immediately, or we will destroy dwellings in the community closest to our ship here. We noticed that they lock up at night and don't go out — hyper-sensitive to cold apparently. We made the threat against structures rather than people, not to create an irreversible situation."

What do you know about irreversibility? thought Adam bitterly, remembering the focuser and the sex spa. "How did the Xarbians respond?"

"The who?"

"The Xarbians. That's what they call themselves."

"They just said that things happen very fast here, and turned on their heels."

"They are happening rather fast, don't you think?" asked Adam with an edge of sarcasm. Rollo looked at him fearfully. It was clear that neither he nor the other expedition members had an inkling of where their actions would lead.

The laws of inertia are taking over, thought Adam. "What are all these preparations for?"

"We're going to carry out the threat. We're adapting our weapons to various usages in case these buildings don't respond to ordinary heat pellets. We figure they should work, though, because the structures are molded from this highly metallic soil. With a well-embedded pellet, the whole shebang should melt down. I'm boosting the launcher circuits in case this stuff is too tough to allow an injection at normal emission speeds. If that doesn't work ..."

"Do they know what you are preparing for them?"

"They have the ultimatum."

"But if they have no weapons they can't anticipate an attack like this."

"They've seen us fell that animal. And besides, I think they must have weapons, or at least equipment for agriculture."

Adam's frustration mounted into rage, but he was helpless to stop this action whose results were so unpredictable. The feeling of impotent anger was a familiar one, something he had not felt too intensely in this lifetime but remembered from somewhere before. Now he felt it on behalf of the Xarbians, who, because of his beloved, were closer than kin to him. "Have the people evacuated the buildings? Are they taking protective or defensive measures?"

"Not a thing that we can see. It is spooky. If their agriculture and technology are all underground somewhere, who knows what retaliation they have in store for us. We don't know what they meant by their 'law.' I'm scared, Adam. This assertion that things happen fast sounds too self-assured to be a bluff. Since we came this distance they must figure we have the technology to carry out our threats. Why aren't they backing down? Why don't they show at least a sign of fear?"

A better question, thought Adam, *would be: Why are we making threats, viable or not?* He began to ruminate on all that had led up to this moment, drawing on his knowledge of history and psychology. He recalled rifts on Earth that had been patched over through concerted efforts to colonize in outer space. How disagreements over fundamental moral issues lay buried under loose heaps of optimism about wresting abundance from colonies. The assumption had been that if the appetite for resources was satisfied in space programs, Earth factions would reconcile. But extraterrestrial resources had never materialized. Space exploration had been put on hold — until the present endeavor.

Technists had never relinquished the dream of resources to be uncovered far afield, chafed under the failures to fulfill it. Their technology proved to be a top-heavy burden, a dinosaur's armor, as long as there was no call for warfare or other derring-do. The seeds of aggression lay dormant. Adam berated himself mentally for not realizing how ready those seeds were to take root. He should have perceived the extent of animosity underlying polite flyting bouts, the tally of petty resentments. The Technists were ticking and ready to explode. *They need the outlet so badly*, mused Adam, *that they prefer not to even imagine the consequences of this aggression.* "When will this display take place?" he asked glumly.

"Tomorrow at noon. That will give them time to find cover by nightfall."

A thin skin of rationalism, Adam observed: *how typical!* "What if they don't abandon their houses?"

"That's their problem. They've been warned."

A barrage of thoughts raced through Adam's mind. At first he shuddered to think of Xarbian casualties. But then he remembered how they could xarp and fly and disappear — and who knows what else — and figured that they would take care of themselves. His real obligation was to this band of fools that he had chosen to join for ulterior reasons. How could he deter them?

In a flash he realized how his contempt detracted drastically from his ability to help. Deep down he wanted them to reap the results of their folly. He was being swept into a moral swamp by anger and a poisonous trickle of fear. He was too upset to speak clearly and forcefully. Even with the intention to dissuade, he knew his inner instability would render him ineffectual.

Then another picture arose horrifically in his mind. He saw himself attempting despite his handicaps to appeal heroically to his companions to desist. Instead Xof gaining their goodwill, he draws their anger onto himself. Their frustration and covert fear of Xarbian powers are unleashed on a safer target as they claim the right to execute a mutineer: him.

In final analysis, he lacked the courage to stand up and risk retribution. And since he would not draw their fire, the innocent Xarbian village would. What if he was wrong about their occult abilities and the Xarbians could not protect themselves? Could such a peaceful society conceive of demonic inventions like heat pellets, laser guns, and sound barrages? If Xarbians were consistently reasonable and unselfish, maybe their laws had never needed enforcement.

Adam grew cold all over. The sweat that should have formed evaporated instantaneously in the moisture-less air and left him icy and shivering with terror. He was paralyzed by moral impotence. To speak would be to offer himself as sacrifice. He knew it beyond a doubt. Even if he were sure the Xarbians were defenseless, would he dare to put himself on the line? He doubted it. And the Technists might not stop at destroying a few buildings. Would they progress from menden to menden in genocidal frenzy? They might decimate the whole planet. The history of Earth was rife with instances of factions drunk on power that ransacked whole nations. And what of him? In his impatience to rejoin his beloved, had he drawn down destruction on her?

In the toils of turmoil, he began to asphyxiate and dashed for an inhaler tube. The tubes, however, were all occupied. Panic beset him for a moment. But when he saw his former friends eyeing him suspiciously, he made an immense effort at discipline and conquered his respiratory failure with Ahim breathing techniques.

That afternoon he listened tensely for sounds of evacuation from the Xarbian village. But not a murmur was heard above the buzz and hum of the spaceship machinery. At length night pounced, frigid and black as the bottom of the ocean. Far off he could hear the dismal echoes of predatory bird cries in the tall fantastic forests.

At noon next day, Adam took refuge in the spacecraft to observe the attack. He was not sure why. On the one hand, it seemed preferable to witness the worst rather than imagine it. And again he hoped to gain the courage — or better, the power — to speak up against the whole mad plan. He should have cautioned against the expedition before it left Earth — but then, he wanted it for his own purpose. Again his half-hearted subscription to Technist activities had sucked him in beyond his depth. He wondered with a dry and hollow feeling in his chest how he would pay for this caper.

As the group wavered with weighted feet toward the village, all of them panting from over-wrought metabolism in the refined atmosphere, something nagged on the fringes of Adam's mind. He was supposed to remember something. What was it? Something concerning Althea? No. It was something grim and foreboding. It had emerged in uncomfortable circumstances. His pre-initiation examinations!

Which one? The first or the final? Then it struck him: He recalled how he confessed to his guides that a soothsayer predicted he would join a warrior race. Now he was among warriors deploying an attack on a peaceful village. His destiny was descending on him.

As equipment was set up and aimed at the targets, the sequence of artillery ranged cold-bloodedly in order, Adam watched from a porthole and waited, wrung with grief and self-loathing. Suspense produced a dual effect: fear for life and sanity; and – yes — a lively, excited curiosity. He had to own up to this shameful response.

Before his agony reached a crescendo, Adam was astounded to see an orange flare spreading across the sky in rapid waves, moving out to the stratosphere as the orange phased into crimson close to the planet and pale saffron at the far fringes. *Summit save me*, he thought. *They have fired!*

He forced himself to look out, fearing to see a conflagration, houses melting, Xarbians fleeing as flames tore their bodies. But the community was as before, intact, not even discolored. The flare of color emanated from a pellet launcher that had burst like a bomb. About it, the charred remains of other equipment smoldered and dripped. The intense heat had apparently disintegrated the five persons in the demolition squad, for they were nowhere to be seen. A circle on the ground had been burnt free of moss and showed itself slick and metallic, still hot. The edges of some nearby tree leaves were singed. Otherwise, Xarbo appeared unscathed. Its plants and structures stood impassively as immortals whom upstart titans have attempted to attack, harming only themselves.

Oh life between lives, Adam gasped. *Things happen fast! Can this be Xarbian law? We should have known the attack would backfire. We couldn't even light a cooking fire here, heat is conducted so fast. The pellet must have dissipated its heat in this super-conducting atmosphere. Only those closest to the launcher were affected — drastically.*

A cry of horror went up from other watchers in the spaceship. Dimly, Adam heard hurried orders to launch off, sounding like faint wails and whimpers, muffled as they were by several partitions. There was nothing to do but flee. They had pounced with their trump and it had proved ineffectual. They lost. Their weapons were destroyed. They had been all too thorough in leaving no other avenue open. The deployed pellets lay dripping by the defunct launcher.

As the horror wore off and the orange faded from the sky, Adam realized that his loyalties were with Xarbo after all. Why else should he be glad that it proved impervious to Earth weapons? All he had to do was get off that vessel before it sped away. He plunged through a labyrinth of passageways and valve closures to the nearest exit. He stumbled down the landing ramp just before it was retracted, and ran, half hopping, toward the pinkish metallic maze of the Xarbian village.

25

ADAM AND ALTHERIN

ALTHERIN UNEXPECTEDLY FELT JOY at the sudden return of her visitor. Their second Being Alone Together had come to a disconcerting conclusion. In fact, they got off to a bad beginning. She had no trouble in making him understand that the first step was an exchange of gifts. But the crudity of his offering took her aback. At first she felt offended. But when she realized that he had performed to the best of his abilities, she felt embarrassed for him. He presented her with a tracery dug with a stick in the moss. It showed a couple reaching to each other across space. The concept was poignant, but the execution hopelessly gross. Again, he proved to be primitive, incapable even of moleculation, helpless to build a home — or even to lock and unlock one. It occurred to her that she should terminate the process of Being Alone Together. But she felt compelled to at least present her gift.

He was awestruck when she sculpted a mound of soil by telekinesis and it fused into the likeness of her own visage with an expression at once of wonder and bewilderment: her reactions to his arrival. He was eager to go on to the next stage of communication, and she let herself be persuaded.

The exchange of words — which they both augmented with mental images — went somewhat better. He told her, as best he could through his unskilled xarping, of his existence as Abraham, filled with vague longings, intent only on being initiated into Ahim Powers but as yet unsure why he desired them so strongly. As he told how he became aware of her, first in dreams and later in recollections, he began to choke with passion. She helped him regain composure through breathing exercises. He went on to explain how he resumed his old name, Adam, because he had made no progress since his previous lifetime — incompetent without her. She felt an odd prickling when he told her that her name had been Althea. The sound of it vibrated in her yeldom, confirming that he was indeed linked to her by fate.

He confided how he feared many times to lose her due to his own willfulness, inertia, or pride. Again, she sensed an ambiguous ring to his humility and resolved to question a zilding on the matter. When he tried to express his feelings upon finding her, he almost lapsed into unconsciousness.

Altherin herself had no such personal commitment to share. Again, she felt the discrepancy between them and wondered if she should call off the whole interchange. But an Oracle had pointed him out as a partner in her destiny. For some reason, she must be required to bring him into her life. She tried to tell him about her travels and recounted the short sojourn on Earth. He was clearly thunderstruck to learn that she had been taught in simple stages how to accomplish a voyage to which he had devoted a lifetime. He told her so. When she revealed her fearful revulsion on viewing food consumption and childbirth, he did not seem surprised.

"Why doesn't it bother you to xarp my frailty?" she inquired.

"You have limits, as I do. And we both have knots of destiny to unravel. We will have a grand adventure together."

Altherin felt suddenly estranged by this irrational outburst. How could one be glad that there were knots to dissolve? She knew that such was the lot even of Xarbians, or they would not have entered a pearl and been hatched. But the theme of life on Xarbo was to overcome rapidly all personal obstacles so as to be fit to help other beings with theirs. One's limits hindered this. How could this Earth creature rejoice in her weaknesses? It was not only irrational but perverse, wrong-hearted. Why should anyone want to prolong the period of Commensuration, when one's imperfections call down retributions? Altherin began to have the uneasy feeling that this creature himself was an obstacle that had been set in her path due to her past misdeeds.

Altherin made an immense effort to show Adam the purpose underlying her travels in space. She wanted him to understand the importance of attaining Completion and choosing an arena for purposeful activity. Although it was counter to her training, she took a hypothetical case for his instruction. She reviewed her horror on witnessing childbirth. This, theoretically, could be an area where she would work to relieve suffering and accelerate evolution. She let him envision her as a guiding spirit who would lead Earth females from their age-old habits of pain and dread, which marred the advent of their offspring.

Adam understood and confided that he felt jealousy when he pictured her helping others rather than him. In this respect, he was at the infancy phase of personal evolution by Xarbian standards. Again, she resolved to interrupt the process of Being Together. But he begged her to describe her other travels. She felt that to refuse him would hinder his chances for growth. Perhaps she could give him a perspective on the far-flung needs of beings in the cosmos.

She told him then of Cannibal Island, which devours itself, as Earth beings devour each other, but with such rapidity and so voraciously that one is appalled to see it. Never is a being on this planet free from appetite. Eat it must at the expense of its neighbor. Everything on this planet, she showed him in startling vignettes, is held constantly to the most basic exigency of existence. Cannibal Island appetites were so far removed from her own state that she had no inkling of how she could be of use there.

She went on to envision for Adam the highly artistic Zeklings, who had been to Earth and mingled their genes with Earth beings many centuries earlier. She showed him their sophisticated technical methods for reproduction — all of them being males — and hinted at their deficiencies in the heart, their inability to sympathize with or feel compassion for the weak or ugly. She pictured for him their craftsmanship and confided how she felt a personal kinship for this planet, filled with magnificent artifacts and handsome men, although pervaded by a profound coldness.

Adam told her that he heard her confession with a sense of dread. If they were to share a life project, she must feel some affinity for him, some heart connection — but in her eyes he was weak and ugly.

Altherin felt an unaccustomed confusion and melancholy on xarping Adam's apprehension. She was beginning to feel chained to this grossly limited being.

Still dominated by the heavy feeling as of some inevitability clinging to her, Altherin forged on to describe her other travels: to Clone Island, where androids manufactured from human tissue grind on in a mechanistic existence unleavened by spirit, devoid of innate prospects for evolution, cut off from donors who bequeathed them their brains but not their minds, their abilities but not their potential for growth. She gave him a whirling glimpse of Ectoplanet and of several others that she had visited recently. It began to dawn on her that she was avoiding a description of Oracle Island.

At last she blurted out a full admission of what had happened in that watery plain. She let Adam see the giant brains among the mollusks. She pictured the striated currents of unmixed waters that live and give the brains their extraordinary powers. She had to use a mind-steadying xena before she could tell Adam how the Oracle gave her foreknowledge of their encounter.

Altherin was not prepared in the least for Adam's reaction to the oracular vision. When he saw himself from her viewpoint, presented as the image of her destiny, he broke into dry sobs of relief. No tears would come, but his whole being was clearly rapt in joy. If he had been a Xarbian he would have bounded to the treetops, fluting shrilly. Being limited to grosser earthly faculties, he could only embrace her.

Altherin was surprised that he seemed to know the next stage of Being Alone Together. Spontaneously he was touching her. This seemed to show an advanced state of awareness. But her pleasure soon gave way to alarm. He was pressing his prickling body painfully to her flesh, stinging it cruelly in every delicate pore. Unable to merge by more subtle means, he apparently was trying to blend with her physically, smearing her against him with an excruciating rubbing motion. He interrupted the rubbing only to crush her spasmodically to him with his arms that seemed to have a stiff core to them like mogdon boughs. His face was losing its color and its humanity as the blood flowed into his vitals. He was metamorphosing rapidly like an apparition from Ectoplanet.

Altherin cast about for a means to terminate their Being Alone. She felt a great coldness like a lump where her heart should be. When he uttered, "Althea, Althea" throatily in her ear, she understood that she was reaping the embrace Adam had stored for a lifetime to bestow on his lost love.

She submitted for a moment to his advances as to a detestable medicine. But the more she submitted, the more intense he became. She sensed his sacro-helix, which was buzzing uncontrollably like a giant wasp from Cannibal Island about to devour its prey.

A terrible fear gripped Altherin, something never before experienced, even when she thought she would perish alone in the Xarbian night. She felt drawn down to identify totally with her body. She was like a morsel on Cannibal Island about to be engorged by a predator who had a predilection for her flesh. This Adam with his hyper helix would induce in her the same rate of vibration and draw her into more irreversible acts. Chains of surrender, self-loathing and Commensuration unfolded before Altherin's inner vision. She must break loose at all costs before this process went any further.

She cast about desperately for the word or image that would awaken him from his bestial stupor. She finally blurted, "Adam! I have chosen the celibate life."

Marvel upon marvel! He understood and disengaged himself, shaking his head as one does on recovery from a faint. On his face she could read emotions wrestling: bewilderment, disappointment, regret, shame. He turned tail and left.

•　　•　　•

When he returned only two days later she was surprised. And amazed at her gladness to see him. The very pain that he inflicted had left a memory print — as Grandar had showed her once that any pain will do. She therefore questioned her gladness as a perversity. Yet there was no doubt that she was bound to this man in a fatal network of emotions and memories both fresh and time-lost.

Adam came back to her with the humble air of one who finds himself still in paradise, although he has obviously lost his rights to it. He confessed his cowardice in not resisting the scheme to demolish the menden, his fright and self-hate as the squad laid siege to the Xarbian village. "I knew the Technist mentality; I should have objected to the launch before it left Earth. But I had such hopes of finding you that I ignored my scruples."

Altherin imagined that Adam must both love and loathe her, considering how his passion made him forsake his principles. A passion as highly pitched as any Xarbian might entertain. And she recalled how she too had once experienced a tormenting combination of desire and dread, directed toward her zilding Grandar. Then she had the expert guidance of a Completion to induce reversal and help her pass through the straits of conflict. Now she was cast in the zilding role. But she was not a Completion. She had not even chosen a life project. Things were going very fast. Too fast for her to react.

She listened as one in a trance to Adam's confessions, his confused love for her. Thoughts came too fast for her to choose one viable for action. He drew her into a vicious circle of speculations, fears, and hopes — drawing her down to his mental level, a bewildered state abhorrent to the Xarbian constitution. Worst, she knew that she must deserve to feel this empathy with an inferior being, must have earned it in her past lifetime. However, it was fruitless to persevere with Adam alone. He was in no position to help her outgrow her old identity as Althea. She sent him from her and petitioned a zilding for help.

Father Loxzar made a show of impatience, although as a Completion he was free from deeply embedded defects. He made clear to her that he would not tolerate idle curiosity concerning her previous existence. She was not to indulge in sentimental attachments to past images. Nor wallow in self-pity or guilt for past mistakes. She was to learn only what was useful from her investigations, if she wanted help from him. He made that extremely clear. His wholesome firmness was just what she needed. Again, her current guide seemed the most helpful, wisest, the most attractive of all her zildings.

As Loxzar helped induce recollection of herself as Althea, Altherin was hustled past images of her body enlaced with Adam's, their child's chubby fingers, their home and garden. All that had been dear and beautiful had to be discarded mercilessly.

She knew that. She accepted. She had already relinquished Adam and that old life. But obviously she was not done with him, still had an attachment. It would be false and cold-hearted to cut the connection prematurely.

After the flood of images, Altherin was awash in a sea of contrasting emotions, like the currents on Oracle Island. She sensed that she represented a strong and confident entity giving warmth and guidance to her companion. Adam was a dependent, childish being tagging at her side, tugging at her to dispense whatever he needed to sustain him. As she settled into the warm current of her own former role, Altherin felt another trickle intruding, forcing her to recognize something she always tried to ignore. It was a cold and bitter edge nudging the warm wave with which she identified — a bilious snaky thought that sidled on the edges of awareness. She relaxed to allow a reversal and admitted the alien insight into her thought stream.

She was jolted to discover that she had despised Adam. She rejected him in her deep heart of hearts. Even while giving him her apparent all, while waiting for him and fulfilling his real and imagined needs, she kept a reserve of contempt. Like the golden heart of an iris, her deepest self was always off bounds to him. This is what the insidious stream was saying: She had been false.

To Adam, she had seemed strong, based on her greatest weakness! She gave in to his whims and tantrums because she lacked the fortitude to refuse him, respect him as her equal. She had put aside possible life projects to make his goals her purpose. But he did not know where he wanted to go. The blind leaned on the blind — and blamed each other for not seeing.

The insights were painful, discouraging. "Am I no better than this crude Earth being?" she almost screamed at Loxzar.

"Your contempt keeps your heart as low as moss. His can be no paltrier than that."

I have fallen in a trap, thought Altherin with a shudder. *I've been in it for two lifetimes without recognizing it. My pride is my downfall.*

"How can I escape from myself, Father Loxzar?"

"This is a question for Mother Rozden. It is her role to help you sort out the tendrils of your destiny. It may comfort you to know that all Xarbians suffer dismay and shame when they gain access to their previous existence on Earth. It is by nature a degrading experience, a step backward. But we take it in order to step more confidently onward. However, you need only discover what remains unresolved from your past life: no need to revisit ailments that have been already laid to rest. May the Summit sing in your yeldom."

With this sacred phrase, Altherin was dispatched to Mother Rozden, who talked to her as her egg mother, Zalda, had done when she was an infant, listening to her doubts and questions. "Do you see any similarities in your behavior with Adam and with Waldin?" she asked, after hearing of Altherin's dilemma.

Altherin was quick to see that she had given in to both of them through a confused sense of responsibility for their welfare. Her zildings had chided her for pretending to know what was best for Waldin, who had more experience than she. It was condescending and false-hearted, they said.

"Yes, yes, I have not been faithful to my yeldom." Altherin squeezed the words out of her narrowed chest. "I didn't listen to my inner ear. I listened to their requests, their pleas, their appeals. I let them control me while pretending to control. I handed them the power. When my life with Adam went astray, I blamed him, for a lifetime. With Waldin, I had to face my error immediately."

"Quite right. Now you must undergo a reversal together with the person most closely involved: Adam himself. Do you have any idea what such a reversal will involve?"

"I mustn't give in to his desires if they conflict with my best values."

"Right again. What might some of those desires be?"

"I get a funny feeling when he confesses his faults. He is being humble. But I sense a creeping on my skin as if Sol is low on the horizon and the chill is settling down. There is a hidden desire under his confessions. His humility contains another element that I don't grasp."

"Recollect it and hold it steadily in mind. You will be able to isolate the disturbing element."

"Yes," Altherin cried after xarping the recollection, "he shows me his humility for a secret reason. He wants me to know his faults not so I can help him overcome them, but hoping I will take over his burden, absolve his guilt. I did that in the past — when I should have stung him to effect a reversal for himself."

"Very good. Now, do not lose yourself in regret. Look for the nature of the reversal you must now undergo together with him."

"If I subverted my highest values to his lowest needs, I must perhaps learn how to put his lowest needs in the service of my highest values?"

"Excellent!" The older woman danced with childlike glee. "What more specifically might you do? What are his lowest needs?"

Altherin described Adam's display of bodily craving, his painful rubbing and clutching motions. That must surely be an expression of his basest desire.

"Very fine, Altherin," her zilding applauded the insight. "You must harness this energy of his to help you fulfill the highest aims of your life project. But you do not have a project yet. Choose one. Do not fall into sloth as you did during your life on Earth."

"Then I must go on seeking my aim throughout the planets?"

"And make Adam join in your destiny! You were depressed on seeing your partner was so lowly because you falsely assumed you must be an accomplice in a destiny of his choosing."

"But how will I persuade him to abandon his body craving and his cowardice and shift his desires to align with mine?"

"By giving him a foretaste of the bliss that your life goal can bestow."

26

ROLLO'S WISH

When Adam broke away from Altherin, his sacro-helix continued to vibrate unbearably. The pulses that had not found expression in coupling with her seemed to reroute themselves with malicious and vindictive intention to punish him. Obsessive ideas stampeded through his mind and body. The compelling images were of excruciating vividness. Forming and dissolving incessantly, impulses flashed and spread in aftershocks like the orange flare from the dying pellet-launcher. And the shocks penetrated every cranny of his body, stimulating all the glands. Adrenaline flowed like a fountain in spurts that jolted him to act.

Before he could resolve his dilemma with Altherin, he knew confusedly that he had to deal with his fellow invaders. They infringed on his awareness through recurring images of their spaceship. What happened to it? Had it departed? If not, were the Technists still plotting another onslaught on Xarbo? He could imagine the ship's risking an oblique takeoff, just to strafe the obdurate village. He envisioned a molten menden. Then he conjectured that the craft might have crashed or failed to lift off, that his former companions crawled among the high trees in an isolated part of the planet, subsisting on moss and huddling together for warmth in the night chill. The face of his friend Rollo haunted him particularly. He fought off scenarios where Rollo lay dead or dying. Instead, he conjured the young man laughing and confident as he had been in his sipping salon at home, secure in his castle fortified with electronic toys.

Adam realized that his mind would not be at ease until he returned to the launching area. He could not rest anyway. His blood was racing, powered by the continuing shots of adrenaline. He walked across the mossy outskirts of Altherin's menden and pointed himself toward his destination. A group of youths gathered for courtship ceremonies spotted him and made a frolic out of transporting him to his goal.

As the band of young Xarbians with Adam in tow approached the attacked but impervious menden, he was appalled to see the spaceship still standing exactly where it had been. As they drew closer, he saw that its tail end was charred. *Galaxies galore,* he thought, *the jets backfired. Of course! No flame is sustained here. Heat is conducted — and dissipated — instantaneously.*

The landing apparatus was still down and the pneumatic chute-gate open. Adam approached cautiously, afraid of what he would find inside. His Xarbian bearers sailed off, not curious in the least to check out the alien vessel. He could hear the high chirping sounds of their good spirits as they resumed their games in mid-flight.

The spaceship proved empty — a temporary relief, but one filled with insidious forebodings. Adam was afraid to approach the menden. What if the local Xarbians had become hostile? They had every reason to be. Wouldn't he be taken for one of their assailants? What if other sorties had followed the pellet-launcher fiasco? He climbed to the nose of the craft as outlook, hoping to spot someone in the distance. He detected what looked like a pile of garments near a grove.

He raced for the exit chute and ran to the spot. There he found a blanket bundled around a plasti-suit. With trembling hands and eyes bleared with fear, he uncovered a horrendous mummy, freeze-dried from alternate dry heat and cold, almost weightless. The cadaver was too dehydrated for him to recognize who it had been. Its mouth was caked with a black substance that shone slick against the dull coffee color of the skin, which was stretched over the skull in a taut grin. No doubt the clothing had been bundled on to fight the night cold. The person must have been on his way back to the spaceship when he or she succumbed.

In the grove, Adam found other similar corpses. He began to count them. He had accounted for more than half the crew members when he heard a groan. He scurried over the dense moss, kicking up great fallen leaves like elephant ears in his haste. They crackled and crumbled into dust as he sped about, giving him the eerie feeling that he was swimming in a dry sea afloat with human pelts.

At last he came upon a small group that was still crawling feebly beneath the towering trees. A large local bird with toes like sharpened jasper watched them at a discreet distance, shifting from one scaly leg to the other.

"What happened?" Adam blurted. Then, "How can I help you?"

"Too late," said one of the five survivors, fixing him with the disinterested stare of the doomed.

"What's caked on your mouth?"

"The wine of death, my friend," said one with a ghastly grimace, then turned his eyes in their gaping sockets and gasped, "Adam!"

Adam started. Who had called him by name? These emaciated humans all looked alike — impersonal relics of an ill-conceived endeavor. Then he recognized Rollo by the little notches that fringed the tops of his ears. The familiar, endearing trait seized him by surprise. Adam ran to the gaunt figure, which had propped itself against a tree trunk, its mouth disfigured by a black line like the others, all the more repugnant for having been familiar. Adam could see, as his friend spoke, that the tongue too was coated with black ooze.

"Thirst, Adam. There is no water here. The Xarbians' yavers create moisture for them."

"What's on your mouth?" Adam asked. Rollo pointed to a pile of fur and bones. "You ate these animals? Raw?"

"Yes. Blood, you know. Liquid."

"To quench your thirst. And hunger. What went wrong?"

"Overdose. Too much. It reacts with something in us."

Adam was about to ask why they had not tried the fruit, but remembered that it had to be ferreted down from trees by Xarbians. The Technists did not have their helimonopters. It was a frugal flight.

"Adam, before I go, answer what I asked."

"What was it?"

"Why did you change your name? You used to be Abraham."

"It will seem very strange to you. Promise you won't laugh?"

Rollo shook his head but chuckled nonetheless in anticipation, a convulsive snicker that shook his desiccated frame like a hoarse wind in a tunnel.

"I was Adam in my last life, Rollo. I didn't grow up enough then, so I had to go back to being Adam again."

The leathery visage seemed to twitch as Rollo digested this testimony to reincarnation, officially rejected by his clan. At length, he absorbed the facts and asked for confirmation: "Adam the father of Alther?"

"Yes. Your grandfather. I died before you were born. Isn't it funny that I came back to be your friend? I guess you needed a grandpa to baby! We Ahims believe in that kind of trick of destiny. Rollo! Try to come back as an Ahim on Earth." Adam was about to add, "Or better, on Xarbo." He peered intently at his friend for some sign of understanding.

Rollo did not answer. He lay very still and grave, staring ahead as if trying to absorb the knowledge, desiring perhaps not to waste energy on overt reactions. Adam let him be, but at a short distance knelt and recited the Rite of Passage that his Algonquian guide taught him. When he looked over, the intelligence had gone from Rollo's eyes. Adam continued to kneel by the wasted remains, conjuring the years when he had been friends with a cheerful little person called Rollo. Memories flooded in: Rollo yelling to him over his microphone as he hovered in his helimonopter, Rollo bending over his plants to dust them tenderly with a tiny anti-entropy gadget, Rollo offering him the best of his food supply, Rollo afraid to offend while tending advice.

Adam made the rounds of the other explorers, all dead or on the verge of dying. He tried to engage them but they were unresponsive, so he recited the rites for them too, but could recognize no individuals. Once the last of the survivors fell limp, Adam left. He did not try to bury them in the metallic silt of Xarbo. It seemed fair in a strange way that the Xarbian beasts should claim the corpses, to counteract the fact that humans had tasted their blood. Now it would be returned to the planet's ecology, and only the towering grayish cone of the spacecraft would bear testimony to an intrusion. As he walked away, Adam could see from the corner of his eye that the large bird was approaching the carrion, its jasper toes tossing tufts of moss as it bounded.

There was nothing to do but go back to Altherin, who had been Althea. A bitter, ironic thought settled in and pervaded his brain as his helix quieted and metabolism returned to normal. *A celibate!* he thought angrily of her — and derisively of himself. *A lifetime I've looked for you and now … now you tell me that you have vowed to be single. You didn't wait for me. You found your Xarbo: a pretty, lethal place poisonous to man.*

Adam rummaged through recriminations until his metabolism rose to an insupportable degree. He could not sustain anger in this rarefied atmosphere and had to perform an emergency breathing exercise until he could take stock of his situation objectively. It was not an encouraging picture. What were his prospects? Stranded without an operable spacecraft and unable to fly, he was at the mercy of this woman whom he both desired and feared. In fact, she could starve him if she wished to!

Why did he resent her so much? Because he deserved a reward after his long perseverance and she seemed determined to punish him instead? He had sacrificed not only time and effort but ethics to reach her. He deserved something. Her! Atavistic attitudes welled up in him. She was his well-earned booty. He wanted to carry her off as ancients did their captured brides. But where would he carry her? The thought stopped him cold, and brought him back to his senses.

When Adam saw Altherin again he carried a concealed weapon: his rage and desire to dominate lurking in him, ready to explode with the proper catalyst. Meanwhile, his behavior was subdued. He could do nothing without her cooperation. He could only beg her to help him overcome his inadequacies. There was no other solution, repugnant as it was.

"Give me knowledge!" he demanded. "At least teach me a shortcut to flying, if not space travel. It can't be too hard in this atmosphere. I almost float already. What would happen if I kicked off? Would I be able to get down again?"

"I can teach you nothing, Adam. I am not a teacher but a learner myself."

"You have to help somehow. At least find out if I can go on eating this fruit without being poisoned. You must be able to focus on molecular interactions. Even Technists have focusers. Of course, the party I came with didn't think of that in time. Lots of things they didn't think of, obsessed with finding fuels. I would never have signed up for such a crazy trip if it weren't for you. You have to help me." His voice broke with emotion.

"I didn't ask to have you come."

Stung, Adam wanted to fling back a hurtful reply, but then he saw she was perplexed, had not intended to offend him. "Forgive me," he said dryly, "but for Summit's sake have a little pity! Don't you know how I feel on this planet? Everything is pristine and crystal perfect. I need to be touched. Please! Touch me!"

Adam wrenched off the clothing he had brought from the spacecraft and tried to press as much of himself as he could to her delicate skin. Instinctively she winced. Her involuntary revulsion angered him and piqued his lust at the same time. In him, the wheel of inertia started to turn and drew him insensibly into its coils. For lifetimes he had reacted to resistance with insistence. Something about a refusal stimulated unconscious energies, beyond his control. He had found this Xarbian girl's frailty unattractive; he had tried to remember her as Althea: earthy, strong, and brown of limb. But now Altherin's fragile structure aroused him. He wanted to crush and punish her, make her fear him. Elude his embrace, would she? He would give her something to elude!

Adam grabbed the tiny woman by the dappled upper arms, somewhat repelled by the fine scales that came off on his fingers. He drew her to him forcibly and strafed her breast with the wiry hairs of his own. He would throw her to the ground and pounce on her. Her expression of pain and dismay stimulated some deep atavistic lust for power, a cruel exultance of the will to utterly defeat the will of another.

Just as he was about to be drawn irretrievably into the gravitation of power and old lust, he noticed that her expression had changed. She had lost the pitiful look of a young girl afraid for her modesty and safety. She seemed to have eliminated all concern for her body. Her gaze was cool and disinterested but not passive. She wanted to speak, but he was clasping her too tightly, constricting her chest His face was an inch from hers. He drew back in order to hear what she would say, thrown off guard by the sudden change in her.

"If you do not release me," she said evenly without any expression of threat, "I will do something that will surprise you very much. Something that will displease you immensely. Our fates are intertwined. Let us not impose more Commensuration on each other."

Adam let her go. She reminded him of his Second Mother. She no doubt had his interests at heart as well as her own. He deserved frustration and impotence for the countless lifetimes when he had had his way, dominated ruthlessly. Most of his subjects had probably been women — and the Summit had sent women to deliver his comeuppance.

"Is this frustration what you mean by Commensuration?"

His thought was so intense that she immediately xarped his query and replied, "Yes, Adam."

For a moment his face flushed with rage and his breath grew ragged. Why should his dedication to this person through two lifetimes and on two planets be rewarded with utter rejection? Why could she not have returned to Earth in a human body receptive to his kisses and caresses? Unsure where love ended and lust began, filled with confusion, he sat and turned his attention from the object of his frustration and steadied his breathing with an exercise.

When his metabolism returned to normal he saw that she was watching him with what seemed a tinge of pity phasing into curiosity and maybe even approval that he had the means to reverse his hysterical state. She held out a hand and helped him undo the tether that kept him grounded. She held it to stabilize him and indicated with a tilt of her head that they should go outside. Soon they were strolling in a mogdon grove, lightly holding hands, already feeling a bit like earthly lovers who have had a quarrel and rediscovered tenderness. Adam again asked her, trying hard not to sound as if he were whining, "Can you do anything to help me get along — to survive — in this homeland of yours?"

"I will take you to elders who may consent to be your zildings. They are our teachers. Like our egg mothers, they care for us."

Adam again recalled his Second Mother and told Altherin that similar mentors exist on Earth. She in turn encouraged him, saying she was sure that the vibrancy of his sacro-helix could be adapted to develop xenas, even though he lacked a yeldom — the inmost ear — and several other Xarbian organs.

"But what can I do with these feelings I have for you? During the in-between time, I learned that, with Althea, for the first time I was husband to a woman, and not only a seducer. But there was still that old urge to make her dance to my tune. There is so much to work out between us and I'm afraid I made you hate me. How can you go off on a whole new track — as a celibate! — and leave me stranded without a mate on this Summit-forsaken paradise?"

Altherin laughed. "Don't complain so bitterly. A bit of acceptance! This place is top priority for Earth beings to grow in. You sneaked in late by a fluke — but still you are here; you have been allowed to stay. Your companions have all left their bodies under the phenamon and mogdon trees, while xaltherin still gladdens your nostrils.

"Whether I remain a celibate or not depends on my next journey to the inhabited Islands of the galaxies and the choice of a life project. The vision from the Oracle shows that it will involve you. Whether I am to be your mate should not be of prime concern. But I have to give you credit for finding me through such primitive and risky means!"

Adam listened impatiently to the soft reasonableness of her arguments. She had said "next journey"! That meant she would leave him. His mind raced like a scout rocket and her words, soothing as xaltherin, bounced off his hectic thoughts. "You're leaving! Why at this crucial time for me? Don't you have a heart in that puny breast of yours?"

She seemed not to be offended by his slur on her physique. Her self-confidence piqued him, yet he was glad that one of them at least seemed to know what she had to do.

"When do you leave?"

"Before Sol sets tonight. It is the best time to go to Oracle Island, which is my first destination. This will be my last and definitive tour of the galaxies."

"So soon! But no arrangements ..."

"Things happen fast on Xarbo, Adam. I will leave you with one of my zildings who will find zildings for you. While I am away you can make progress in the xenas. Then you will be able to help me in my chosen project."

"Help you! What's that mean? That I'll be some sort of Technist lackey, a mere specialist to consult on minor issues? I'm to be your partner, not your apprentice. Why should I consent to help in some esoteric 'project,' when I should be your project, as you are mine?

"Please!" he cried. Again his tone changed, now petulant and bullying as it had been in countless other lives. His voice echoed among the giant trees and caused browsing creatures to take cover: "Please! I'm not ready to be alone here without you. I just can't! I'll drink dandon blood and die like the others. I'd sooner do that than wait in uncertainty for you to come back and make me your big stupid assistant."

Altherin did not respond to his objections. She assured him only that a zilding would come for him in the grove and give him shelter for the night. Later, his training would begin. Then she gave him a swift foretaste of what it is like to be a charged channel instead of a contentious polarity. As she gazed at him intently, she conveyed the taste of a xena, and a great sense of surrender overcame him, not a languor but an unexpected surge of energy, a transformation of tension into harmony. He yielded a moment to ecstasy. Then he rallied, afraid to be lulled, and tried to seize control of his destiny.

"Wait! You can't leave yet! How long will you be gone?" She gave no reply. "Tell me at least what was that 'surprise' that you could have pulled to give me 'immense displeasure.' "

"I would have disappeared from between your hands."

"But you are disappearing now!" he wailed.

Already she was bounding off without looking back and soon was speeding through the air. He was bobbing a hands-breadth above ground, tethered to a green shoot where Altherin had secured him. Before she flew out of earshot, he yelled, "I know your name! Someone told me. You are Altherin. Altherin. I will call you from the galaxies. Remember that. Sound can pierce you to the yeldom!"

27

ALTHERIN'S LAST JOURNEY

ZILDINGS INTIMATED THAT a proper life project might be based on a positive potential within a negative context. Altherin kept this idea in mind as she recollected Father Grindil's instructions for inter-galactic travel: to make a thought-print of yourself as when passing through ordinary walls and 'remember' to materialize yourself at a pre-determined location. "Transfer is instantaneous," he predicted. "You will not be flying, which is movement through space, and therefore time." And so again Altherin traveled with the infinite speed of thought, and transferred herself in zero time to her first destination.

Oracle Island induced a vague sense of discomfort in Altherin. When she begged for more knowledge from the great brains, they advised her not to press for further forecasts concerning her destiny, warning that such previews can actually hinder the flow of events. Their metaphor was, to know a Xarbian night while on Earth. Yes, some matters require preparation and Altherin was still suffering aftershocks from the foreknowledge that Adam would figure in her future. When she insisted, "Give me an inkling. Show me something!" she was thrown suddenly off balance. An unsteady motion as of ground tremors disoriented her. Unable to move freely, she felt trapped. When asked for clarification, the Oracles conveyed telepathically that they foresaw an experience of joggling helplessness but could not interpret what it represented.

Puzzled and frightened by this partial prediction, Altherin arrived shaken on Cannibal Island, where she perched high out of reach of the constantly foraging inhabitants. The collective sounds of feeding rose loudly and multifariously. Millions of tiny pincers dug into flesh while carapaces creaked and flexed. Rodent worms, fastened lethally to prey, gnawed their way through vitals. Thick-limbed arthropods clamped down on the backs of the worms and sipped on their gelatinous flesh with loud sucking noises. Swift as dragonflies, winged predators descended on these in turn, snapping off the lobster-like limbs and flying away with torn segments. No screams or groans arose; none of the beings possessed vocal chords. Only the sounds of guzzling consumption prevailed: gnawing, sucking, crunching of bone, flapping of muscle torn from its mooring.

Overcoming her revulsion, Altherin admired the variety of methods displayed here in catching and devouring prey. Evolution showed much imagination in the species on this Island. Could this be the constructive element in a negative context that she should cultivate for her life project? Exercising rigorous reversal of her instinct to turn away, she xarped the feeding swarms and enjoyed the warming trickle of imbibed body fluids. She gave way to the expansive sensation of simple body pleasures not pricked by pangs of conscience — only the final pang of death when one's turn to be devoured rolled around. This was a most egalitarian society; no one claimed to be the last link in the food chain. Every life ended in sacrifice to another. Originally Altherin had viewed the Cannibals only as voracious takers. But they were also ultimate givers. This, Altherin learned. However, her goal was to be of service — and she could see no way to use her powers constructively here.

•   •   •

Altherin took a special interest in Earth, where she lived before as Althea and where Adam lived so recently. The complex truce arranged between Ahims and Technists invited investigation. The latter, she noted, still had a taste for meat, an atavistic tendency toward the consumption she witnessed on Cannibal Island. Altherin was curious as to how this practice played out on Earth.

She discovered that animals for meat were bred in captivity and executed swiftly by Technists in temple-like slaughterhouses First, Ahims induced the animals to accept their fates through rituals of consent. However, Altherin xarped that these creatures never truly lived. Penned, they had no outlet for their instincts, could not pursue happiness — the legacy of all, according to Xarbian wisdom. The wild voracious hordes of Cannibal Island seemed better off than these captive victims of supposedly humane measures.

Altherin found that Earth was filled with paradoxes like this one: compromises instead of solutions to complex issues. Ahim and Technist values were essentially incompatible, yet they agreed to share the planet peacefully. Technists retained an urge to devour — not only meat but also fuels and colonies and information. They loved to consume energy, delighted in electronic displays, in extravaganzas of technical virtuosity. They craved facts above all, and fed facts into their computers as avidly as the Cannibals tore gobbets of flesh from their prey.

Ahims disapproved of fact-collecting for its own sake, and even more the idle theorizing that facts give rise to. Above all, they abhorred experimentation. All of the processes in which Technists delighted involved what Ahims considered a blind and blundering interference with systems. When the expedition to Xarbo ended in such spectacular failure, Ahims hoped this would teach Technists a lesson: to proceed more slowly with time-tested ancient traditions that would eventually allow for intergalactic travel without harm to visitor or host. But the Technists saw failure only as a challenge to increase their efforts. Already they were gearing up for more expeditions that would include more options for surface exploration, take-off methods, and so on.

Altherin watched as the impasse between Ahims and Technists became more aggravated. She sensed that the latter were deterred from destroying the former with their advanced weaponry only because they considered certain Ahim powers to be useful, at least peripherally. Altherin felt impelled to help resolve the conflict. She grew impatient as she observed how tools mastered their masters. Technist goals seemed childish. She buzzed around Earth repeatedly, feeling ever more frustrated. Her zildings had taught that she should not buck a system, but encourage positive aspects latent within it. The positive elements on Earth were all associated with Ahims. But to boost them was to risk escalation of the conflict with Technists, all too ready to interpret any sign of power as a threat.

Altherin left Earth reluctantly and thought-printed herself to Clone Island, where she predicted that problems would be simpler. She wished she could have a zilding along to advise her — but all of this, this last journey to many Islands, to choose her life work, had to be solo. Xarbians have to grow up fast.

Clones, she knew, had been created from tissues excised from Technist geniuses, selected especially for their inventiveness. It turned out that, although Clones inherited their donors' cleverness, they were devoid of conscience. Ahims were not surprised; these were not creations of the Summit, but by-products of biology. They called them 'secondaries' because they were once-removed from the creative impulse of the Summit; more like products than progeny. Ahims rejected genetic engineering as too radical a remove from the primary Intelligence that imbued the natural world with its own qualities. The ruthless behavior of virtually all Clones seemed clearly to back up this explanation.

However, as Grindil explained to Altherin, Technists refused to accept the existence of the Summit as the ultimate creative energy and intelligence that animates the world. They simply said that something had gone wrong technically — that science was not advanced enough to make a good humanoid Clone. Meanwhile the race of Clones had proliferated and wreaked considerable havoc. Finally, the ungrateful children of technology were shunted off to an uninhabited but habitable planet and left to their own devices.

Having seen the beautifully structured animals who were clones on Earth, Altherin imagined that the humanoids of Clone Island would be magnificent specimens. She was surprised to find virtually no signs of physical presence. She could xarp that signals were zinging through the air and through many-storied structures. She detected humanoids in the high-rises and in small vehicles that emerged from slots in these and traveled swiftly through pneumatic tubes. Once she located the Clones, she was amazed by how much they had riddled their own bodies with devices. For instance, she could xarp how they neutralized the effects of too rapid tube travel by an implant in their inner ear. It adjusted automatically to dizzying spirals and rapid speeds for which a biological ear was unfit. Other implants enhanced sensation and cognition. In fact, the Clones seemed to derive more satisfaction from problem solution than from sensual pleasure. Their genius surpassed that of their earthly forebears, since they improved on their faculties with bionic add-ons.

As Altherin observed this Technist dream come true, she realized that these entities lacked something essential. They possessed biological life and inventiveness but lacked the subtle attributes of self-direction, which Ahims identified by the ancient term kriya. Without a central guiding instinct, they were virtually determined by their environment — which was increasing in complexity as they solved more technical problems. Ironically, they in turn were subjected to increased data feedback. In effect they had created an unending cycle of conditions and conditioning in which they were both manipulators and manipulated. They were subject utterly to laws of cause and effect, but incapable of recognizing any overriding purpose or meaning behind the laws. They existed entirely in a field of mechanistic reactions.

Altherin followed one Clone, who had checked into a sort of sanitarium for 'restoration.' There a device massaged each muscle. A recorded hypnotic message directed his mind to re-simplify itself and be fresh for more data. His sexual appetite was renewed through an injection of hormones and a dietetic regimen. An electro-magnetic implant in his brain was recharged. All this struck Altherin as extremely ingenious, and yet fundamentally profane: a display of intellect without inspiration, satisfactions ever falling short of joy.

She was about to depart, seeing no way to dispel the delusions of these limited beings. Then she was arrested by a cry of grief issuing from somewhere in the sanitarium — a cry utterly out of tune with the complacency of the Clones she had witnessed. She traced the sound to a detention chamber, where she saw a normal Earth being of the smaller variety and xarped the person's memory. She had been exiled by mistake, as an infant. She was the offspring of a great scientist, mistaken for her Clone rather than her child. Her human instincts impelled her to search beyond Clone systems. She was judged insane in her pursuit of a transcendent happiness beyond problem solution. Altherin longed to help this misplaced person, teach her xenas, transport her to Xarbo — but such an undertaking was beyond the scope of her mission — and her ability. She had to find her life project elsewhere. Reluctantly she moved on.

Altherin's last stop — and last hope of connecting with her destiny — was Zekling Island, another planet she had visited before. There she could appear visibly and interact for mutual enjoyment. The Zeklings loved beauty and devoted themselves to artistic work as well as animated conversation and fashionable sports: to anything done daringly with flair. Altherin cherished friends among this all-male society who treated their bodies as sculptures to perfect and polish, so to reflect the coppery light of one Sol and the silver sheen of another.

"Altherin," cried the first to see her, with a wide smile intended to mimic the flash of Xarbian yavers.

"Hahiahii," trilled Altherin; "you do mimic us well."

"No one can aspire to your exquisiteness, dear Altherin," he responded. "If I should ever resort to female company, as many of our ancestors did on Earth, I would choose you above any queen in the galaxies."

All of Altherin's Zekling friends liked to tease her and, because she knew they were joking, she felt at ease with them. On this Island she would not be faced with dread decisions of courtship.

"Tell me about your connection to Earth," Altherin addressed a special friend.

"An ancient visit. Our traits are still discernible in some of its people. Come ride with me and we'll talk."

Zabor reached down a whorled pole that he used to guide his six-legged mount and helped Altherin settle next to him on the gafter's broad hairless back. "We call this pole the 'unicorn's horn' — a piece of Earth lore that our ancestors brought back with them. And we call our gafters Zekling unicorns because of their single antenna." Zabor steadied Altherin beside him and goaded the creature into a swift pace, its long neck poised and unwavering like a great snake.

"Pardon me if my question is rude — but how could Zeklings have spread their traits to humans if ..."

"We reproduce asexually like bacteria? It seems an oddity occurred when we visited Earth. Our oldest poem fragment says, 'A new passion awoke/Not for polished stone and metal/But for limbs of polished flesh./They engendered progeny, expending substance/On the alien factor.'" Zabor looked archly at Altherin, adding, "Perhaps you don't much like this song. The 'alien factor' is of course the female."

Altherin laughed. She loved bantering with her Zekling friends. "I can see traces of Zeklings among Earth's Technists," she countered: "their love of poetic flyting, their salons, fanciful toys and conveyances."

"Oh no," Zabor grimaced. "We're not like those machine-mad little maniacs, are we?"

"Tell me what you are like."

"We love our father and hate our mother."

"But ..."

"Yes, they are both within us. Biologically we are all male, but the female mentality is always latent, nagging."

Altherin was mildly annoyed, yet amused, and asked, "Is the conflict ever resolved?"

"Perpetually, in our art — the one outlet for the enmity we bear ourselves. Our mother-hate is expressed in our war against all weak and flabby forms, in our adherence to strong lines. We hone everything down to its essence. We hate excess and dross — so we delve for the statue within the stone or the bone."

"But your art is refined — a feminine trait."

"Yes. It is needed, but we have more than enough of the feminine in us. That is why we must fight it, to keep equilibrium. 'To balance on the gafter's back,' we say. That is art. But before you can have balance you need two complementary elements with which to work it out. What if the gafter had only his left legs?"

Altherin laughed. But she knew she had no role to play on this planet. She could see what was lacking: the heart-rending reversal that marks a moment of insight when a conflict is resolved. Here, conflicts are retained, cherished, elaborated. *Like the irritating grain of sand that inspires an oyster to create a pearl,* she thought. *Yes, the Zeklings sublimate all annoyance into art form. Their chests never crack with the ache for destiny and the ambiguity of love.*

For a moment Altherin had a cowardly thought: why not hide out on Zekling Island? Join in its endless ceremony of beauty? Why return to Xarbo to face the dilemma of choosing a life project — a dilemma that had to be resolved quickly in the Xarbian way?

Zabor, as if intuiting her hesitation, tempted her with an invitation: "Won't you demonstrate the Xarbian art of moleculation for us before you leave?"

Altherin agreed to create a structure, molding matter by telekinesis to fit her concept. The Zeklings applauded wildly, their tattooed arms gleaming in the copper sunshine as they saluted her. Immensely excited, they begged her to stay and produce more marvelous architecture. She felt a tug. Here, she was much at home. The air was light, the people refined and vigorous. They were austere at heart — like her — brothers all, hailing her for skills she had mastered. She would be a princess here, an artist of renown. She would ride fantastic beasts and delight in Zekling aesthetics, wit, and creativity. And be celibate without conflict.

With reluctance, Altherin declined the invitation. She was after all a Xarbian, at least in this incarnation, and was compelled to look to the knot that had formed in the thread of her destiny; to deal with this Adam from Earth, who the Oracles foretold would share in it.

Back on Xarbo, Altherin's zildings convened to help her 'pass the night,' the period of indecision about one's life project. "What have you gleaned from your travels?" Father Grindil prompted.

"That there is no way to interfere constructively in another system." It was a bold statement, a sort of confession to failure, and she said it defiantly, expecting a reproach.

Instead, they all looked at her encouragingly. She continued: "Yes, it would be wrong to deviate Cannibals from their fierce instincts, or the Clones from their addiction to problem solution, or Earth beings from compromises."

"Good, Altherin!" her elders exclaimed in chorus.

"But how am I to choose a life project?"

"Calls for help will come from other planets. You will use your skills only where they are called for."

"But why these many visits?"

"To focus your attention on being useful. To familiarize you with foreign values. Above all, to convince you not to tamper with them."

"You mean I was supposed to be stymied?"

"Yes."

"Then everyone is frustrated in the search for a life project?"

"Right."

"Because there is none?"

"Exactly. In a sense. There may be any number of projects, depending on how many calls you receive."

"So my main concern is not with other planets at all. It's to clear my chest of turmoil so I may receive calls!"

"You have found the truth, Altherin."

"Ooh. Then Adam was right!"

28

ADAM'S XENAS

Never since his time in the in-between state, when Althea left for Xarbo, had Adam felt such utter helplessness. Altherin/Althea, his only reason for being on this strange planet, had left him to be cared for by her strange zildings, ethereal beings who looked like dandelions. Even as he had hurled it, Adam knew his threat to Altherin was an empty one: "I know your name; sound can pierce you to the yeldom." He was only fooling himself. For all his dire need and numbing desire, he did not have the technique by which to conjure anyone or anything by name. The ancients on Earth had known the ritual, and apparently Xarbians did, but Adam was a dropout from Earth's schools and an alien to Xarbo's. In fact, he had every reason to believe that the urgency of his need was a hindrance to acquiring the required skills. Paradoxically, those who wanted the Powers most were the first to be excluded — by their own uncontrolled metabolism!

While ruminating bitterly on these ironies after Altherin left, Adam was vaguely aware that soon the temperature would drop drastically. What should he do about it? In a fit of self-pity, and a wish to inflict Altherin with remorse, he left the menden and stomped into the nearby grove, half-hoping, half-deciding to let himself die of exposure. As shadows grew longer, visibility blurred. Dusk came on quickly with a breath of gelid air. There was no wind, of course, but warmth seemed suddenly to be sucked from the grove. In the chill twilight Adam imagined that he saw underbrush, although he remembered none. The forest had been clean and clear as a cathedral, the straight trunks soaring high above the mossy floor. Now he looked up. Against the violet sky filling with stars, something was spreading its wings. A canopy of vulture bats? Dread clutched him. Immediately he regretted his resolve to die, but knew that every house would be locked.

The bat-like wings spread wider. The stars were blocked from view. He seemed to make out long necks swaying, perhaps peering at him from high in the trees. He crouched at the foot of a large phenamon to make himself less conspicuous. Among the huge trunks, the underbrush seemed to be foraging. What was it and where had it come from?

He was certain now. Something stirred in the grove. Bushes walked abroad. He peered around. They were converging. Maybe fifteen of them! He sank his head between his knees and tried to concentrate on a calming technique. There was nothing he could do against the unknown. Perhaps he could elude the interest of predators if he made his vibratory output extremely faint. It was his only hope.

Suddenly he was startled from his exercises in breathing and galvanic skin response. Something brushed his skin and made it crawl with the electricity of fear. He screamed. And his scream lost itself as a puny echo among the giant trees. He opened his eyes and saw a bush of fur closing in on him. It approached without hesitation and engulfed him. He imagined in an instant a squid's beak hidden deep in the fleecy fibers, probing for him. He pushed against the deep pile but it gave way to his thrust and he sank farther into it. It was like the morass of a nightmare, the monster Sticky Hair of epic comedies. All too quickly he lost all his learned resources for coping. There was nothing to do but fall unconscious.

When he came to, the horizon was bitten by the bright fuchsia blur of Sol. For a moment, he thought it was setting and he still had the night to contend with. But quickly the air warmed. Then he remembered the furry bushes and his fear. However, they had vanished like apparitions induced by some Technist chemical. He stretched his cramped muscles. His rage had vanished. He was drained, neither glad nor sorry to be alive. His mind was like an empty vessel waiting. What would this new day bring to fill it?

As if in answer, he saw a figure approach him through the grove, which was rustling with the sound of giant leaves folding for the day. He thought that he recognized the stately person whom he had met with Altherin, but these foreigners all had a similar strangeness that overshadowed their differences.

"I am Grindil, Altherin's zilding," the Xarbian addressed him courteously.

"What were those … things?" Adam blurted.

"Dandons and thalapers and several other species who know how to pass a night comfortably."

"They … they did not … want to harm me?"

"I sent them, my friend." Grindil touched Adam's shoulder with a hand as small and soft as a bobcat's — and as sure of quick power.

The gentleness of the sender did not seem to tally with the frightfulness of his emissaries. "Why did you set them on me? Are you friend or enemy?" Adam took a direct, courageous stance.

"I am your friend and guardian. You will pardon the intrusion. I xarped your night-time of the mind and your location in this grove. To perish deliberately is a grave matter, with far-reaching consequences. I am sure you would have regretted it."

"But those dandy thapers — whatever you call them? They almost scared me to death."

"It was the only way to protect you from the cold. I made you a gift of a privilege I have. From birth, we Xarbians have the right to call on the other species once, in an emergency such as yours. They will provide haven in the depths of their fur. I have never needed to use this privilege — Sol be praised — and I am old now. I passed it to you, for I xarped that you truly did not wish to die."

"Good thing I blanked out, or I would have died of fear!"

"Possibly. The important thing is you are here, and I am prepared to teach you precious xenas and bring you to others who will teach you further. You will be glad for all this when light returns to your mind."

As Grindil spoke, Sol cleared the horizon and lost its reddish hue. Clear rays struck Adam and humility returned with their clarity. He touched Grindil's chest in an Earth-honored gesture and was pleased to feel a heart beating there where a human heart is. Still, his own cardiac area felt sore and disjointed. *Why*, he wondered, *does everyone else know what is good for me better than I do?*

Adam was apprenticed to a female Xarbian, formerly an eclectic on Earth. She reminded him of his Second Mother: wiry, tough, and uncompromising. Full of surprises. Utterly self-assured. Formidable. Adam had the distinct feeling of picking up where he left off with his earthly teacher and wondered: *Must all unfinished business be picked up somehow somewhere in the universe?*

Although the tenor of the relationship was so similar, this Xarbian, whose name was Xenda, used methods very different from those of his earlier instructor. She avoided trauma to his system. She did not try to manipulate his diet or even his posture. Although she was aware of the latent energy in his helix, she concentrated her efforts on his mind.

"The mind is like a globe," she explained. "It is like Earth or Xarbo. It contains all phenomena you can imagine: all animals, all plants, all elements. To experience them, you may circle the globe, meander to locate them. But if you locate yourself at the center, like a springster at the focal point of her web, you can have access to any point on the surface. You travel by the shortest way, which is in no-time, to any destination. That means any space and any time that you choose. Accuracy in reaching your destination — which may be a piece of information — depends on your ability to sustain awareness at the still center of the mind."

By speaking with new Xarbian acquaintances, Adam was able to affirm his guess that this new training was the key to all xenas. For the first time in his lives, he was entrusted with the best available knowledge. He was not on probation, not shunted off with half-way measures, and so he acquired unprecedented confidence. A happy feeling accompanied every training session. He mentioned this to his teacher.

"Yes, my child," Xenda said with a kindness Adam had not realized these god-like beings could entertain: "no need to suffer. Are self-denial and discipline still valued where you come from?"

"Well, Technists value them. But they compensate for their pains with a great deal of self-indulgence. Ahims are generally more lenient with themselves, but learning disabilities like mine are still regarded as a kind of inborn stubbornness. And extreme measures are sometimes used to correct them. I could tell you stories about my Second Mother! Yes, self-denial and discipline are still used on Earth."

"I know you desire the technique of self-transportation. And it will not be denied to you. Ability to visualize your target is essential. Since your spacecraft is a familiar object, you can practice on that."

For a moment Adam was transfixed with panic. What if he remained in the in-between state between departure and arrival, failed to re-materialize? Xenda laughed: "You should be so lucky to stay in no-space and no-time! But that will not happen until your tasks on this planet or another are completed. Only then can you rest in the great Stasis."

Adam was amazed when, after following Xenda's simple instructions in thought-printing, he found himself in the spacecraft's coil library. It had been so easy! He was filled with delight, beside himself with happy amazement, and gratitude. A power for which he had struggled for two lifetimes was bestowed here quickly, graciously, with dignity. He did not have to beg or submit himself to humiliating interrogations. There were no cumbersome calibrations of pulse and brainwave. With minimal fuss, he learned how to transport himself. He visualized the spacecraft and soon found himself in it, together with his teacher. It was true that things happen very fast on Xarbo. Even for him! Unable to shrill his jubilation like a Xarbian, he fell back on a homely earthly gesture and grasped his mentor in a bear hug. He was surprised at the warmth and vigor with which the diminutive person returned his embrace.

Adam was inundated by a wave of tenderness — for himself and for the race of wise and generous beings to which his beloved now belonged. Also, for humanity on Earth still struggling. He was so overwhelmed with gratitude and compassion that he could not thought-print himself back to the menden. Xenda had to load him with the coils he had selected and the portable coilcorder into an air carriage and tow him. When he came to after an exhausted sleep, she admonished him from indulging in emotional orgies. "It is beautiful," she admitted, "to give in to waves of joy. But until you are strong enough to sustain them, you should not allow them to overwhelm you."

Adam nodded, but still felt an urge to exult and exult again over the immense contrast between his past frustrations and the utter simplicity with which he could now fulfill his greatest desire: to travel without a vehicle.

Adam was listening to the coil-corded voice of an ancient lyrical poet when his second zilding approached. The lyrics helped him to get in touch with his roots. The age of lyrics had been long on Earth and had given way only slowly to the rebirth of epics. Lyrics spoke of individual impressions, personal emotions. One might know these things were trivial and yet be attached to them. Such was the condition of most Earth beings still in Adam's day, although it was no longer fashionable for poets to express intimate truths.

"I am Grandar," the zilding introduced himself. "I will be your teacher for some small xenas. Perhaps Altherin has spoken of me. She too is a dinzil of mine. I was an adept of the sacro-helix in my Earth-life. Here, the helix is not the great power, but since you activated yours, it cannot be kept dormant without danger. We must channel its powers, to accomplish some minor needs."

Adam was taught by Grandar to extend the prophetic powers of his helix, to consult it for knowledge of distant places. It would serve as an adjunct to learning space-travel, helping him to visualize at immense distances, through dense atmospheres — and to choose the rate of vibration at which one could safely re-materialize on a given site.

The helix also aided in communication with other species. Adam surprised his teacher with his strides in this area. "Originally rites of consent," Adam explained, "these techniques were used by archaic societies to induce game animals to submit. For epochs hunting fell into disuse, but after the Wedding of Science and Religion there was a Rebirth of World Cultures. Rites of consent were revived, not for hunting of meat, but for other reasons. I used them to persuade bees to relinquish honey."

"On Xarbo we have a similar ritual: the one Grindil used to bring dandons and thalapers to save you from night exposure. As he must have told you, we can use this call for help only once. We cannot manipulate other species at will. The laws are very strict. Simple but inexorable. All Xarbians know that by binding another, we bind ourselves as well. We avoid unnecessary chains of action and reaction. It would be sheer perversity to destroy other species for their fur, for instance, when we can moleculock our houses at night."

"I would never kill for fur." Adam bridled slightly.

"I did not imply that." Grandar's brilliant crimson scales glowed when he showed vehemence. Adam was awed by the unearthly magnificence of this Xarbian. "However," the zilding added, "we can communicate with other species for the joy of it."

Adam learned to command the attention of Xarbian creatures to share his sense of well-being, his human cleverness. And the strange beasts gained a new gleam in their eyes and sighed with deeper breaths as they acquired some subtle qualities of the human. Thalapers seemed especially affected. They reminded Adam of giant rabbits, about waist-high to him and covered with fine reddish fibers. Inadvertently Adam communicated to one the impression it made on him of an oversized toy with gaudy plush plumage. The thalaper was visibly rebuffed. In exchange, it conveyed a crude yet vivid image of how it saw him: a great two-pronged root, obscenely naked. Worse: dangerously naked, for to be without furry tendrils on Xarbo is a fatal deficiency if one is locked out at night.

When Adam saw how his confidant saw him, he laughed aloud. A naked root! A walking parsnip. Why had he not imagined it? When the thalaper tuned in to the source of Adam's merriment, it reciprocated, flashing an image of itself as a raspberry-suited bunny, and laughing at itself in turn. Of course it did not have the larynx to produce human laughter, but Adam perceived a bubbling, enlivening wave pervading its mind and body and knew that he had taught an alien animal to have a sense of humor.

Adam shared many intimate experiences with Xarbian acquaintances of several species. He met a dandon whose mate had been killed and eaten by the Technist party. At first it shunned Adam as a member of the invading group, but finally confessed its despair. Adam was reminded inevitably of his own bereavement. He felt pity for the beast and tried to inform it of rebirth and possible reunion with its mate. Clearly, such concepts were beyond the dandon's grasp and he succeeded only in confusing it, as when a trainer plies a dog with too many signals. Adam was overcome with remorse. As he tuned in again to the creature's loneliness, he was wrenched with profound compassion and shook with dry sobs. The dandon responded sympathetically. It convulsed and heaved awkwardly, casting out its fear and grief as it would poisons. Thus, through shuddering retches, it purged itself of the haunting hollowness of bereavement.

When Adam realized he had made it possible for the dandon to exorcise its grief, he was immensely moved. He felt his chest writhe with new sensations. When he told his mentors how he had been enriched through empathy with the dandon, they whooped like school children, flew gaily around him, and clapped him on the chest in congratulation. Even Grandar, whose dignity would seem incompatible with such displays, flew joyfully without restraint, like a comet, and piped a jubilant song. Adam realized then that dignity had nothing to do with restraint, although on Earth it was too often confused with it.

"You are fast becoming a Xarbian," Xenda proclaimed. "Altruism is the highest value here. I can see your chest is fairly cracking from expansion. This calls for a celebration."

Adam was amazed and, again, moved by the child-like eagerness with which the troupe of sages prepared for a ceremony. And surprised too by the simplicity of the affair. No feasting or speeches freighted this un-solemn occasion, only music and flight and exchange of gifts made quickly by moleculation. And the haste did not detract from the beauty of the garments and other objects created. Deftly, with the strokes of a sure imagination, vivid colors, strong forms and rich textures materialized — all embodiments of the happiness shared by teachers whose pupils exceeded their expectations.

For some days after the ceremony Adam found he could fly higher than ever before. His whole body seemed less dense. He could have been a tube — a trumpet with a golden hollow that emitted tender and delicate new tones.

Then unexpectedly, through the same wide open channel within him, wisps of emotional smoke wafted, interfering with the broadcast of happy messages. Adam had the distinct impression that Altherin was calling for help, was in a state of discomfort or danger. The sensation came first as a bare edge of ill ease that interrupted his basking in the approval beamed from Xenda's eyes. He let his attention drift toward the discomfort and knew it was not emanating from her or from him, nor was it the by-product of any familiar failing. It was not guilt or impatience or frustration. He had learned to monitor his own weaknesses even while on Earth. No, this was a communication, not of a specific message, but a sharing of crisis. It could be coming only from Altherin.

With this vague knowledge, he went to Grandar. "Yes," the Xarbian confirmed, "you may well be tuning in on Altherin's condition, wherever she is in her travels. But at this phase of her training, not even her zildings interfere. You have made a great stride toward knowing how others feel. At this point it is important to sustain caring without trying to take responsibility for the other. The greatest respect is to stand by ready to assist if asked, but allowing the other to cope in her chosen way."

29

THE FIRST CALL

A LTHERIN DECIDED to drop in on Adam. She knew it would startle him, but could not resist the temptation — and she felt he could sustain the shock. After all, he advocated dealing with personal problems before all else. He should be able to handle a little surprise. Then they would laugh about his momentary bewilderment and celebrate their reunion. Altherin snickered in anticipation, imagining what Adam would witness: a haze expanding in the ceiling as with a light that burns its way through — and then her form materializing almost instantaneously from the blur.

In fact, Adam was taken off guard. He fumbled about looking for cover, soon realizing there was none. But then he saw that it was Altherin who had taken shape by his side. They embraced gently and began to recount what had happened during their separation.

"Yes," Altherin confirmed, "you no doubt picked up on my discomfort somewhere. Probably on Cannibal Island. It was very frightening — and I think I sensed your concern, but didn't respond to it until I was out of there and with the Zeklings. I almost stayed with them; I belong with them in so many ways, at least superficially. But something brought me back to Xarbo to unravel my destiny. Perhaps it was the call of your caring."

Adam's breath quickened and tears rose to his eyes on hearing his beloved acknowledge his love. He had to reciprocate. "And you," he voiced his gratitude hoarsely, "you sent your wonderful mentors to pull me out of suicidal self-pity — without even a rebuke for my foolishness in staying out at night."

"You tried to kill yourself?"

"In a moment of confusion. But your mentor Grendel ..."

"Grindil. "

"He sent a pile of walking fur balls to tuck me in for the night."

Altherin chuckled at the image. "And Xenda and Grandar also lent a hand?"

"Hand and heart. I was used to trial by ordeal on Earth, but they reversed my expectations. Which made it easier for me to reverse my behaviors."

"Have you learned to be self-sufficient?"

"You think dependence is my worst habit?"

Altherin laughed at herself. "Perhaps my worst habit is casting you in one role. What did you learn?"

"Gratitude for gratuitous giving — to me, a recipient who may never reciprocate. For those dandons and karuners and thalapers who saved me and didn't linger for thanks. In the past I might have plotted to exploit them further. I am learning also how to let experiences flood in without resisting or manipulating them — without twisting the tail of destiny. And, strangely — this is the biggest reversal of all — the less interference I exert the more control I have!"

Altherin xarped Adam's inner state and found him indeed profoundly changed: humble, receptive, innocent. His heart had become malleable from alternate constriction and expansion. The nerves in the cardiac region were newly alert and alive. They had been root-bound; now they were loosened and thriving. They were finding nourishment in all of Adam's contacts, with both superior and inferior intelligences. The tendrils of his heart were reaching out, seeking what Altherin would provide — but without the urgency that had previously frightened her away.

"Adam, what are you doing to me? It feels so good inside you that I want to lock myself in there and ride with you like a baby in an air carriage."

Altherin was surprised to hear herself enthuse. She had never used such childish expressions, even as a child. She felt silly, a bit disassociated from herself. And yet she was sincere. A new Altherin was sprouting inside the old one. It was as if Adam's candor had evoked a sympathetic response. Her austerity was breaking down. She did not try to hold onto it. Like an insect in metamorphosis, she simply witnessed her involuntary transformation.

This Adam, she thought, *who seemed so primitive, a shameful reflection of my crudest self, what is he now? A catalyst for my biggest reversal!* She had developed a shield against the pains of Commensuration imposed when she spurned Waldin's courtship. Now the shield was cracking. The cold igloo of her celibacy melted. Her limbs were flooded with warmth.

With the innocence of the newly awakened, she pressed her body softly to Adam's. She performed an impromptu courtship dance close to him. Earlier resolves were cast aside with abandon in a reversal free of second thoughts. This Earth being had taught her to open; she would trust him to teach her how to be his mate!

But he was not responding in kind. He drew away. "Altherin," he said, his voice breaking with passion, "my heart rejoices as yours does. It is bright as xaltherin. All colors dance around your beloved image. The wish for union with you has been the impelling force of two lifetimes."

"Then why do you retreat from me as if afraid?"

"I am afraid. Sometimes my impulses have led to regrettable mistakes. I do not know if our two species can mate. If I give way to my passion, I may harm you. I should go to our mentors before I unleash my desires on your delicate body. I sense you are inexperienced in this."

"Yes," confessed Altherin, suddenly sobered but only slightly abashed. Adam's concern for her awakened still deeper layers of affection for him. "Yes," she repeated: "I cut myself off from these matters when I tried to take the lead in a courtship situation. It was presumptuous of me and I hurt my partner and I paid for it with great anguish. I am still paying with my ignorance. I have visited many Islands and learned many things but the female life urge in me is blunted and blind. My impulses are less reliable than yours. At least you stopped ..."

"Let us not make the mistake," said Adam with hoarse emotion, grasping her small strong hand, "to think our impulses are evil — as many of our ancestors did on Earth — because they have caused pain. Let's learn how to live rightly with them. Can one of your teachers help us?"

"Yes, my first zilding, Mother Melda, is an adept of Being Alone Together. We should seek her help. I should have known I would go back to her; I failed to learn what she tried to teach me."

Adam grasped Altherin's hand and restrained her flight. "Let's wait just a little. I want to relish a few precious moments together. What if your zilding tells us we can't be mates? Let me spend at least one night in hope."

"Maybe I know already how we could judge for ourselves if we can be mates."

"How could that be?"

"Has Xenda taught you how to sustain a blank state of mind, where all channels are open?"

"Yes, but I'm not very good at it. Can't linger there very long."

"When you can, you'll have a failsafe way to undertake anything, to know anything. The trick is to start from neutral and you will not go astray. It is the purists' way. Your intentions will be instinctively pure if you always start from the still mind."

"I'm not at that level yet. I guess we'd better not tempt fate. Let's look up your zilding tomorrow."

The next day Altherin and Adam met, intending to visit Mother Melda. As they walked through the menden, they sensed an unprecedented mood of foreboding. Consternation creased every face, yet no one could specify what calamity had befallen or who had reported it. Finally, by questioning everyone, they tracked down the fateful rumor. Santor, a Completion of mature age, invited them to join him in contemplation, to help avert an impending disaster.

"Do you know who the Oracles are, my dears?"

"Yes, I've visited them and heard their divinations," Altherin replied.

"One of them has been captured. I was composing my mind this morning to leave this body forever. In the increasing quiet, I sensed a vibration of extreme urgency. I was in a state of maximum receptivity, yet it took some time to trace the signal accurately. Many details are still missing. The Oracle itself is disturbed, concerned not only for its own safety but for all who might be affected if its stores of knowledge are pillaged."

"But who? Why?"

"Someone clever enough to find and abduct an Oracle, who wants information that's off-limits because dangerous in the wrong hands. Someone not wise enough to ask fruitful questions. Someone driven by unruly impulses."

Santor stopped pacing but continued to gesticulate, frustrated. He had just shared the unwelcome news with the population at large. Anyone with information relating to the crisis should share it with Santor. Altherin was the first. "I was with the Oracles recently," she began, "and received a disturbing but vague prophecy — or so I thought. It involved a shaking of the ground and an oppressive sense of confinement."

"That must have been the Oracle's foreknowledge of its own capture, jiggling in a tub, isolated from the source of its living waters, at the mercy of a Clone or ... "

"Not a Clone, Santor," Altherin guessed. She stilled the impatient elder with a hand on his pale shoulder.

"You are no doubt right, my child. Clones are too busy with their limited successes to cast an eye elsewhere. The discontents of the galaxies are that race of experimenters on Earth. Our erstwhile brothers." Santor cast an eye toward Adam — not accusatory, but rather hopeful. If the transgressors were indeed from Earth, Adam might know how to deal with them.

"It is a great coincidence," Altherin marveled, "that just yesterday Adam and I made clean moss of our hearts. We are free of personal muddles; we can help. My fate is clearly involved: The Oracle shared a foreboding of its capture with me."

"Not really coincidence. You will see that as you grow, child. The closer you come to Completion, the more quickly you will be tuned in to everything that concerns you. You'll have to be prepared for reversals right up to the end. Look at me. This morning I thought I was ready to leave life on this planet, forever. Then this signal caught me at the crucial moment. My destiny must be connected with yours, or we would not be speaking now."

"I wonder why my destiny is connected with the Oracle's. It is a terrible responsibility."

"Have you been to Earth lately?"

"Yes."

"The abductors may have accessed your knowledge vaguely through some kind of mechanism or primitive xarping. We must be cautious, always. As other species mature, they may pick up on hints of powers from us. Until they gain the ability to handle them, they will inevitably pervert them. A little power is a dangerous thing. Anyway, you are prepared to counteract. And you have your partner."

Altherin and Adam did not reach Melda that day. Altherin was dispatched immediately to Oracle Island and Adam underwent intensive thought-print training in preparation for a sortie to Earth.

On Oracle Island, Altherin was affronted by an incredibly crude and cruel sight. A spacecraft had landed and set up a scaffolding over the shallow striated waters, which curled and gurgled around the pilings. Atop the scaffold lay a tank. Altherin knew without looking that one of the great brains was sequestered in it. A spigot at the bottom of the tank thrust forth its snout as a mute threat to what was arguably the highest intelligence in the galaxy.

Remaining invisible, Altherin approached. Near the tank an electronic device had been installed. Leads from it entered the space capsule. Apparently the invaders could not breathe the atmosphere of Oracle Island and remained in the capsule, accessing their device by remote control. What was its purpose? Altherin drew on science she had acquired on Clone Island, wondering if in fact her visit there had been fated, so she might glean data useful at this dire time.

The device, she divined, was a translator that received brainwaves from the captured Oracle and relayed them as language to the captors, whose thoughts in turn were conducted to the great brain as frequencies that it could decipher. Altherin could not but admire the ingenuity of the system, especially the intermediary element that neutralized the invaders' random thoughts. She wondered who discovered that a mind cleared of chaotic waves is a perfect receiver — and recalled that a little knowledge can be dangerous.

Were the discoverers Clones or earthly Technists? As she eavesdropped on the questions directed at the all-knowing brain, she concluded they were the latter. They grilled the Oracle for knowledge about pools of fuel, worlds ripe for conquest, and the outcome of earthly conflicts. They must be desperate to try such extreme measures as this. Adam had told her that any former

Earth colony was considered fair game — and Oracle Island was an abortive colony. The brains, after all, were flotsam from a Technist shipwreck.

Altherin tuned in now to the Oracle itself, which was aware of her presence although its captors were not. It continued to send a powerful signal for help, refusing to focus on the questions transmitted to it. Thus, the abductors had no way of knowing whether their questions actually penetrated the great brain's awareness. Refusal to respond was its only way to stall for time and, hopefully, help. Meanwhile, the demands volleyed forth with increasing urgency and specificity: "Does such-and-such a planet have fuel deposits? Is such-and-such a former Earth colony?"

By refusing to focus on the questions, the great brain would not betray even an unconscious hint of an answer. This, Altherin quickly surmised. Meanwhile, the interrogators, initially dismayed and frustrated, became increasingly annoyed and finally hardened into a resolve. They opened the spigot on the tank enough to let the living water leak slowly. This, they clearly thought, would call the Oracle's bluff. And yes, it had to admit it understood their intentions, communicated through the device. The translator was working; the great brain knew its life was threatened. And it decided to die rather than submit to the demands. A half-evolved race, incapable of simplicity in its own society, wanted to spread its complications and depredations throughout the galaxies. This contamination had to be stopped at all costs.

Even accustomed as she was to the expedition of all matters on Xarbo, Altherin was amazed at the speed with which the Oracle made the decision to lay its life on the line. It was withdrawing into silence, preparing for departure from its material form. Perhaps it had already abandoned its body in the tank. If Completions could drop their forms at will, why not an ancient Oracle?

Altherin struggled with an impulse to somehow destroy the destroyers, rescue the source of wisdom. But all her mentors' advice had been to never buck destruction directly but rather discover a constructive sub-current and give it her support. Now where could she look for a positive element, however minor, in this situation? And how could it be strengthened quickly enough to save this Oracle — perhaps all the Oracles — from extinction?

30

FOX AND LION

WITH THE EXIGENCY of participating in a mission of universal proportions, Adam learned fine points of thought-printing for space travel rather quickly. It was an advantage that he was to visit his home planet. He could clearly visualize many familiar areas. It was harder to memorize the alien constellations by which to navigate en route. Guides who had frequently travelled to Earth xarped their images to him until he had them firmly in mind. Some constellations were shaped like gargoyles, some like dragons, others like disks of hard candy spiraled in cinnamon and green apple colors. Finally he was ready.

"Remember," Santor adjured him, "once on Earth, you must seek out a constructive factor and further it. Do not try to mount an attack on the attackers of the Oracles."

Adam nodded, at a loss as to how he would accomplish the mission but eager to test his new Powers. In the no-time of a thought, he spanned the breathless depths of the universe, pausing in time to recognize a signpost way-station, and finally recognizing Earth's solar system. He zoned in on the neighborhood where he was raised, amazed yet not surprised. It was almost as if he had returned to childhood. But there was no time to waste on musings. He sought out sipping salons he had visited with his Technist friend Rollo.

Soon he learned that Rollo's father, Alther, was rumored to have reverted to Ahim ways and was organizing non-violent ploys to recall the attack on Oracle Island. Adam remembered too well who Alther was — his own son when he had been old Adam, a son whom he neglected, engrossed as he had been in his wife, Althea. He remembered also how Alther had seemed to recognize him when Rollo introduced him reborn as Abraham. Again he realized how right his teachers had been: better to forget one's earlier incarnations, lest one invite entanglement in complications. But, too late: He knew who he had been and whom he had loved, whom he had fathered. When he met with Alther again, would his still youngish son think of him as the formerly neglectful father — or as the innocent young friend of his lost Rollo? Above all, would Alther accept Adam as an ally in a great undertaking?

Adam decided to use subtle, indirect ways to locate Alther. He broadcast through crude earthly underground communications that he was interested in an alliance. Let Alther come to him.

In fact, in short order a casual meeting was arranged in a park where Adam had taken on physical form after his long thought-voyage and bivouacked. The two approached each other cautiously but hopefully. Alther extended a hand and Adam grasped it gratefully.

"You are Rollo's Ahim friend!" the man exclaimed warmly.

"Yes," Adam replied tentatively, wondering how much more would come to light. He did not mention his own name. How could he now say, yes, I was Abraham?

"And yet it seems I met you in another ..."

"Yes," Adam says, still afraid to admit that he had once been the older man's unresponsive father.

"Weren't you on that expedition where Rollo was lost? How in the name of Heisenberg did you get back here? We assumed that ship was destroyed."

Suddenly Adam sensed what he had to do. He took Alther by the arm and recounted all the wonders that he had known on Xarbo, describing it in detail with emphasis on the xenas, especially the ones that brought him back to Earth.

"Then Xarbo must be like Ahim paradise!" Alther exclaimed. "But not for poor Rollo and his buddies," he added sadly.

"I mourn for Rollo too. He died by my side. But you are right about Xarbo as a prime destination for Ahim souls in search of reincarnation. Your mother Althea went there directly, as to the old-fashioned heaven of the Age of Superstition."

"How do you know about my mother?"

Adam took a deep breath and, placing an arm around Alther's shoulder, explained how he had been his father, reincarnated as Abraham, renamed Adam to resume the tasks old Adam had flunked.

"And ... and you were able to find my mother, Althea?" Alther was clearly trying to absorb the stupendous information that was coming his way. "You could tell who she was? But you say the Xarbians don't look much like people from Earth. What does Mother look like now?"

At this point Adam glimpsed the solution to their mutual problem and felt a truly Xarbian jubilation thrill through him. He first satisfied Alther's curiosity about Altherin, then divulged the plan that was emerging in his mind for how they could abort the attack on the Oracles. "Listen, dear Alther, partner in this great mission: Don't you see how we have evidence in my very presence of how Ahim powers are real and practical? How the Technist type of aggression is not only wrong but impractical?"

"You mean we should broadcast your whole story of surviving the landing on Xarbo and returning without access to a spacecraft?"

"Yes, but let's go directly to those in command. We can't waste time while the Oracle is in jeopardy. If you can put me in contact with some of the higher echelons, I'm sure I can establish my identity. All my old mentors, even Technist friends I frequented with Rollo, will recognize me."

Thus Alther revealed the identity of the native-stranger who returned to Earth by mental means alone. The Technist-Ahim team in charge of space travel agreed to examine evidence, meet with Adam and those who vouched for his identity. Although the Technist members were initially skeptical and considerably disappointed, they saw no alternative explanation for Adam's safe return. If Adam's mind-travels were made public, it would be clear that fuel sources would eventually be unnecessary. Then what excuse could they offer for holding the Oracle hostage? They had to relent in grilling the great brains for information about planets harboring fuels.

After several intense sessions with the space travel team and the inevitable amazement and head-scratching, Adam and Alther were successful. The team recalled its fact-finding spacecraft from Oracle Island. People were amazed at the sudden return of the craft, unaware of why its search for colonies had been aborted. Tension that had been mounting between Earth's two factions was suspended. All held their breath for resolution of this mystery. A tribunal of one hundred members was set up to examine the motives of the sortie and determine future policies of space travel. Both factions would have an equal voice. The reversal of the aggression on Oracle Island opened the way for peaceful talk and averted a mounting crisis. Adam was invited to address the gathering.

Before his turn came to speak, he was electrified to find Altherin by his side behind the scenes. "I thought you might need a little more evidence to back your case," she communicated to him. "Since the Oracle was released — still alive, by the way — I figured I might as well help out here."

Adam came on first alone, backed by his panel of old teachers, who attested to his identity. He described in detail how he survived on Xarbo where the Technist crew had failed with their crude methods. He explained as best he could the techniques of thought-printing and space travel — "not after all so very different from the so-called magic employed by ancient shaman-healers on Earth and revitalized by Ahim adepts."

The tribunal was virtually convinced, although several expressed doubt about how fast the xenas could be assimilated on Earth. Then Altherin stepped up to the podium, her dandelion hair on end, rainbow eyes flashing fiercely with delight. The hundred gasped in unison at the sudden appearance of an extraterrestrial so close, sparkling, tiny but intense next to the robust earthly Ahim. And yes, she was a former Earth person: Althea, mother to Alther. Members of the tribunal were electrified and fascinated, their silent wonder giving way to a hubbub of speculations.

The tribunal broke up, but the news of Xarbian powers spread quickly — Altherin herself cropping up here and there like a magical mouse whose roar is heard around the globe, irrefutable evidence of fuel-less flight. Knowledge of the Powers, it was conjectured, could be accelerated if guides from Xarbo were invited. Past and future seemed to fuse as she appeared like a goddess of old to predict Earth's future, a world beyond the known worlds.

31

FACTS OF LIFE

ADAM WAS ELATED. And yet, almost frightened by his achievements both in the public and private domains. Old myths aroused superstitious fears. On Earth one could never hope to proceed so fast in fulfilling one's deep desires. The gods would avenge themselves for stealing their powers, sending armed angels and beaked eagles to punish. Cautionary tales informed ancient lore. Yet so far, since landing on Xarbo, Adam had accomplished all his desires unpunished. He had found his beloved, won her to his side, learned xenas despite his lingering weaknesses. He had traveled by thought-print back to Earth, not only to vindicate Ahim faith in psychic techniques, but to collaborate in the rescue of an endangered genius. Rapid and elegant accomplishments, independent of weapons or political machinations, were the norm for Xarbo. It was time he began to think of himself as a Xarbian rather than an Ahim, and cast off the old earthly superstitions about limits imposed by gods jealous of their might.

First, he examined thoroughly his fears. Were they aroused by his conscience? Had he achieved a limited good by ignoring hidden evils? Did he take inordinate pride in his accomplishment? Did he benefit the few, or himself, at the expense of the many? No, his conscience was clean. He had engineered rescue of the Oracle without even injuring its captors. All had profited from his intervention in the crisis.

Now he was to join his beloved in a final ceremony of Being Alone Together. He was at last free from the attitudes that marred his past liaisons. He was not eager to dominate Altherin, nor fearful of being judged unworthy of her. He came in trust to meet with her and Mother Melda.

"Let us visit a nursery," said Melda. "Before Being Alone Together you may want to know of long-range results of your union."

At the nursery a private ceremony was in progress. In a little chamber that reminded Adam of Earth's ancient chapels, a mystery was unfolding. It was closed to their view but Melda explained what was happening. An egg was being fertilized. A woman had brought it after gaining permission from zildings and other elders. Only a Completion could become a mother. Also, her prospects had to be examined. She must be willing to stay in her material form long enough to oversee the raising of her child. Once permission to fertilize was granted, the woman chose a father.

Adam was confused. "How did she produce a baby — an egg — in the first place?"

"Patience. You will have your basic biology lesson in good time. First things first," admonished Melda.

"Does the father have to be a Completion too?" asked Altherin.

"Not necessarily. He will not rear the child. The mother and zildings will, as you know. But it is a great honor to be chosen to fertilize an egg. The mother picks the father for personal reasons. Perhaps she likes his physical aspect. Perhaps he was significant in one of her lifetimes. Or she may choose a father for his altruistic bent."

Adam tried to evaluate how the criteria for parenthood might relate to him. It seemed fathers were supernumeraries. After fertilization of the eggs, they went their ways with no parental duties or joys. There was no family on Xarbo as on Earth. No need for a helpmate in providing food or other goods. Everyone cooperated for mutual growth. Expertise in the xenas seemed the only 'profession' and this did not pertain to one sex more than the other.

Yet the sexes were, in a certain way, more clearly defined than on Earth. The females were quintessentially feminine, the males masculine in a way that, while refined, exuded a raw energy that Adam found slightly intimidating. Fortunately, martial arts on Xarbo were relegated to celebratory display. Fighting for a mate was a vulgarity some might recall vaguely from past lives on other planets, but never one to employ on Xarbo.

"So," Adam ventured after reviewing all he knew of Xarbian courtship and conception, "is sexual intercourse not ... necessary here? Not done?" he added awkwardly in his eagerness to know.

Melda and Altherin could not restrain a hoot of Xarbian mirth. "Do not fear," Melda gasped at length; "congress with your beloved will be more rewarding than anything you might have experienced on Earth."

"There are gradual steps one takes in Being Alone Together," Altherin essayed.

"You mean like visiting, bringing gifts, going places together?" Adam tried not to betray impatience with what might prove a long process.

"Not exactly, although as you know we make gifts for each other and ..." Altherin broke off. Adam could not know she was recalling her mistakes from earlier courtship exercises with the boy Waldin.

Adam, still dubious, asked again, "If eggs are fertilized later, intercourse can't be necessary. Isn't it contrary to the Xarbian way to do something that's not needed just because it can be done?"

Melda laughed with a flash of large translucent yavers. "You have become more Xarbian than a Xarbian," she exclaimed. "The zeal of the convert! The fact is, we do not consider any occasion for joy and innocent pleasure to be unnecessary. These good feelings are the reason for life! As long as painful complications are not created, we rejoice in touching, gift-making, communing with each other.

"What you say about egg fertilization is true. However, no Xarbian woman produces an egg unless she has had a powerful sexual encounter. Some choose a celibate life. But if she is to become a mother, she must first experience what it is to be female."

"Are all eggs fertilized then?"

"By no means. Some are simply reabsorbed by the woman's body."

"Does the man ..." Adam chose his words carefully, "help the woman to produce an egg?"

"You will learn that together with Altherin."

"Our physical differences will not be a barrier? Old Earth texts warn of incompatible types, of Elephant Women and Mice Men. It would seem I am a Bear Man and Altherin perhaps a Deer Woman."

"What?" the two exclaimed in unison, puzzled.

"Sorry. The symbolism is based on Earth animals. The idea is, for instance, that big and cumbersome can't fit with small and delicate."

"Don't be concerned with grosser physical aspects," Melda reassured him. "Here, intercourse is a harmonizing of every cell and mental vibration, not simply interpenetration as on Earth. Compatibility is established on subtle levels of mind and spirit. It is literally impossible to be intimate with an incompatible — or indifferent — person."

Adam suddenly was thrust back into the feeling of disorientation he experienced on arrival. He was unsure what Melda meant by "subtle levels of mind and spirit," but was quite sure he was inadequate to participate in this obviously refined and esoteric aspect of Being Alone Together.

Actually, he realized in his confusion, this was the latest of a series of insecurities he had suffered since arrival on Xarbo. First he had despaired of flying at will. Then he resented his need to eat and dispose of his waste while the locals subsisted on xaltherin. He had been barred from dwellings that lacked apertures until he finally mastered moleculation. At each step, his fear of failure gave rise to some repressed resentment of the highly refined natives. He saw arrogance in their celebrations of themselves. Their shrill music grated on him. Their free passage through air and matter alike seemed flippant. He equated their airiness with frivolity, snobbishness toward him, thick and cloddish as he was. Then, as he was granted xenas and mastered the Xarbian skills, he shared in the gusto and joyous self-celebration.

Now, again, he saw himself as gross and ignorant. How could he court a Xarbian woman? Claim her as his? What if he proved insensitive on the subtle levels that made Xarbian relations meaningful? Even after learning the great powers he had coveted for lifetimes, he was still inadequate to make love to the woman he loved!

A bitter pellet of self-knowledge slid from his brain to the pit of his stomach. With cold, derisive irony, he reviewed his long journey to catch up with his beloved, winning her with his few scraps of wisdom and achievements — his survival pitifully dependent on Xarbian animals, his knowledge bestowed by charitable mentors. After all that, would he prove impotent to consummate his passion when the telling time came?

Adam's self-laceration went unnoticed by Melda and Altherin. When he emerged from brooding, Altherin was asking her zilding, "Why did I suffer so much when I terminated courtship with Waldin?"

"I'm supposing you proceeded far enough to have produced an egg, which you re-absorbed. Since you cut short the impulse to intercourse, the energy aroused was turned in against you. That was the physiological commensuration. Being Alone Together is an undertaking with immense potential for joy — or suffering." Turning to include Adam, she added, "You must never persevere in that ceremony beyond what your heart dictates."

Adam gulped audibly, aware now of a pitfall he might encounter. Again, the women laughed and Melda reassured him, "You must have faith in yourself and your guides."

"On Earth," Adam observed, "we experiment with a lot of sexual games. They get serious only when we want to become parents. But here ..."

"Yes, here parenting comes later. It is a most deliberate act of fertilization — and the father may not be the mother's mate."

"But the mother welcomes the child as if it were?"

"Who is the child, really? It is a consciousness that comes to inhabit the developing egg."

"Where does it come from?"

"From beings in the in-between state, which you no doubt remember. Once an egg has been fertilized and is growing, we hold a ceremony of invocation. We call for a conscious entity to enter the egg so it may join us here on this blessed planet. Those who are ready for it will hear the call and speed to us. Usually one who had prior connection with the mother will win through. Or perhaps one whose achievements on Earth were great. From then on the egg may be said to have not only life but destiny."

"We are seldom born with such a clear sense of purpose on Earth," Adam observed. "In fact, some entities try to avoid or stop their conception in such a dubious environment."

Adam recalled vaguely the flaming rebellion with which he had entered Earth's atmosphere to be born as Abraham. Rather like a meteorite, he noted, that may burn itself out before impact. In fact, if he had had the power to reverse his descent to Earth, he would have done so.

"Now," said Melda, "you have had quite enough of reproductive theory. Tomorrow you will resume courtship."

32

LOVE AND DEATH

WITH ONLY DIM AWARENESS of what marriage might mean on Xarbo, where no one worked and parents did not raise their children, Adam approached courtship exercises with a torrent of emotions held in check for a lifetime. His first desire was to convey to Altherin what her freckles meant to him. Seemingly a superficial aspect of her appearance, they constituted a tenuous connector from one lifetime to another. They represented the lively spectrum of manifestation — the beautiful 'dappled things' that lured one from the in-between state to take on a new body and continue one's millennial progress.

How could Adam suggest all this with a simple gift? There were no models on Xarbo from which he could draw, except her lightly speckled upper arms themselves, their bright colors rippling as she moved. What from his memories of Earth would serve him? Suddenly it came to him: the image of a leopard lily from the swampy gardens of his native planet. By moleculation he would attempt to recreate this flower, subtly shading it with Xarbian colors, with iridescence that shimmered and lent it an aura of mystery and power. Adam's product was crude and schematic, but Altherin was delighted with this gift that hinted of her and the image he held in mind as he sought her out.

To him she gave a tapestry that portrayed the fabulous beasts of Zekling Island. She showed one, a gafter, laying its head on a maiden's lap as the fabled unicorn was portrayed in ancient tapestries from Earth. Through myths from his own world, she spoke to Adam of creatures at once frightening and magical, who laid their strength at the service of innocence. She explained how she exorcised her original loathness to be near him, the prejudices his strange appearance aroused, the disgust at what seemed disfigurement to her. Through the symbolic weaving, she showed how now she saw him as something more than human, rather than less.

Adam was so moved he could scarcely contain his courtship dance. He felt impelled to hasten the process of Being Alone Together. But they followed the ritual as prescribed. They spoke words on all the registers they knew from epic stories to sardonic flyting. Finally, when the last word dropped into silence, they stretched out their hands. With yearning tempered by tenderness they touched each other, savoring contrasts. Theirs was a bridge between worlds. Their differences had threatened to divide them, but they had transcended the divisions. Like the clear and milky streams that nurture the Oracles, the two distinct beings curled around each other, united in desire.

Deep thrills of sexual passion spurted like underground springs to buoy their spirits and increase their joy. They became for each other the archetype of male and female, of all complementary forms in the galaxies, the very source of creation. For, deep in the heart of all matter lies the tension of a polarity, and the polarity of sex is one of its types. Embracing each other, they embraced the universes.

At last Adam rose from Altherin's arms as a rocket from a launching pad. Abruptly he broke the mystical mood and reverted to a comic muse for his courtship dance. He zigzagged through the air impersonating a spacecraft blundering from planet to planet in search of colonial conquest. This way he symbolized for Altherin his own past lust to dominate his beloved. As she laughed at his antics, she purged all her earlier resentments.

Then abruptly Adam changed guise. After speeding high as if shot by jets and crude fuels, he stopped abruptly in mid-air at the height of the mogdon leaves. Imitating their motion as they fall, he let himself float down to Altherin's arms. This gesture was compact with wit, for it told her many truths at once: that he understood how to make reversals; that he was now ripe as a leaf that relinquishes its grasp and yields to the lure of the land that beds it at last; that his frenzied search was over, fulfilled by a Xarbian surrender to superior powers.

The courtship dance must put to rest any lingering doubts about the rightness of a union. In this case, the doubts inhered in Adam's past defects. By his comic parody of power plays, he proved he had given them up. Beyond that, he played Altherin on all her scales: humor, compassion, devotion to achieving Completion. When the light in her eyes reflected the fullness of her being, he drifted down to lie close to her. Ever so slowly he let himself float down, wavering as a leaf does, exercising the greatest control, which seems no control at all. Tenderly he brought himself to rest on her breast. Finally they breathed together as one being in the fiery purity of their passion. Not a muscle did they move to disrupt their ecstasy. They lost all awareness of limbs and surroundings and lay together in a mutual foretaste of the Stasis that leaves the body aside forever.

The affair of Altherin and Adam was unique on Xarbo. Although many Earth beings reincarnated there and sought out former lovers or mentors, no one before Adam had voyaged there in human form to re-link strands of destiny with a beloved. This rare and marvelous occurrence appealed immensely to the Xarbians, to whom meaningful coincidence signifies harmony with the Summit. Zildings saw Adam and Altherin as candidates now for wedding, seldom performed on Xarbo, where none of the earthly reasons for it exist. However, when a couple overcomes extreme obstacles to be together or undergoes many incarnations working out a relationship, the union has to be celebrated. Besides, these two were popular heroes who had rescued a kidnapped Oracle. Their cooperation in this enterprise marked them as partners.

The wedding of Adam and Altherin was attended by inhabitants from mendens all over the small planet. They converged on the temple of Sol with pipes and dancing, high flying and exchanges of gifts. The apex of festivities involved the performance of a music tale — Altherin's account of the Oracle rescue. From modesty, she couched it not in serious mode, but in mock epic style, she and Adam in animal guise, sniffing out the source of trouble. She portrayed the aggressors as kragils with their feet on the prey. Adjured not to fight might with might, Adam goes underground, burrowing like the fox to unearth a resistance group to join. Slyly he digs out information desperately needed to free the Oracle, barks a signal to call forth the resistance leader.

Here the story took on mythic characteristics, for the coyote who steps forward recognizes the fox as his reborn father. His eyes blaze in amazement when he hears family secrets only his father could know. Together they convince the marauders to withdraw their forces from Oracle Island. The very presence of foxy Adam among them is proof that thought-print powers are real, more valid than fuel-dependent propulsion. To cap the climax, Altherin tells how she strode forth boldly, flaunting her other-worldly beauty.

After the recitation, the wedding guests whooped with approval and clustered around the couple to congratulate them. They especially appreciated that Altherin and Adam had recounted a factual story of generous action and not a fantasy. They were filled with admiration and joy for the two. Only, they wondered, what are a fox and a coyote?

The celebrated pair were conducted to a newly — and quickly — constructed home filled with weavings and statuary created as gifts, many with a whimsical theme of fox and coyote as interpreted by Xarbians from the couple's descriptions.

Adam and Altherin enjoyed their home for only a few days before Santor arrived to speak of his final parting, and to reveal his identity as Altherin's father. She was pleased but not altogether surprised to learn who had the honor of fertilizing Zalda's egg. Now the legend of Oracle Island became a family saga, for it was Santor who had picked up the distress call and launched the rescue mission.

Adam, however, was not so pleased by the interruption of his hard-won domestic situation. An old resentment welled up to sully his temper, fueled by obsolete concepts of family. "Why," he asked, "must you show up now when you neglected Altherin for a lifetime? Fatherhood failed is not —" he flailed about for alliteration to finish his phase in the flyting mode — "fulfilled with facile farewells."

Santor made no pacifying gesture but pointed out some complications that surround the father figure on Earth: "Daughters may fall in love with a father, sons compete with him. He is resented as the family ruler. Here, the only authority is the law of Commensuration. Here, however, a male Completion may be called on to raise his child if the mother wishes to cut short her term on this planet."

"Why would anyone willingly leave this place? Especially after wandering in the limbo of in-between? This is a paradise."

"Patience, Adam. All things in the galaxies change. Even our minds! When you reach Completion, you will find what was beautiful before is yet more beautiful — and nonetheless you will be prepared to give it up. All the magnificent worlds are but a manifestation of the unmanifest Summit. Completions yearn for nothing but the Summit. They have only to decide when to make their merger."

"This planet is Summit enough for me. It is perfection."

"No, Adam. It is merely the ground on which perfection can be attained. The laws of Commensuration provide the conditions for it. If obeyed they can transport you to bliss. But the cost of breaking the laws is high."

"You spoke of a sign that tells us it's time to leave this place," Altherin reminded the elderly sage.

"I thought you said we chose when to die," Adam interposed.

"You are both right. Xarbo is the last place where we take form. Things happen fast here, even for someone who came through the back door, like you, Adam. But we may achieve Completion well before completing our projects. Mothers, for instance, are Completions who linger to bring a pearl of time to maturity — through their generosity, you see. They do not need to stay for their own destiny, but for another's."

"And for emergencies like the Oracle's?"

"Yes. But once all calls are answered, the Completion is free to go."

"So," Adam guessed, "it's like vacation after finishing all jobs?"

"Not quite so simple. There is a sign. A harbinger appears: someone whom we have wronged in the past. This messenger must be released from the ties of destiny imposed by our past deeds; in sum, the harbinger must forgive us. Our last act is to neutralize a process started in error."

"How can you say we choose when to leave, yet have to wait for this messenger from the past?"

"Once you are a Completion, Adam, your desires are identical with the laws of destiny itself. No Completion would choose to leave before righting all errors. Such a person has only selfless desires. A sign is no more than the fulfillment of an inner wish."

"I may not even know what my inner wishes are."

"Perhaps. But things can happen fast here, remember. Now I will tell you something wonderful. Since I have wronged no Xarbian, I could never imagine who my harbinger might be. It is you, Adam! You have come as if by summons of fate from another world to release me. On Earth, in another life, I deterred you from progress. I was a professor of history who revived Utopian literature and was much admired — although I knew that history was a useless field. My research proved that mankind learned nothing from observing old mistakes. I toyed with the idea of Utopia although I knew that no manipulation of environment, genes, or social structure would ever answer the most profound yearnings. I had no idea where the answers lay. And I was envious of the young, my students, who might yet find better ways. So I callously encouraged them to stumble in the same sidetracks I took. I misused your admiration to direct you into a futile quest, a lifetime of useless intellectual speculation. Fortunately for you, Althea came along and converted you into an Ahim."

"Professor Stinson! But all that is past now, of no consequence."

"Yes. In fact, if you were still suffering from the wrong I inflicted, you would not be able to forgive and release me. But you are free — and so I am free to leave you now."

Adam easily forgave the former professor for misleading him as old Adam, the student. He and Altherin prepared a simple departure ceremony for Santor, reciting the parting chants and decking him with a passage shawl. He composed his mind as if for a night's rest. And as he withdrew his attention he withdrew also his physical form, which disappeared from their view. He dematerialized his body as for thought-print travel. This time he left it in the unmanifest state.

33

HARBINGERS

A LTHERIN AND ADAM settled into conjugal life with a clear goal in mind: to help each other attain Completion. They grew in efficiency as well as magnanimity, displaying both strength and delicacy, and proved virtually infallible in their enterprises. As Altherin's Zekling friends would say, they were balanced on the gafter's back. Often they took on seed projects where benefits from their acts would mature after their lifetime. Occasionally they traveled to Earth, where they subtly induced mental equilibrium in decision-makers, thus ensuring a continuation of non-violence and non-intrusion — and an eventual persuasion of more inhabitants to follow the Ahim way to Completion.

Adam, to his surprise no less than Altherin's, reached Completion before she did. He was on Xarbo, flying home from a small mission in a neighboring menden, where he had become the zilding to a child. Adam mused on how solutions to problems were becoming easier — in fact, often presented themselves spontaneously. And that was the last of Adam's observations. All musing stopped, like a sonar coil that has played to its end. No unnecessary thoughts sprang up to tire his mind. It was as if he stepped inside a dwelling, locking out all noise, his mind sealed in silence, and in that silence all things gained dimension. The beautiful planet rounded out before his eyes and took on a deeper edge of beauty, and all that he saw assumed greater familiarity. The trees and animals became suddenly more dear, close to his heart, as he passed them on his way home.

When Altherin greeted him, it was as if for the first time. He truly saw and appreciated her, where before he had stood at an angle, observing her indirectly through his own desires and doubts. He felt a sense of relief, an immense relaxation replacing a habitual but almost imperceptible strain.

When he told her what was happening, she felt a surge of joy, for she recognized what her mentors told of the oncoming of Completion. Then she felt a small twinge of separation. He had gone before her — despite their expectations of somehow reaching their goal simultaneously. He was catapulting into the new condition by himself. His tendency to inertia, to not turn back once en route — that which had held him back through so many incarnations — was now working to his advantage. Thus he redeemed his worst defect and let it carry him through to his final goal. "It's so simple, Altherin," he enthused. "It's total ease. I've stopped resisting because now there is nothing to resist. I was clenched, and the effort of clenching made a hardness like a shell, closing me off from what I most desired. When I strained to be with you, resisting rejection, I alienated you. But the irony beyond this irony is that my fumbling eventually brought us together!"

Altherin, who was not altogether free of fears and desires, was envious of Adam, just a little. Although not capable of tears, often she felt her breath become a bit rough as Adam rejoiced in his new condition. And a new obstacle loomed in her path. Watching Adam while he rested at night unsleeping with closed lids, she perceived him as an alien creature. Not as before, when he seemed an insensitive and ungainly intruder from a primitive planet, but now as a superior oblivious to her in his rapture.

"Adam," at last she blurted in her trouble, and he emerged from his quietude as a newborn emerges from the spume of an egg. "Help me," she begged, "through this time of crisis. You are strange to me and I despair of joining you. I rebel at the injustice. After waiting for you so often, now I am left behind."

"You will not be left!" Adam promised. "I will not depart from this planet and this body until you are ready too."

Thus comforted, Altherin gained a bit of confidence and with it, in the Xarbian way, she quickly recovered. She and Adam xarped each other at length until they brought her mind into harmony with his.

The sign that she had achieved Completion came in a way unexpected by both. After many xarping sessions, she had gone out for some flying recreation. Suddenly an urge to help someone overwhelmed her. She was unaware of any appeal, but her spirit overflowed with the bounty received from Adam. She was full to bursting like a temple that cannot contain the zeal of a ceremony, her desires shooting forth in sprays of generosity like celebrants winging through its walls. She was free of all need to further herself. She was completed and filled forever. She had only to share her freedom by freeing.

She celebrated her release privately with Adam, not to flaunt her good fortune before others. They embraced in the old Earth way and felt all boundaries dissolve. She confided how she wished to share her good fortune by taking on the sacred duty of motherhood. "But not alone," she assured Adam. "I want to have you with me all the way."

He agreed and she petitioned zildings for permission to collaborate in parenthood with Adam, to in fact have an egg fertilized by him. The sages all shook their heads. An Earth being was not capable of fertilizing a Xarbian egg. She would have to find another suitable candidate.

As Completions, neither she nor Adam fretted over this obstacle. Adam knew that only physical traits are conveyed in fertilizing an egg. Whoever was to inhabit its nucleus would be an entity from the in-between. They were both surprised at the speed with which solution to their query came. Even more, at how it came. Altherin received a call for help, a request to meet someone in a grove. She went alone. When she saw a familiar figure waiting, she felt a thrill of foreboding, which was also a shiver of anticipated but unknown joy. Coming closer, she recognized Waldin and remembered how, many years ago, she had wronged him at her first courtship. She forgot him as she had progressed in the skills of living. But he had not forgotten her. "Waldin! I wondered what became of you. My zildings would not tell me. They said I would find out when I was capable of caring. And here you are!"

"Yes. I got word that you reached Completion — and am glad of that. I have been spending much time with my zildings sorting out the strands of my destiny, my connections with others. And one strand does not mesh, one relationship has hindered my progress toward Completion. It's my irrational attachment to you, Altherin. Surely now that you are freed you can help me."

"What happened when I left you that time in the grove? As you know, of course, I suffered for my folly."

"Yes, I heard that with Grandar you went through what I did, yearning for someone who eludes you, wasting your substance in wishing. Strange, isn't it, how unrequited passion constructs an idol in the image of the desired person? But Grandar was a wise zilding. He brought you through the madness to a reversal. I have been trying for years to attain that safe haven, but have just been playing hide and find with myself. I overcame the pangs of physical desire but other demands sprang up. I cannot resign myself to your loss, it seems. I know I cannot be your mate, yet feel that by Law of Commensuration, you owe me something."

"Do you hate me, then?"

"Not exactly. I just feel you owe me something. I demand a favor from you, proof that you somehow care for me. Without a token from you I am incomplete; a strand of my destiny dangles loose."

"What can I do for you? I do care, of course. Any need to a Completion is felt as her own need."

"I need you to need me. But how could that be, when you are already a Completion?"

Altherin felt confronted with a riddle as in the ancient Earth myths. She listened for an answer from the recesses of her mind as he prompted her, "What service can you do me that will be not cold charity but a benefit to you as well? What honor ...?"

Suddenly certainty arose in Altherin like an image transmitted by an infallible Oracle. She knew without doubt what honor she must bestow on Waldin. He would be the father to her egg! She would show him that she had not forgotten the qualities that had first attracted her to him, that she valued them enough to want them for her offspring. She would repay him fully for the wound she had inflicted.

When Adam heard of Altherin's decision, no jealousy arose. He wondered only that they should live so long as to rear Altherin's child. He had been sensing that they were ready to leave now that Altherin had come to Completion. He was ready to withdraw. Yet he would not leave her alone to rear a child.

After the fertilization ceremony the three embraced — Altherin, Waldin and Adam in one circle. As they drew apart, Waldin looked them in the eyes in turn, with new significance, and said, "I have it. It has come to me. Completion. While our breasts pressed together just now I felt my boundaries melt away. I became one with you. Now we have stepped apart, but the awareness of union has not lessened."

Altherin was ecstatic. Since reaching Completion, however, she expressed her joys less dramatically than before, as mere ripples in a constantly joyful state. She simply laid a strong, soft hand on Waldin's arm and led him home with her and Adam to celebrate.

When the egg had developed enough to invite a ceremony of invocation, Adam went to the nursery to speak with the crier. He asked if a particular entity could be called to inhabit the egg. The crier agreed, noting however that the entity would respond only if it were advanced enough to be ready for Xarbo and, of course, had not already incarnated elsewhere.

"Good," Adam agreed. "I want to give an opportunity to an old friend who both detained and furthered me in my life projects, but who always wished me well. Who had a great deal of inborn generosity. If for nothing else, he should become a Xarbian for this. Mother Altherin has agreed to this choice. His name was Rollo."

Adam communicated what he could of Rollo's intimate nature to the crier. It was the best he could do to help his old friend. He thus did a benefit to one who had wronged him in some ways. It was a surprise that Waldin, who should have been Altherin's harbinger of death, was giving her a new life project by fertilizing her egg. Deep within, Adam doubted they would live to raise her child. And so did Altherin. Neither mentioned these doubts to the other.

After the invocation ceremony, Waldin lingered to talk with Adam. He remarked how Rollo, soon to be reborn as his and Altherin's son, had been with the invaders who threatened Waldin's menden. He recalled how the Earth people died a horrible death and wondered if some of those were less guilty than others. If Rollo was an innocent victim of Xarbian Laws of Commensuration, should he not have a compensation?

"Adam," cried Waldin with sudden illumination. "It is I who must rear this child to be! If this Rollo, who suffered collateral damage due to our laws, comes to live on our planet, I must be his parent! Not just his egg-father, but his guardian."

Adam turned to Altherin. Their eyes met in understanding. Nothing more needed saying. It was settled. Waldin had indeed been Altherin's harbinger and, Adam now understood, Altherin had been his own! Over centuries he had wronged her and within this lifetime had repaid her. Bringing her to Completion was the last of his obligations. They were par and perfected.

As they prepared each other for the ceremony of departure, Waldin was their witness. He would inherit their home and bring his and Altherin's child, formerly Rollo, to live there with him. As Adam and Altherin embraced for the last time, they smiled in joy. They knew what each other knew. Two bodies were hugging but there was but one essence. It was no leave-taking at all. They were together forever. When the bodies disappeared, as soon they would, a temporary haze would precipitate. Nothing more. And yet they honored the veils they had worn for this lifetime; without those bodies, they would not have learned what they needed to grow and inhale the universal breath. For the last time, Adam formed the air into a name: "Altherin," he said, piercing her to the yeldom.

They closed their eyes and took leave of the worlds they had known. They traveled back in memory, reviewing in an instant myriad actions and images meaningful during their quest for Completion. Altherin recalled the temptation of the Zeklings' fair planet with its elegant structures and clever, gay inhabitants. She remembered her mother Zalda and her other mothers from lifetimes past. She recalled how it was to be Althea and acquire patience with her husband — tolerance that later became an impediment to her growth and his. She saluted the worlds she had visited, all evolving in their own way — even Cannibal Island and the complacent yet ruthlessly busy world of Clones. She relived briefly her first impression of Earth from her Xarbian point of view, with its air-like substance that flowed. She envisioned that former homeland as now it flourished under the nurturing influence of Xarbo, its two factions coming to unity as she and Adam had. Everywhere she went in her mental farewell, she saw herself reflected as in a full spectrum of the worlds.

Adam ranged far and wide in his mind, too, although he had not visited so many planets. He remembered the great gardens of Earth, the electronic hum of its cities. He conjured the striated waters lapping about the Oracles and retraced the events by which he had been instrumental in the release of the captive brain. He perceived how history was bent by a revolution within one's heart. He saw the unloved face of his son Alther and loved him now wholly. He saluted Alther and the reversals that culminated in the recall of a spacecraft and the promise of a platform for peace on Earth.

Adam saw himself again as an initiate in Ahim ways, smiling now at his ignorance, his sense of impotence that impelled him to cheat on exams. Little did he realize then that an individual can revolutionize worlds through personal reversals. Knowing now how all desires are finally fulfilled, but not always as one expects, he went back to times when he wanted many different things. He recalled his ambition as a historian to crack the secrets of the world with the intellect — crude and vain as attacking a hologram with a screwdriver! He pictured himself in sipping salons, risking the fine nerves of his body with focusers and sex spas, with wild adventures miraculously survived so that even though impaired this body served as his last.

He took leave of all bodily sensations with a memory of a distant incarnation when he had crouched among stinging grasses to stalk prey. He remembered too the enticing sting of his beloved's hair. The sting and caress of the world had been a great and joyful celebration — at least now in retrospect.

Thus, together, Adam and Altherin reviewed in an instant their lifetimes. The moment was brighter than any spark that flares before it pops out of existence in the volatile Xarbian atmosphere. Memories ceased and, as they left forever the great spiral of Time, they perceived it as a structure. It was not a loosely connected string of events but a form that they had created. They had constructed patterns together with innumerable other beings as they worked out their destinies. Now their contribution was complete. They departed from Time as from a great whorled conch that spews its creators to dissolve beyond it. Now, together, they were leaving their Time in the created worlds, as their artifact. Exempt from all requirements of Commensuration, they would hear no more calls for interaction. Simply, they merged with the Summit, whose abode is within and beyond the rarest xaltherin.

XARBIAN VOCABULARY

Dandon, karuner, palanthin: animals

Dinzil: pupil

Kragil, minglin: birds

Mogdon, phenamon: trees

Moleculock: render impervious on a molecular level

Phylane: cartilaginous skeleton

Sintor: celibate

Yavers: quartz-like 'teeth'

Xaltherin: air, atmosphere

Xarp: intuit through a *xena*

Xena: metaphysical technique

Xin: musical scale

Zilding: mentor

Yeldom: organ beyond inner ear

ABOUT THE AUTHOR

Diane De Pisa's early publications include three articles on Black Elk Speaks, the topic of her doctoral dissertation directed by Scott Momaday at UC Berkeley, and twenty poems in several journals. In 2014-2021 the *Berkeley Times* carried two serialized and condensed works sequentially: a satirical novel titled *As Sour Grapes Ripen* and her text for photos of Berkeley in the sixties by her late husband titled "Telegraph and Beyond."

De Pisa's account of grief and recovery, *Love of Finished Years*, was published by Wipf and Stock in 2021. Her "Bird Tracks: A Pantoum" won a Poetry Society of America award for a surreal poem, and a short story, "Visions Etched in Ice," earned the grand prize at a Canadian festival.

Diane lives in Albany, California. You can find out more about Diane's works and world at her website, *dianedepisa.com*.

YOU MIGHT ALSO ENJOY

CITYFALL
by Lorna Hopkins Keith

After Samanda Lar destroys her ex-husband, the Volen hand her the mission of saving the people of City and establishing their new home.

MEMORY AND METAPHOR
by Andrea Monticue

Civilization fell. It rose. At some point, people built starships.

THE WORLD'S SHATTERED SHELL
by Laurence Raphael Brothers

It's the end of the Age of Kali and our world is dying, its bounds shrunken to encompass a single city.

Available from Water Dragon Publishing in
hardcover, trade paperback, and digital editions
waterdragonpublishing.com

With a heaving ocean and magical fog
as background, *Marriage Dance* tells an extraordinary story of inner revelations. Pfister gradually enters the soul of every character peeling away their masks and elaborate lies until finally revealing their virtues, failings, and yearnings. The swaying images and pirouetting circumstances endear the reader from beginning to end. All of this is told in precise language underscoring Pfister's mastery of the narrative medium. A delicious dance not to be missed.

Jorge Armenteros,
author of *We Are Not But We Are*

Here is a noir-esque page-turner par excellence. Pfister's protagonist is a stumbling marriage counselor in Monterey. "But I am polarized. Like everyone else, I oppose myself." Glistening seascapes undercut the staid melancholy, and a whirl of dust motes and strapless lace revolve us in the genre.

Sarah Riggs,
author of *The Nerve Epistle*

***Marriage Dance* is no waltz or tango** of love. It's an emotional, spiritual mosh pit, a jitterbug of truth and deceit. It even manages to dance a twist at the end.

Terry Wooten,
Michigan Notable Book Award

Pfister's novel blends noir with magazine journalism, achieving not only a riveting story but a mesmerizing philosophical discourse on love. The result is lyrical, precise, and fast-paced, without sacrificing heart or wit. This is one of those rare books you can enjoy at the beach or savor in a hushed library corner.

Christine Stoddard,
author of *Water for the Cactus Woman*